VIGILANTE VAMPIRE

BO BLACKMAN
BOOK FIVE

HELEN HARPER

Vigilante
Vampire

Book Five of the Bo Blackman series

By
Helen Harper

Copyright © 2015
All Rights Reserved

Helen Harper

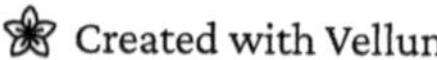 Created with Vellum

CHAPTER 1

MONSTER

I perch myself on the motorbike seat then reach inside my jacket pocket. Pulling out the lurid green lollipop, I carefully unwrap it then give it an experimental lick. Gooseberry. Figures. I shrug to myself and go all in. The tingling on my tongue isn't entirely unpleasant but it would be nice if they made these in O neg. Perhaps I'll write a letter to the company.

Across the street, the graveyard is bathed in eerie orange light cascading down from the lampposts. The same light is reflected in the puddles underfoot. It makes it easy to see the cluster of witches, even as they huddle together with their backs to me. Their chanting rises and falls. I could interrupt them now but I'm vaguely curious as to what they're up to. Or rather, I know what they're up to; I'm just not sure about why. Raising the dead takes a lot of effort.

A car pointlessly equipped with a modified exhaust roars past. It's designed purely to draw attention to itself. No doubt it's been blazing a loud path through the streets of London for some time. I roll my eyes. Boy racer. Even the witches don't pay it any attention. I crunch down hard on the lollipop, the sour shards melting into nothing in my mouth, and jog after it. The lights up ahead are red so, unless the driver is prepared to ignore every rule of the road, I'll have a few moments to deal with it. The car comes to a screeching halt but remains on the clutch, cylinders firing. It's a hell of a noise.

On the off-chance that the occupant is looking in their mirror, I waggle my fingers in a friendly wave but whoever is inside the tinted windows is more concerned with themselves. No one exits in an angry fugue and no one notices when I reach the rear and crouch down to give the shiny exhaust a sharp pull. My skin sears as I touch the metal and there's the faintest tinge of burning flesh. No matter.

In theory, I should use a wrench to detach the bolts from the engine cylinder but I've got vampiric strength. With two sharp tugs, I pull away the exhaust. The edge clatters down to the tarmac, with the remainder now barely clinging to the car's underside. I step back as the traffic lights switch to green and the car accelerates away. The noise is even louder now but there's also a satisfying array of sparks.

The car lurches to a halt less than fifty feet away and a white guy with unbecoming dreadlocks stomps out. He glares at the car, then flicks a glance in my direction. I toss the lollipop stick to one side and examine my fingers. The blisters are already starting to heal. I prod one with detached curiosity; there's a zip of pain across my palm. I shrug and cross the road. Whatever. Time to deal with the witches.

The four of them remain preoccupied with their graveside efforts. Although the hapless driver shouts at me, his garbled rage makes his words indistinct and neither the witches nor I bother to look round. I vault over the iron fence and weave through the graves. Considering how much it's rained lately and how soggy the earth is, I suppose they've done well to reach the coffin this quickly. A hazy purplish smoke is rising up around them and there's the crackle of magic in the air. The witch nearest me flings back his hood and raises his arms up. There's the sharp sound of splintering wood – I guess the corpse is finally ready to make an appearance. I glance round and note the ring of salt. At least these guys aren't completely stupid.

It's got to be a money thing, I decide, as the remaining three witches edge closer and peer down. If they were raising a body to do their dirty deeds for them, they wouldn't bother with the salt. It creates almost as effective a barrier as any expensive spell and the corpse would be unable to pass across it. That means they just want to talk to it. The trouble with the dead is that unless their spirits remain tethered in ghost form, they don't usually make much sense. I lean back on my heels and wait. The reek of rot and decay is already strong.

The chanting grows, reaching a crescendo just as I catch a glimpse of the corpse itself between the witches. A woman. Her flesh is falling away from her skull in strips and there's definite ooze. She's been dead for at least a couple of months.

'Who is my father?' demands the first witch.

I raise my eyebrows. Not money then. I've stumbled across a coven with daddy issues.

The dead woman moans. Her lips part and her jaw works as if she's trying to speak. I peer closer. Her tongue has all but rotted away. Even if a spark of intelligence remained, she wouldn't be able to talk. Oh well.

'Who is my father?' he asks again, his voice rising.

I sigh. All four of them snap round, finally realising that they're not alone. They gape at me while I fold my arms. 'You're obviously not going to get an answer,' I inform them.

One of the witches breaks away, advancing towards me. From underneath his hood, I can make out his pulsating tattoo. It's throbbing with the same ire that's reflected in his eyes.

'I like the matching outfits,' I drawl. 'Are hooded cloaks a prerequisite for midnight grave incantations? If so, I'm afraid I'm rather under-prepared.' I unzip my jacket and take it off, dropping it to the side.

He snarls, lifting up one pale white hand. He murmurs to himself, clearly preparing to shoot out a vicious spell in my direction. It's a wasted effort; he's already spent far too much of his energy on the necromantic magic. I dodge the stream of light with ease. Then I smile.

'Just for that,' I say, 'I'm going to make you hurt.'

I whirl round, leaping into the air and lashing out with my foot. I connect with his chest and he staggers backwards. I thrust out with the base of my hand and slam it into his nose. There's a satisfying crack and he collapses to his knees, blood everywhere.

A second witch approaches. She's smarter than her buddy. Rather than attempting a feeble spell, she draws out a sharp curved blade that glints against the orange light. The other two rush me from opposite sides, lunging for my arms. I duck and roll backwards and they collide with each other. The witch with the blade ignores their pained cries and continues to advance.

'I know you,' she hisses.

I lift up a shoulder in a show of studied nonchalance. 'I'm famous.'

'Am I supposed to be impressed?'

'I'll give you my autograph when we're done.'

Her lip curls. A half beat later, the knife leaves her hand and flies towards me. It's no throwing dagger and it's certainly not aerodynamic. She has just enough magic juice inside her to murmur a few words to help it on its way. I spin as quickly as I can. Rather than embedding itself in my stomach, it hits my side.

I frown and twist back to face her. 'I think you nicked a kidney.' I glance down. The hilt is made of bone, carved with a pretty inlay. I brush it with the tip of my index finger. 'Human? That's pretty icky.'

She flings herself at me with an ear-piercing scream. Hampered by the blade which remains in my side, I allow her to body slam me. We both fall to the ground. Her hands flail, her nails scraping into my exposed skin. I lift my head up and thrust my forehead into hers. Dazed, she falls back and I push her off me then get to my feet. I take out a cable tie from inside my jacket and loop it round her wrists.

The two who smacked into each other are back on their feet. They look from me to their friend and back again then they share a single mutual glance before turning and fleeing. I don't think so.

I crouch down and pick up two smooth pebbles, hefting them in my hands. I take aim and let the first one launch; it glides through the air with perfect precision, striking the first witch on the back of the head. He crashes to the ground while the other keeps going. Not wasting another second, I throw the other pebble. Unfortunately this time my aim is slightly off and it hits his ear. It must have done more damage than I realised, however, because he veers off course, smacking into a gravestone and flipping over it with a groan. He doesn't get back up.

The reanimated corpse has emerged entirely from the hole in the ground. She stands on the edge, wavering and scowling. A single maggot crawls out of her eye. We stare at each other for a moment. Hello. Her jaw moves, as if she's trying to remember how to speak. When no words come out, she lifts her shoulders in a slow, stuttering facsimile of a shrug. She remains standing for one more long moment then turns her back and drops down into the open grave. I sidle over and peer down as she slides back into the broken wooden box, closing her eyes and falling still. At least someone around here knows their place.

I bind the wrists of the remaining three witches and drag

them into the salt circle, arranging them around their own handiwork. I keep an eye on the half-destroyed coffin but there's not even a flicker of movement. All that work, I think, for such a short-lived and pointless spell.

The witch who wanted the information groans and glares. 'We weren't doing anything wrong.'

I tut. He obviously thinks I was born yesterday. 'It's against the law to bring the dead back to life.'

He spits. 'I only wanted to know who that whore had slept with.'

'You're planning a family get-together?'

He snarls. 'I'm dying. If I can find my real father then I have the chance of a transplant. You've just sentenced me to death.'

'Aw.' I jut my bottom lip. 'That's a crying shame.' I nod to myself. 'Still, it's useful information.'

'Why?'

I shrug. 'I'm hungry and I don't fancy tainted blood.'

His mouth drops open as I take hold of his nearest companion, pulling up her body so I can reach her neck with ease. I let my fangs lengthen then run my tongue across their sharp tips. A moment later, I sink them into her jugular and drink. Witch blood isn't the tastiest; the magic tends to give it an overly sweet edge, which isn't pleasant. It'll do though.

Once I'm done, I let her drop back down again. She moans pitifully. I take out my camera and snap a picture of all four of them, sending it off with a quick text. The police can take care of the rest. I stand over her for a moment, frowning. There's something I'm forgetting. Then I click my fingers as I remember.

'I promised you my autograph,' I tell her. 'I do apologise.' With one swift yank, I pull the knife out of my side. Sticky blood leaks out, making my skin itch. I ignore it and bend down, grabbing hold of her arm. I carve an initial into the soft flesh of her forearm. It's a bit wonky but it's unmistakably the letter B. Tears leak out of her eyes. I add another B right next to it then lean back to admire my handiwork. Not too shabby.

'What's wrong with you?' the witch shouts as I pick up my jacket, turn round and start walking back to my bike. 'Don't you have a heart?'

I climb back over the fence, albeit rather more slowly this time. 'Nope.'

The souped-up car is still in the middle of the road. There's no longer any sign of the driver. Either he vanished when he saw what was happening in the graveyard or the daemon leaning against the shadowed wall has eaten his heart.

'Was that really necessary?' X asks.

I cock my head. 'They were breaking the law. I thought you wanted me to clean up the streets.'

He pushes himself off the wall and steps into the light. He's not using any kind of disguise and the dark tattoos covering his face are writhing like snakes. 'So far tonight, there have been three rapes, nineteen burglaries and one attempted murder. And yet you're bothering yourself with a group of petty black witches.'

Guilt swirls up in my gut. I slam it back down again. 'I can't help everyone. And you know as well as I do that necromancy of that level requires human sacrifice. They killed someone for that little chat.'

He quirks an eyebrow. 'They killed an elderly man on his death bed who had only hours left. Who did you actually help tonight?'

'A dead woman who deserves to rest in peace.'

X's black eyes watch me. 'This vendetta isn't healthy, Bo. You shouldn't be concerning yourself solely with the witches.'

I glare at him. I don't like the witches and I'm not psychic like X. I can't read people's minds and dart all over London whenever a crime is taking place. If I had known where the more serious offences were occurring, I'd have gone there.

He folds his arms. 'I am not a wizard. I know your thoughts because you are in front of me. I don't know what is going on in every corner of the city. You're the investigator. Investigate crimes.'

I mirror his stance. 'I just did.'

Something glitters in his eyes. 'Go for a week without approaching any witches,' he says.

'I'm already your dog, X. There's no need to shorten the leash.'

'And I'm not your enemy, Bo,' he replies softly. For a brief second his pupils flare and I wonder whether he's lying. It's not as if I'm likely to call him out on it, though.

I blow out air through my cheeks. 'Fine,' I sigh. 'I'll stay away from the witches.' I hook one leg over the bike and start the engine. 'Was there anything else? Because those crimes aren't going to stop themselves, you know.'

He tosses me a ball of paper. I catch it with one hand and smooth it out. There's an address on it, somewhere in the East End. 'What's this?'

'A stray thought I caught earlier today. Something's going down there tonight and I thought you would be the ideal person to check it out.'

I glance at my watch. 'I have things to do and it's already after one.' X doesn't speak. He simply regards me with silent intent. I wrinkle my nose. 'There's no need to be so intimidating.'

He doesn't even blink. 'I didn't say anything.'

'You didn't have to,' I mutter.

He flicks a look at my side. 'Doesn't that hurt?' I don't answer. X licks his lips slowly. 'You like the pain,' he says.

I meet his eyes. I'm not ashamed. 'It keeps my mind sharp.'

I wait for him to answer but his face is an inscrutable mask. What are you thinking, X? You know my thoughts. What are yours?

'Check the address out, Bo,' he repeats. 'Medici will keep for another hour or two.'

I can't keep anything a damned secret. 'Yeah, yeah.' I rev the engine and take off, accelerating into the inky blackness of the night.

THE ADDRESS that X has sent me to is in a decidedly seedy part of town. The damp air has given way to a steady drizzle and I can already feel irritating drips of cold rain dribbling down my neck and under my collar. I pull the bike up outside and eye the flashing neon sign with disgust. 'Girls. Girls. Girls.' How wonderful.

I watch the entrance for several minutes. It's not exactly a hive of activity; in fact, if it weren't for one man edging nervously up with the club in his sights, I'd think the place was closed. As it is, when he catches sight of me, he abruptly changes his mind and hurries past instead. I nibble on my bottom lip and make a decision. Forewarned is forearmed, after all.

Jogging after him, I jump in front and effectively bar his path. His shoulders droop and his cheeks are still stained with the flush of embarrassment.

'What's your problem?' I ask.

'N-nothing,' he stammers.

My eyes drift downwards. No wedding ring and no tan line where a ring should be so it's not adultery that he's ashamed of. 'Tell me about the club.'

'What club?'

I give him a look filled with exasperation. He shuffles his feet and attempts to sidestep away from me. He's not getting away that easily. I reach out and draw the tip of my finger along his rough cheek. He flinches. 'Come on,' I coo. 'You know which club I mean.'

He backs up just as a car with headlights on full beam sweeps past us. Both our faces are momentarily illuminated. The man cowers. I smile nastily.

'You're the Red Angel.'

I move in even closer until I'm crowding him and invading his space. Even with the scent of rain all around us, I can still smell the bitter tang of his sweat. 'You don't have to be afraid of me.'

'I'm not afraid!'

I part my lips, permitting the tips of my fangs to protrude ever so slightly. His Adam's apple bobs up and down as he swallows. 'Good,' I purr. 'Tell me about the club. Is it a floor show?'

He nods with such vigour that I start to wonder how his head remains attached to his neck. 'Yes. Yes. There's a floor show!'

I lean my head to one side and drop my eyes, fixing them on his neck. He starts to tremble. 'Are there private rooms?'

He squeaks.

'Sorry,' I murmur. 'I didn't catch that. You'll have to speak up.'

'Yes.'

'Why this club?' I inquire.

'I ... I ... don't know what you mean.'

He's at least a foot taller than me but he seems to be diminishing in size by the second. I push myself up onto my tiptoes and force him to meet my gaze. 'Why are you visiting this club? Why not another one?'

His eyes dart around. 'It's the nearest one to my house!' he blurts out.

'Really.' I delve into his pocket and, before he can react, take out his wallet and flip it open. 'But it says here that you live in Brighton. That's almost fifty miles away.'

'I meant hotel! It's close to my hotel!' A flush rises up from his neck. Lies, lies and more lies.

Growing bored, I grab his collar and slam him against the wall. He struggles against my grip but it's a feeble effort. 'I tell you what,' I coo. 'I'm willing to let you go, Mr...' I glance down at his wallet '...Archer. I've already fed tonight, after all. But you need to start talking – otherwise I might decide I need a little dessert.'

He stares into my eyes, his body sagging as he acknowledges the truth of what's written in them. 'They're young,' he mutters eventually.

'The girls?'

He nods.

My stomach tightens. 'How young?'

'S-sixteen. Maybe seventeen.'

Above the age of consent. How handy. I seriously doubt there's much in the way of consent on the girls' part, even if he's telling the truth. I eye the unfortunate Mr Archer and wonder whether he's fooled himself into believing the girls inside are happy to take on board what he's offering. There's no end to what people will make themselves believe in order to salve their consciences.

'Who's in charge?'

'Of the club?' He visibly relaxes when he realises I have bigger fish to fry than one dodgy punter. 'The manager is called Malpeter. I've never spoken to him myself,' he adds hastily.

'Is he a triber?' I ask. Considering X sent me here directly after his warning to stay away from the witches, I'm assured that Malpeter isn't one of their ilk. It doesn't mean that he's not a bloodguzzler or a daemon, though.

Archer shakes his head. 'Human.'

'Bouncers?'

'They're human too.'

Interesting. I nod and release him. He staggers away from me in haste, almost tripping over his feet in a bid to get away. I watch his departure with detached curiosity and shrug to myself. Then I pivot round and head back to the front door of the club.

I push open the door and am immediately confronted by the thump of music. A burly guy in a monkey suit narrows his eyes at me, obviously surprised by my entrance. A beat later, recognition lights his expression. I launch a sharp, vicious punch to his solar plexus and he collapses, groaning.

'I see my reputation precedes me,' I tell his foetal-like shape. 'It's a shame your reaction time is so slow though.' I bend over and reach inside his coat pocket, sliding out the poorly concealed gun. It's scratched and battered; this is a weapon that's seen some action. I eject the clip and throw the now-useless hunk of metal back down. It bounces off the back of his head and he grunts. Oops.

Stepping over his body, I walk down the narrow corridor. The walls are covered in lurid red paint and there are framed photos of smiling girls. Smiling girls with dead eyes. The distinct smell of marijuana fills the air. I have no doubt that I'll find evidence of stronger stuff too. All the better to ensure pliability. I curl my nails into my palms until I draw blood.

The corridor opens out into a larger space. The music here is louder. To the front there's a slightly elevated stage with a pole and a woman in a g-string, stilettos and nothing else gyrating slowly round it. She's not even making an effort to sway to the beat. There are a few tables in front which are occupied by men whose eyes are almost as glazed as hers, and a brightly lit bar which seems to sell little more than vodka and Scotch. Behind it there's an open door leading to yet another corridor. Red light glows from within.

From one of the dark corners, a shadow pushes off and approaches. He swaggers past the lighted bar and his features become more distinct. Ugly bastard. There's a jagged scar down one side of his face and his nose is squashed and bent as if it's been broken one too many times.

I quicken my step, swiping a glass from a nearby table and smashing its rim against the edge. The music continues but the woman on the stage freezes and stares. All the other punters turn in my direction. A few stand up then seem to think better of it and sink back down again. One or two glance at the empty corridor behind me, already planning their escape. I ignore them and keep my focus on the advancing brute. His muscles bulge against his ill-fitting suit as he lunges for me. I spin to my left and strike out with the glass, drawing a beaded line of blood down his cheek. Now he'll have a match for that scar. His hands automatically rise up to the wound while I kick upwards, aiming for his groin. He screams and falls forward.

I vault over the bar and wrench the nearest bottle out of its optic, then I arc out the vodka in a fine spray and casually pull a lighter from my inside pocket. I flick it open and light it. The seated customers start to panic and get to their feet, ready to bolt. I throw the lighter down and there's a roar as the alcohol catches fire, effectively creating a barrier of flames between me and them. The cheap carpet underneath my feet adds fuel to the fire while they all back away towards the wall. I walk round the other side to the woman and offer her my hand. She stares at me with rigid, wide-eyed fear.

'I'm not going to hurt you,' I tell her.

I'm not sure if she can hear me over the music. She shakes

her head and stumbles backwards, the heel on her left stiletto snapping. She kicks off both shoes and turns to run, flitting behind a dirty red curtain. I let her go, picking up the undamaged shoe.

The fire is licking at the tables and chairs. The alcohol may well have burnt out within seconds but these are cheap furnishings. One of the men on the other side of the flames has a mobile phone to his ear. If he's calling the fire brigade, they might get here in time. Then again, they might not. I cast a look over the lot of them, registering all their faces just in case. To a man, they look terrified. Good.

I spin round and head for the other corridor which is lined with doors. At the far end, a fire exit swings open. The woman from the stage, with several others in tow, runs out into the night. Good for her. I leave them to it and focus on the door nearest to me, kicking it open. There's a stained mattress and little else.

Above distant shouts, I hear an unmistakable click and duck just in the nick of time. The plaster in the far wall crumbles as a bullet smashes into it. Before my would-be assailant can try again, I turn on the balls of my feet. It's a short, weedy guy wearing a grey suit.

'You should pay attention to who you're attempting to kill,' I say conversationally, as I wrest the gun from his hand. 'Guzzler reflexes are no match for humans.'

'What do you want?' he hisses.

I take a gamble. 'Oh, Malpeter. There's so much that I want.'

Judging by the expression on his face when I say his name, I'm right. This is the club's manager. I give him a nasty smile and get behind him, then shove him inside the room. There's a rusty bolt on the outside of the door so I slam it shut, locking him in. He yells loudly. I ignore the noise and examine the lock. Perfect. With one sharp, well-placed kick I manage to destroy it completely. Now no one's getting in or out that room without a battering ram. By the time the fire-fighters get to him, the smoke will have destroyed his lungs. He's toast.

I hear him yell again. I shrug, not bothering to answer, then head towards the other high-pitched shouts, which are all coming from the far end and another locked door. I pull open the bolt and peer inside.

The shouting stops abruptly, as if someone has hit the mute button, and twelve pairs of unblinking eyes face me. I can see several of them wondering what fresh new hell is now coming their way. The room reeks of faeces and vomit and most of the girls are wearing nothing more than dirty underwear. One of them lets out a small whimper. I doubt any of them has seen their sixteenth year yet, despite Archer's assertion to the contrary.

'Don't worry,' I say softly. 'Help is on the way.'

I leave the door open, allowing them free exit if they so desire. None of them makes a move; they're already too conditioned by fear. I try the other rooms.

There are ten in total. These ones are obviously kitted out for business, with actual beds and real sheets. Two are occupied. The first has an obese sweaty man who's so involved in his sordid fantasy that he's not heard any of the commotion from outside and is continuing to lick the pale, half-formed breasts of a dark-haired girl. I glance at the stiletto shoe in my hand. From underneath him, her eyes meet mine with a flicker of dull hope. I throw the shoe and it embeds itself in his neck. With nothing more than a groan, he collapses. She pushes his dead weight off her and gets to her feet, then she kicks him. He doesn't move. She kicks him again, absorbed in her actions. I leave her to it. We're far enough away from the fire here.

The other occupied room only contains a girl. She's shackled to the bedpost and there's an ugly welt down the side of her face. Her face is streaked with mascara. From underneath the caked-on make-up, the eyes of a teenager gaze out at me. I suck in a breath and stride over, unpicking the lock and freeing her swollen wrist just as sirens start to filter in from outside.

'You're safe now. The police will take care of you.'

She starts to tremble. I place a reassuring hand on her shoulder as her shaking grows more violent. 'No,' she moans.

'Don't worry. Everything will be alright now.' My words fall empty. Both of us know that everything will never be alright. I turn to go.

She gasps. 'No.' Her accent is strong. It's unlikely she knows much English. She's probably been trafficked here with the promise of a better life. A hard knot forms in my chest. The things we let happen on our own doorstep.

'They'll help you,' I reiterate, my voice strong.

Her hand shoots out, curling round my wrist. 'No polis.'

'They're the good guys.' I have no way of knowing whether she understands me or not.

Her grip tightens. 'No polis.' Her voice drops to a plaintive whisper. 'Please.'

I don't have the wherewithal to deal with a broken girl; I can barely deal with myself. I look from her face to the hand-cuffs and back again. A memory tugs at me of another room and another captive, drenched in blood. I helped him. I shake my head to clear the vision. The police have trauma specialists, they have people who care. I open my mouth to tell her again that they'll look after her.

'Come with me then,' I end up saying, without really knowing why.

She stumbles to her feet. I unzip my jacket, drape it over her shoulders and help her out into the corridor. It's filled with smoke now but I can already hear calm orders being given as the fire brigade take control out in the bar. The girl and I lurch out to the right and the fire exit.

The others are still huddled together in the last room, too afraid to move. I flash them a reassuring smile as we pass. Then there's the sound of booted feet running towards us as I push open the last door and burst out with the girl by my side. She gulps in the cool night air.

'Wait here,' I say. I head back in to the others and throw Archer's wallet to the nearest one. 'Give that to the police,' I tell her.

She bites her lip. 'Thank you,' she whispers.

I meet her eyes. 'Don't thank me. I'm a monster too.' And then I leave them to the real rescuers.

CHAPTER 2
SHADOWS OF A FORMER LIFE

I take the girl to my place. Her arms cling to me on the bike and her tiny frame is apparent even through the bulk of my leather jacket. When I unlock my own door and she blinks at the impersonal rooms, I wonder what she's thinking. It screams of money, with polished marble floors and gleaming mirrored surfaces. I have no idea what it actually costs. X pays those bills. Frankly, I hate it. I use it for little more than sleeping. I won't let myself miss my small flat above the New Order offices though. This is my new life. Regret isn't going to help anyone, neither will pointless yearning for the past.

I point out the spare room and shove a bundle of towels at her with a mutter about the bathroom. She clutches the towels to her chest. I can see the questions in her eyes. Why am I helping her? What am I going to want in return?

'You're going to need something to wear,' I mutter. I'm barely five foot. This girl might be far younger than me but she's also far taller. Anything I own will look simply ridiculous on her. I pass her my bathrobe for the time being. The rest will have to wait.

'Is there someone I can call?' I ask. 'Parents? Mother, father...'

Her face whitens. She shakes her head in mute denial.

'Are you sure?' I prod. There has to be someone. She can't be completely alone.

'No.' She tilts her chin upwards in a surprising show of stubbornness. 'Is no one.'

I look her over. I have no idea whether she's telling the truth or not. Hell, for all I know it was her parents that got her into this mess in the first place. I could force it out of her or I could just respect her wishes. I purse my lips. 'You can stay here.' I turn and head for the door again.

'Where...?' she swallows, her voice faltering.

'Out,' I say shortly. 'I'm going out.' I don't look at her.

I'm running out of time. Dawn is still a few hours away but I wanted to achieve more tonight. I speed across the sleeping city, pull up across the street from the Medici headquarters and gaze at the shadowed building. It looks quiet but I know better. Inside it will be a hive of activity. That's what happens when you fling open your doors and recruit a bunch of newbie vampires.

For a very long time, each of the five vampire Families held to the rule of five hundred: five hundred vampires each. They would only recruit when those numbers dwindled. It kept the different Families stable and equal so that no one Family rose above the others. It also kept the human population's worries at bay. As long as the bloodguzzlers were obviously in the minority, they wouldn't be considered too much of a threat. Considering vampires possess superior strength, longer life spans and are above human law, it was an important rule to accede to. Nobody wanted a war. Unfortunately for all of us, times change.

Thanks to the machinations of Nicky, a Montserrat Family

recruit, there were some brutal deaths at the hands of various vampires. Opinions began to change. The Families went from being glamourised figures to objects of fear and hatred. Protests grew and anti-vampire sentiment spread. The other four Families worked together to combat the growing antipathy but bull-headed Medici wasn't prepared to compromise like they were. Instead of making concessions and breaking tradition to maintain peace, he broke tradition to grow his own power. He smashed through the Families' own rules by recruiting at least one person against their will. He encouraged violence. And then he opened the floodgates by changing the centuries' old recruitment laws.

The latest Medici numbers stand at well over three thousand. For the other Families to challenge Medici would lead to a bloodbath – one they're so far unwilling to engage in, even if older vampires possess far more strength than newbies. The human government has been equally slow to react. Medici is growing stronger by the day and everyone else is standing around and wringing their hands. It doesn't help that the noisiest human protestors have begun to 'mysteriously' vanish. Everyone is running scared.

I've been inside the Medici fortress once before, sneaking through London's underground train network. That way is now blocked. Equally, if I tried to gain entrance through the front door, I'd be cut down before I could take three steps. My face – and my opinions – are far too well known. Instead I come here whenever I can, waiting for Medici to leave his stronghold. He can't stay inside forever. Even alone, he's stronger than I am – but I am very, very motivated. If the opportunity presents itself, I'll do whatever I can to bring him down. I owe it to my grandfather and all my friends. Hell, I owe it to myself.

I don't have to wait long tonight. Less than ten minutes after I arrive, the Medici gates open and a solitary figure strolls out, making a beeline for me. Tonight he's holding a silver platter with a single glass of champagne. From the condensation clinging to the rim, it's even chilled. How thoughtful.

'Ms Blackman,' the bloodguzzler says. 'How are you this evening?'

'Fabulous. Where is your Lord?'

I receive a cold smile in response. 'He is unavailable.'

'He's always unavailable.'

'He's a busy and important person.' His tone makes it clear that he believes I am neither of those things. He bows his head towards the glass. 'With our compliments.'

'No, thank you.' I was brought up to be polite, even to a goddamned Medici vampire.

'It's not poisoned, I assure you.'

I sneer at him and my efforts at politeness flee. 'The day I take anything from Medici is the day I grow two heads and start enjoying broccoli.'

'Such vehemence. We're not doing anything wrong. We are merely reacting to events outside our control in order to maintain our position.'

Yeah, right. 'Tell Lord Medici to react to my presence and stop cowering inside.'

He throws back his head and laughs. 'He's not afraid of you. You're simply too insignificant for him to bother with.'

If that were the case, he wouldn't keep sending out gifts. He may not be afraid of me but he doesn't think I'm insignificant either. Before I can say this, however, the bloodguzzler flicks a glance to the side. 'You have company tonight.'

I stiffen. He laughs at my expression and melts away, taking the champagne with him. I stay where I am, trying not to swing around my head in too obvious a fashion. I should have known I wasn't alone.

'Hello, Bo.'

I curse myself twice for a fool as my heart rate quickens. This meeting was inevitable; I had just hoped I'd have more time to prepare for it, that's all. I glance over and try to relax. 'Lord Montserrat.'

A muscle jerks in Michael's jaw. He's pissed off and not doing a very good job of hiding it. I take note of the shadows underneath his eyes. He might still be dressed as smartly as ever, in the midnight-blue colours of his Family, and his dark hair might be as perfectly coiffed as it's possible to get, but he's been suffering. I push down my twinge of worry. He can look after himself.

'Lord Montserrat?' he asks, his tone cool. 'Since when have you reverted to such formality? And where the hell have you been? I've been searching the fucking city for you.'

I'm well aware of that. Unfortunately for him, the resources of a Kakos daemon like X are no match even for an entire Family of bloodguzzlers. I gesture towards the Medici stronghold in what I know is a flippant action. 'I'm here every night.'

'So I've heard,' he grinds out.

I shrug. 'What's it to you?'

In one swift – although not entirely unexpected – action, he grabs hold of my shoulders and yanks me towards him. 'What's it to me? You ask that? After everything we've been through?' His face looms towards mine.

I pull away. 'Too much has happened. I have my own agenda now and you're only going to get in my way.'

His face twists in barely controllable rage. 'I've been worried about you. You've abandoned everything and everyone.'

'Really? What about you? Because it looks to me like you're abandoning *your* responsibilities. What are you doing about Medici? Are you going to continue to let him get away with all this?'

'Medici is my concern, not yours. What about O'Shea? Your grandfather? New Order?'

'New Order has got four vampire Families behind it. Not to mention people like Arzo. My grandfather is in a coma. Crying over his bedside isn't going to help him.'

'And O'Shea?'

My expression closes off. I fold my arms and look away. I'm not prepared to go there. Not yet.

'Bo, talk to me!'

'I don't have time for this.' He lunges for me again. This time I manage to stay out of his grasp. I take a step back and eye him. 'I know you mean well. I know you're worried but I'm fine.'

'I don't believe you.'

I sigh. 'Then I'm sorry. I'm doing what I need to do and I don't need your help. I've got resources and I'm coping perfectly well. Stop seeking me out.'

His gaze sweeps over me. 'Your name is constantly in the paper. You're no longer the Red Angel, you're an avenging angel.' His mouth turns down. 'Or devil.'

'What of it?'

'Who gave you carte blanche to be judge and jury?'

'I haven't heard many complaints.' I shrug. 'Although there was a smack dealer last week who whined quite a lot.'

He shakes his head in bitter resignation. 'You're going to get yourself killed if you keep this up.'

'If that happens then it's on my head. It's not very likely though.' I lower my voice. 'I'm getting stronger by the day,' I say in all seriousness. 'And I'm doing good.' I look back over the road. 'Can you say the same?'

He runs a hand through his hair. 'We're dealing with Medici.'

'Really?' This time I keep my tone soft rather than accusatory. 'There's not been much evidence of it so far.'

'Trust me.'

I meet his eyes. 'Trust works both ways. You have to trust me too.'

For a long moment we simply look at each other. Silence draws out between us, an unfathomable chasm of things left unsaid. 'What happened to us?' he asks eventually.

'Life's a bitch.' A small, sad smile crosses my lips. 'Speaking of bitches, how is Arzo?' The big Sanguine man helped me out a lot in the past and I miss his counsel but that doesn't change the fact that he was blind when it came to double agents who'd been recruited by Medici to destroy us all.

Michael sighs. 'Bitch or not, he misses Dahlia.'

'I didn't kill her.' Medici had claimed that everyone would believe I had.

'I know.'

I scan his face for the truth. 'I didn't kill Connor either.'

'For fuck's sake, Bo, I know that too!'

I tug at my ponytail. 'Does everyone else know that?'

His expression is stony. 'Go and see O'Shea. He needs you.'

'I can't,' I whisper. 'Not yet.'

O'Shea had been falling head over heels in love with the carrot-headed human. I put a stop to that when I allowed Connor's neck to be snapped by a damned witch. I ruined my friend's life and there are no words in the world to make up for my failings. I can't see O'Shea. Not now and maybe not ever. I do need something to stop Michael from worrying about me, though, otherwise I'll never get any peace. To distract him as much as anything else, I take a step forward and curl my arms round his back, pressing myself against him.

He wraps himself around me and rests his chin on my head. 'I miss you.'

I don't answer. I remain where I am, inhaling his scent. I'm allowed a moment of weakness, I decide. When I finally pull away, however, my jaw is set. 'I'm fine. Stop worrying about me and focus on Medici instead. You have to take him down.'

'I will.'

I reach up and gently brush my fingers against the rough stubble on his cheek. 'Good.' Because, I add silently, if you don't do something soon, I'll have to, whether or not I'm strong enough to take on Medici.

Then I step away and melt back into the night.

I SIT IN THE SHADOWS, scant inches from the shaft of sunlight hitting the balcony in front of me. Taking a deep breath, I inch out my finger. The light scalds my skin, instantly turning it flame red. I draw back with a hiss. I'm determined to keep trying; sooner or later I'll be strong enough to face daytime.

It takes newbie vampires a long time to adjust. I'm simply not there yet and it's starting to eat away at me like a cancer. Stalking through the streets at night is all well and good but it's not just my hankering for golden sunshine that has me desperate to withstand the day. Bringing down small covens of necromantic witches and dens of despicable humans is one thing; possessing the strength to do more would make a huge difference. Not to mention that the pain helps clear my thoughts of Michael's face as well.

There's a tap on my shoulder. I spring up in an immediate attack position. The girl leaps away, her eyes wide and her skin pale but I have to give her credit – she doesn't run. She points to her neck and then to my stomach. I immediately understand and shake my head. It wouldn't matter how hungry I felt, I wouldn't drink from a kid who's already been through more in one short life than most people manage in decades.

She gestures once more. I set my mouth. 'No.'

She looks upset and mutters something incomprehensible under her breath. I can't tell what language it is.

'What's your name?' I ask, enunciating every word as clearly as I can manage. She just stares at me. I gesture to myself. 'I'm Bo.'

She blinks rapidly. 'Maria.'

'Where are you from, Maria?'

She doesn't answer. Instead she draws the bathrobe closer around her in an unconscious movement. She's still scared. I sigh to myself. This is no place for her. Now, with her face scrubbed clean of make-up and only the mark on her cheek marring her skin, she looks even younger, probably only fourteen or fifteen. A vampire's lair – and a rogue vampire's lair at that – is no place for a kid. Bringing her here was a stupid idea.

'Do you have family?' I try. It's worth a second shot.

She doesn't respond. She just bites her lip and turns away, heading back to the spare bedroom and closing the door behind her. I look at it for a moment and make a decision. Taking my phone, I walk over and knock on the door. The second she opens it, I snap a photo of her. She cries out and slams the door shut again.

'Suck it up,' I tell the door. 'It's for the best.'

I tap out a cursory message to Rogu3, asking him to search for her real identity if he's back up and running in the hacker world. His parents confiscated all his equipment after he almost died but I have the feeling they won't have been able to stop him for long. I would rather not involve him in anything I'm doing but it's either that or introduce her to X so he can read her mind and there's no way I'm about to trust the Kakos daemon to that extent. Not to mention that he's made it patently clear on many occasions that I'm not to breathe a word about him to anyone.

I tell myself that is a simple task which Rogu3 can do

standing on his head and keep my message as professional and distant as I can manage, informing him that I'll pay his full fee but that he has right of refusal. He's only to contact me by text or email. I take a deep breath before I send the message, wondering if there's another way. If there is, I can't think of it. I press down my thumb. Done.

When the phone rings a few seconds later, however, I almost throw the damn thing away.

'Good afternoon, Bo,' X purrs. 'I want to congratulate you. After the debacle with the witches, you did some good work last night.'

It's on the tip of my tongue to tell him that what happened with the witches was actually a roaring success but I think better of it and bite back the words. He probably knows what I'm thinking anyway.

'Actually,' he drawls, 'I don't know your thoughts right now. You have to be next to me for me to read your mind.' He pauses. 'But I'm not stupid either. It's not difficult to guess.'

I roll my eyes. 'Well then, I'm going to guess that you're not just phoning to give me a pat on the back and a shiny gold star.' He's not really the type.

'No. I would have called round in person but it appears you have company.' He clicks his tongue. 'That wasn't wise.'

'It won't be for long.'

His voice remains inappropriately cheery. 'See that it's not.'

I wait. When he doesn't say anything else, I sigh. 'So?'

'So what?'

'So what do you want, X?'

He laughs, a melodic sound that still manages to send a shiver rippling down my spine. 'You realise I have you eating out of my palm, don't you? How far are you prepared to go to please me?'

He's taking our relationship a little too far. 'Watch it,' I growl.

'Or what? You'll hurt me?' He laughs again. 'Cut out my heart and eat it?'

That's it. I might be currently working for him but there are limits. I pull the phone away from my ear and hang up. Enough already. A second later it rings again. I scowl at it, tempted to ignore it then I give up and answer.

'That wasn't very polite, Bo.'

'So stop toying with me.'

'Very well.' His tone changes, becoming brisk and businesslike. 'Someone tried to contact you on your old number. I think it might be worth following up.'

I'm wary now. 'Who?'

'A human with a rather peculiar name. Jonesy, I believe.'

I frown. 'I don't know anyone called Jonesy.' Something twitches in the back of my mind. It sounds familiar though.

'He has a daughter called Lisa and he's a big fan of yours. That ought to jog your memory enough.'

Before I can say anything else, he hangs up. I wrinkle my nose. Jonesy? Lisa? Then, in a sudden flash, I remember. He's one of the Tube workers. In fact, he's the caretaker at the station nearest the Montserrat mansion. He helped me sneak in after hours so I could use the tunnels to move around. I did actually tell him he could contact me if he ever needed a favour.

It was only a couple of months ago but it feels like it happened in a different lifetime, to a different person. Still, if X thinks it's worth my time then it's bound to be interesting. It beats wandering randomly around the streets, I guess.

I cast a long look at the closed bedroom door before picking up my phone to make another quick call. Everyone likes pizza, right? I throw down some money on the table so Maria can pay for it and waltz out.

X might have a penchant for all things fine and luxurious but there's another reason why he installed me in this flat. It has a direct line from the basement to the London Underground – and only I have the key. I think he likes the symmetry, as if I'm Batman and this is my Batcave. I don't feel much like a super-hero, though.

I weave through the darkened pillars to the door, jiggling the key in the lock and slipping through. It might be brilliant spring sunshine outside but here it's dark and dingy enough to fulfil every vampire's dreams. I ignore the skittering of distant rats and toss a coin to decide which station I'll use. I try to keep my movements random. It wouldn't do to be predictable. Once I know where I'm going, I jog down the old, twisting tunnels until I finally emerge near the station platform I require. I've timed it correctly and have plenty of time to follow the tracks and hop onto the platform before the next train arrives.

It's not yet time for the evening rush home from the office to the myriad of leatherette sofas which dot the dwellings of the city but there are still a few people hanging around and waiting for the next train. The station guard catches sight of me and blows his whistle, directing everyone else to the far end of the platform. His nervy action is rooted in reality rather than fantasy. Not long after I moved to this area, some dick in a shiny suit approached me for a date. It didn't go well for him. Now all the Underground personnel are under orders to keep the public away from me. I know because I saw the order on a shabby wall in a station across the city when I was killing time a couple of weeks ago. It'd probably be more sensible for them to ban me entirely but they're all too scared. Once that would have trou-bled me; now it suits my purpose.

There's a loud roar as the train approaches, the brakes whining as it pulls to a halt. The doors swish open but the carriages are too busy for my taste. I wait until the train is pulling away again and leap onto the back instead, clinging on with my fingertips. It's not the most comfortable position but it beats awkward glances from the commuters and tourists inside the train. I've given up on wearing disguises, I'm damned if I'm going to hide who I am any more, but that doesn't mean I like the stares or surreptitious snapping of camera phones. I don't want anyone following me either. Anyone who tried would only end up getting hurt.

I switch trains three times. At the last change, a small child holding her father's hand catches sight of me, although he's far too engrossed in whatever delights his phone has to offer to notice. She gives me a wide-eyed stare and then smiles. I bare my fangs. Her bottom lip trembles but she manages to hang on to her emotions. I contort my face into a snarl and the girl finally begins to wail. It's for the best: vampires aren't cuddly creatures. She'll do well to learn that at an early age.

It's irritatingly busy by the time I make it to the station where Jonesy works. From the platform onwards, most of the people I pass have the glazed look of office workers in their own little world so I manage to wend my way to safety without inci-dent. With all hands on deck for the approaching rush hour, the staffroom is empty. I settle down in a vaguely comfortable chair, propping my feet up on the coffee table next to an old newspaper with wrinkled pages. I pick it up and scan through, looking for articles which might provide me with more little tasks to undertake.

I skim past the sections that feature my name. The paper is more than a week out of date, so there's not much to pique my interest. I settle on an interview with a stereotypically smarmy politician called Vince Hale. Unlike many of his more cautious compatriots, who are wary of drawing the ire of the Families, he is openly anti-vampire. I blow air through my cheeks in disgust. He's only pandering to current public opinion. I long for the day when people – especially politicians – have thoughts of their own rather than merely following the tide. Whatever happened to the road less travelled?

Evening is drawing in by the time the door opens to admit a tired-looking woman. At first she barely registers my presence and walks over to the corner to make herself a cup of tea. It's not until she turns to sit down that she finally sees me for who I am. Her cup freezes in midair and her hands start to shake. The cup slides out of her grip and smashes on the floor, hot liquid splattering everywhere. I give her a big grin and she darts out as if hell is on her heels. I start counting to twenty in my head.

I've only just reached sixteen when the guy I'm here to see makes an appearance, putting his head around the door to confirm what the freaked-out woman must have told him once she finally managed to find the words. Unlike her, he doesn't betray so much as a trace of fear.

'You came,' he says quietly, closing the door behind him. 'I wasn't sure you would.'

I shrug. 'I promised you a favour so here I am.' I knit my hands behind my head. 'What do you need?'

'It's all over the news,' he says. 'The stuff you've been doing.'

'I wouldn't believe everything you see on TV.'

He sits down opposite me. 'You killed two witches in the East End.'

I bob my head in reluctant acknowledgment. 'That part is true.' I lick my lips. 'But they were up to no good.'

'You found those arsonists out on Bell Street.'

'They were kids. It didn't seem fair to slit their throats when there was the chance of redemption.' I let my mouth curve into a smile. 'It doesn't mean I'm not keeping an eye on them though. Especially as they're out on bail.'

He looks me directly in the eyes. This isn't the twinkly

station caretaker I remember; something has happened to change his demeanour. Not that I can comment; my demeanour has altered somewhat since our previous meeting too. 'You think you're above the law.'

'I'm a vampire. Of course I'm above the law.'

He doesn't withdraw. 'Some people say you're evil.'

I raise my eyebrows. 'Is that a challenge?'

'No.' He reaches into his pocket and pulls out a photo, tossing it in my direction. A pretty blonde woman beams out at me. 'My daughter.'

'Lisa.'

Something flickers across his expression. 'You remember her name.'

'No. Someone else reminded me about her. Is she dead?'

For the first time he appears nervous. 'No!'

I run my tongue across my teeth. 'So what's the problem?'

He takes a deep breath. 'She's disappeared.'

'She looks like an adult. Eighteen?'

'Nineteen.'

I throw down the photo. 'So maybe she's just run off.'

He shakes his head vehemently. 'Lisa wouldn't do that. She's a good girl.'

I sigh. 'All parents think that about their children.'

'She's not a bad person,' he says stubbornly. 'And she wouldn't run away.'

'Okay.' I don't care enough to argue. 'Why don't you just go to the police?'

'I have. I've been several times. They've put up a few posters but they're not doing anything else.' His shoulders stiffen and I catch a glimpse of his angry pain.

'They know what they're doing. She'll turn up sooner or later.' Even if it's in a body bag.

'You can find her.'

'I don't see how.'

He reaches out and takes my hands. I'll admit I'm surprised at the physical contact. 'Please. I'm desperate.'

'Why would you want someone who's evil to search for your daughter?'

'Not everyone thinks that about you. The police are tied up in red tape and bureaucracy. You're getting things done. Some people think you're a hero.'

'Some people think I'm a murderer.' I lean forward. 'What's to stop me from locating your daughter, drinking every last drop of her blood and then leaving her empty shell of a corpse on your doorstep?'

He doesn't drop his gaze and he doesn't flinch. Impressive. 'At least then I'd know where she is.'

He really is desperate. I retrieve my hands from his grasp. 'Okay then.' His face lights up with painful hope. I wag a finger at him. 'Don't. Don't expect that I'll find her. Don't expect that I'll find her alive. And if she doesn't want to come back, I'm not going to make her.'

He nods vigorously. 'Yes, yes. Thank you!'

'Don't thank me.'

My words don't make any difference. His gratitude is pathetic; I should probably feel something other than vague irritation. I examine myself and realise I don't. I've become colder than I realised.

I take all the details I need from him and walk back out. I swerve round the corner then halt in my tracks. Damn it. There's a very good reason why I've been avoiding this part of town.

'Sir, you can't bring your dog here unless he's on a lead.' The guard's voice has a definite tremor to it – he's obviously aware that he's talking to a vampire. He just doesn't know very much about this particular vampire.

Matt's shoulders droop. 'The lead broke,' he mumbles. He starts to turn away in a dejected slump.

Kimchi's head jerks up in my direction and his tail starts to wag so violently that it slaps against the guard's thigh. The dog barks several times and darts towards me. Matt lunges for him in panic, only just managing to grab his collar before he bounds at me. 'What's wrong, Kimchi? What is it?'

Shit. I duck out of sight just before Matt can look up. I can hear Kimchi's barking getting even louder and more desperate. I cover my ears and walk quickly in the opposite direction. Time to go.

CHAPTER 3
THE CRIMSON WAVE

Blame London property prices for the fact that Jonesy lives so far away from his place of work. With my bike back at the flat, it takes some time to reach his neat terraced house. At least the sun has now fallen so I can move around without fear of frying.

There's no garden to speak of and the house is nothing more than a typical two-up, two-down building but whoever lives here is house-proud. The windows are sparkly and gleaming with heavy brocade curtains just visible on the inside. There's a light on, so his wife is at home. I hope for my sake that she's not the nervous type.

I step up and ring the doorbell. It tootles a merry, chiming tune that's entirely at odds with their family's current situation. I adjust my cuffs and wait. Perhaps Jonesy's wife won't let me in. Then I can go off and find something more ... bloody to occupy my time with.

Someone calls out. I wait another minute and then the door swings open. A plump woman with rosy cheeks gazes out at me. 'Bo Blackman.'

I nod.

She grasps my hand and pumps it. 'I'm Alison. Thank you so much for coming. We're at our wits' end. Please come in.'

I'm startled at her warm words and relieved expression. She doesn't pause for a moment in allowing me access to her home. Doesn't she realise what she's just done? Now I can wander in whenever I want. A lock won't keep me out. I frown at her lack of circumspection; she really should be more careful. Nonetheless, I step over the threshold and give my shoes a cursory wipe on the welcome mat. It's a typical coir version – although this one is inexplicably covered in red hearts. The smell of baking bread rises up from deep inside the house. I must have raised my nose in the air to inhale it because she throws me a guilty look.

'I know it's silly to be baking when Lisa is missing but I have to do something to keep busy or I'll simply go insane.' She leads me through to a small sitting room and gestures at the sofa. I perch awkwardly on the edge. 'It's worse for Jonesy.' She sighs. 'It's always the way, innit? Fathers and daughters.'

I clear my throat. 'Is she your only child?'

Alison Johnson nods. 'Yes. We always wanted more but it wasn't to be.' A rueful expression crosses her face. 'I shouldn't complain. We're luckier than many others. Now, can I get you a drink?'

I somehow doubt she'll be keen to offer me the kind of drink that I want but the woman surprises me. 'I got an online delivery of blood a few days ago, just in case.' She throws me an anxious look. 'It's O negative. I kept it in the fridge. I don't know if that's right or not.'

I blink. 'Um, thanks but I'm not hungry. Don't worry about it.'

Her face drops. 'You don't want any?'

It occurs to me that she probably went to considerable lengths to get hold of the blood. I don't enjoy it when it's chilled and if it's already a couple of days old then there will be virtually no nutritional value. All the same, I find myself opening my mouth. 'Actually, you're right. Some blood would be lovely.'

Her relief is palpable. She beams at me and bustles away. I shake my head, bemused, and stand up. The mantelpiece is busy with framed photographs and I wander over to take a look. Almost every image contains all three of them: Jonesy, Alison and Lisa herself. They give every appearance of being a very happy family – but appearances are often deceptive.

I'm just replacing a holiday snap when Alison comes back in. 'That one's from Spain,' she says with fondness. 'Three years ago. We had such a wonderful time.'

I turn. She holds out a long-stemmed glass. There's a plastic stirrer with a bright purple monkey on the end of it sticking out of the top. I can't stop myself from staring.

Alison coughs. 'Sorry. I thought you might want to stir it. Like tea.' She laughs to herself. 'It's lucky I didn't put one of those little umbrellas in. Lisa loves those umbrellas.' Her expression drops. 'Well, she used to anyway.'

I take the glass and give it a tentative sip. It tastes unpleasantly metallic and stale. I force a smile and gulp enough to be polite then put it down. 'How long has she been missing?'

'Jonesy didn't tell you?'

He did but I want to hear her version of events as well. I fold my hands together and wait.

'Eight days now,' she says quietly. 'She was up at the college. She's doing a catering course there. She called to say she'd be late coming home so we didn't wait up. The next morning her bed wasn't slept in.' Alison presses her lips together. 'We've not seen her since.'

'Her friends?'

'We've asked around. None of them know where she is.'

'Boyfriends?'

'There was a lad from round the corner but they split up in the summer. He was a nice boy but he wasn't enough to hold my Lisa's attention.'

I cock my head. 'Why not?'

She twists the tarnished wedding ring on her finger. 'She takes the world very seriously. Always going on protests and writing to our MP. She wants everyone to be happy. When they tried to close down the community centre at the end of the road, she organised a sit-in to stop the demolition.'

I frown. I hadn't spotted any sort of building like that on my way here. 'Did it work?'

Alison looks away. 'No. People can only stay interested for so long. They have jobs and lives. Sooner or later all of them drifted away and the council swooped in.'

'So this boyfriend...?'

She waves a hand in the air. 'Adrian tried to support her but he wasn't really interested. He liked his football and his friends and going to the pub but he just didn't feel things the way that she did. She took the worries of the world on her shoulders. She was such a good girl.'

I watch her for a long moment. 'You think she's dead.'

She starts. 'What? No!'

'You used the past tense.'

She seems flustered. 'I didn't mean it like that.' She turns away.

I nibble on my bottom lip. Either her subconscious is telling her things she doesn't want to know, or good little Lisa had a change of heart and wasn't always such an angel. It won't be hard to find out. I consider pressing Alison for more information but something about the set of her shoulders changes my mind. Sympathy has nothing to do with it; if I'm going to get the truth that I need, I have to pick my moments.

I paste a smile on my mouth. 'Can I see her room?'

'Of course! I've not touched anything in there, it's exactly the way she left it. The police came round and had a look. They took away a few things but they promised I'd get them back.' Her voice takes on a fretful note. 'I really want to get them back.'

'The police will keep their word,' I say drily. 'They tend to do that.'

She nods then leads me out of the room and up the narrow staircase. There are more photos lining the walls. Each one tells the story of a happy life filled with love and laughter. I rather suspect that anyone with the desire to advertise their happiness probably isn't quite as content as the rest of the world imagines: it smacks of trying too hard. Scratch the surface here and I bet there's a bed of rotting, spitting vipers.

Lisa's bedroom is the first room upstairs. Old stickers with flowers and unicorns adorn the door. Alison laughs awkwardly when she catches me staring at them. 'She wanted to get rid of all those. Said she was too old for them. They're stuck fast though and Jonesy never got around to getting the stripper out to get them all off.'

I nod like I'm interested. She opens the door for me and follows me inside. 'Actually, it would be better if I could look around on my own.'

She deflates. 'Really?'

I take pity on her. 'I stay more focused when I'm alone.' I lean in ever so slightly. 'It's a vampire thing.'

She blinks. 'Of course. Her jewellery box is over there. She has some things in the bathroom – it's next door if you want to have a look. There's a box on top of the wardrobe. Can you see it? It's only got old toys that she can't bear to throw away but if you can reach it, you're welcome to look. You're quite short. Shall I fetch it down for you?'

'Mrs Johnson ... Alison, I'll manage. Honestly.'

She nods. She is still reluctant to leave me alone. I think it's less because of a lack of trust and more that she's desperate to help. I take charge of the situation and gently propel her out of the room. 'Thank you!' I close the door after her and breathe out. Gods preserve me.

Lisa's room is small. There's a single bed with a frilly pink cover, the afore-mentioned wardrobe, a small vanity covered with make-up and bottles, and little else. It's clean, neat and wholly unremarkable. I start with the bed. If I were a teenager – even one already in the bounds of legal adulthood – and I was looking to hide things from my over-protective parents, under the mattress would be a good option.

There's nothing there. Admittedly, it's difficult to tell what the police took away with them and I have no way of knowing how careful they were with their search. I'll cross that bridge when I need to; right now, I want to get a feel for Lisa herself. Is she as good a girl as her parents are trying to make out?

I flip back the duvet. Nothing. Her pillows are plump and the sheets are clean. If Lisa has been concealing anything, it's not here. I move over to the vanity and lift up various bottles. It's all typical girlie paraphernalia; nothing is very expensive although she's clearly someone who takes care of her possessions. There is a tube of lipstick which is almost down to the nub and a few clean brushes. Her perfume has a couple of millimetres left inside it. Lisa doesn't like waste.

I open the drawer underneath. There are a couple of old postcards with nothing written on them and some scented notepaper. I take it out and rub my fingertips over the front of the pad. Several sheets are missing. Rummaging around in my inside pocket, I eventually retrieve a pencil. I shade in the top page, revealing Lisa's last words: 'Dear Gran, Thank you so much for the...' I stop and return the pad to the drawer.

The wardrobe is as neat as everything else. An array of brightly coloured clothes hang there, each one ironed to within an inch of its life. Nothing is very revealing but the colours suggest that Lisa liked being noticed. I run my finger across them, occasionally stopping to examine a garment in more detail. There's a pair of jeans crumpled at the foot of the wardrobe so I pull them out and check the pockets. I find a receipt for a café. Two teas and a coffee – none of this herbal tea or frothy latte malarkey either. It's dated from two weeks ago. I pocket it, just in case.

Despite Alison's concern, a quick jump makes it easy for me to grab the battered box on the top of the wardrobe and pull it down. There's a bald Barbie, a well-loved teddy bear with worn fur, and various bits of plastic which no doubt hold some sort of sentimental value. I pick through it all. If there ever was anything here, either the police took it or Lisa disposed of it.

I leave the box where it is and sit on the bed, taking everything in. Other than the single pair of jeans from the wardrobe bottom, all of Lisa's belongings are orderly. She's thrifty, sends kind notes to her family to thank them for gifts, gets on well with her parents and appears to be nothing more than a nice, prepossessing young woman. I don't believe any of it for a second. Everyone has secrets; I just need to find hers.

When I finally leave the bedroom, Alison Johnson is still hovering outside. I wonder if she's been out here the entire time. I give her a reassuring smile. 'She keeps her room very tidy.'

'Oh yes, Lisa was always like that. Even as a child. A place for everything and everything in its place.'

'Where is the bathroom?'

She points to a closed door to the right. 'It's there.'

I bob my head dutifully and wander in. It's the kind of bathroom which has knitted covers for toilet rolls and embroidered towels. My mouth twitches. This family is like something out of a sitcom.

I open the medicine cabinet above the sink. There's some old flu medication, paracetemol and a spare toothbrush. I rock back on my heels and try to think. I'm missing something.

'Alison?' I call.

A heartbeat later she pops her head round the door. She's still hovering. 'Yes?' Her expression is eager.

'You mentioned the old boyfriend. Adrian.'

'Adrian Leeman. He lives at number 38 on Bow Street.'

I nod. She's remarkably keen to volunteer information about him. Maybe she disapproved of the relationship. It makes the next question rather awkward. Big deal. 'I'm going to assume that they had a physical relationship. Did you and Lisa ever discuss contraception?'

Two high dots of colour appear on her cheeks. 'We did. We had the talk when she was twelve. Some of my friends thought it was a bit too early but I wanted her to be prepared. You never know with girls these days. She was always such a good girl though. We never had any trouble.' She catches my look. 'She still is a good girl,' she says firmly.

I murmur noncommittally and give her a little prod. 'Contraception?'

'Oh, yes! She was on the pill.' She drops her voice to a conspiratorial whisper. 'Her father wasn't very happy about it to start with but it did help with her monthly cramps. She used to suffer terribly.'

My brow furrows. Not only is there an absence of anything to indicate a sex life, there are also no feminine sanitary products. I look Alison over. She's in her early fifties. 'Have you been through the menopause?'

She's taken aback by the question. Her blush intensifies and she looks away. 'Is that relevant?'

'It might be.'

She clears her throat. 'Yes. I had quite a time of it. In fact, there were a few months when…'

I hold up my hand. 'I don't need the details.' I gaze at the empty cabinet for a moment longer. 'Who is Lisa's doctor?'

'Dr Bryant. She works at the clinic just down the street.' There's a flicker of alarm. 'Why? You don't think she was sick, do you?'

Past tense again. I don't pull her up on it. 'I'm sure it's nothing but I'd appreciate it if you could call Dr Bryant and tell her I'll be coming by with a few questions.'

Alison's eyes shift nervously. 'Okay.'

I pat her arm. 'We need to cover all the bases.'

She bites her lip. 'Sure.' She holds out a small card. 'This is the policeman assigned to her case.'

I take the card and study it, make a mental note of the details and hand it back. 'Thanks.'

'Would you like some more blood?'

I try to repress my involuntary shudder. 'No, thank you.'

'Something else? Tea? Coffee?'

'I'm fine. I should get going. I'll be in touch if I have any other questions.'

'Ms Blackman? You will find her, won't you?'

I meet her eyes. 'I will try. There's no guarantee of anything though. You need to be prepared that maybe she doesn't want to be found.'

Her hand flies up to her throat. 'You think she wanted to leave?'

She might have left all her clothes, make-up and jewellery behind but she's taken all her sanitary products and contraception with her. I reckon she's making a clean break. I open my mouth to say this but something in Alison's face changes my mind. Maybe I still have it in me to be nice after all. 'I'm just saying you should be prepared for every eventuality.' And with that, I leave.

I wander back down the street, my hands shoved in my pockets. It's been several weeks since I took the time to ask questions first before taking action. I mull over all that I discovered before veering left to Lisa's ex-boyfriend. It's still early.

I've barely rounded the corner when a dark shape flies out of nowhere, barrelling into me. My fangs immediately elongate and I thrust out my hands to ward off the attack and protect myself. I only just manage to pull the punch in time. Kimchi slobbers all over my face, panting a cloud of doggy breath that has me recoiling. I extricate myself and look over the top of him.

Matt grins at me sheepishly. 'Hey.'

'What are you doing here?'

There's a fleeting look of hurt in his eyes but he quickly masks it. 'Looking for you. I've missed you, Bo.'

Kimchi licks my hand as if to add weight to Matt's words. I sigh. 'How did you find me?'

'When Kimchi spotted you at the station we followed you. I'm not completely stupid, you know.'

I raise my eyebrows. Not that I can speak. I allowed a muscle-bound idiot and a drooling dog that is incapable of little more than waddling to trail after me without me noticing. To add insult to injury, Matt sticks out his tongue.

'You shouldn't be here,' I mutter.

'I need you.'

'No, you don't. Go back to the Montserrat mansion where you belong.' I tilt up my chin, sensing a hovering presence behind him. 'Who else is there?'

From the shelter of a tree, a slim shape appears. I'd recognise those heels anywhere. 'Beth? They let you out?'

She smiles at me. 'As you see.' She walks up to Matt and

hooks her arm round his. 'It helps to have some brawn around though.'

I almost snort. In a fight, I reckon Beth could take Matt down any day of the week, despite his well-advertised muscles. 'Does that mean you can withstand sunshine?' I ask, wondering whether that is jealousy uncurling deep within my stomach.

She shakes her head. 'No, but Ursus thinks I'm close.'

I gaze at her suspiciously. I'm betting there's more about her newfound freedom than she's letting on. Usually no vampire is let out until they are strong enough to get a sun tan. Matt and I are special cases; making another exception for Beth seems unlikely. I wrinkle my nose to show my distaste. 'What do you want?'

'We thought we'd tag along.'

'I don't need company,' I growl.

'Maybe not,' she says lightly. 'But we need you.' She pauses. 'I've just been to the hospital.'

'Bully for you.'

'Your grandfather is stable.'

I fold my arms. 'And still unconscious.'

'When he wakes up...'

'If he wakes up. And what are you doing visiting him? He all but blackmailed you to look after me. I'd have thought you'd had enough of him.'

'He needs someone to be there.'

'No,' I say flatly. 'He doesn't. You know why? Because he's in a coma, Beth. He doesn't know what's going on. Besides, he's an old man. They're probably better off pulling the plug.'

Matt stiffens but Beth is unfazed. She steps over and peers into my face. 'You don't mean that,' she says decisively.

'Yes, I do.'

'You're hurting, I understand that. But you can't keep pushing everyone away.'

'Watch me.' I spin on my heel and start walking away.

'Do it,' I hear her mutter.

'Beth...'

Her tone brooks no argument. 'Do it.'

Matt clears his throat and calls after me. 'Kimchi is your dog.' His voice is filled with reluctance. 'I can't look after him any more.'

I slowly turn. My gaze drifts down. Kimchi is looking at me with an expression that can only be described as doggy adoration. I curl up my fists. 'I'll pay you.'

Beth doesn't give him time to answer. 'It's not a question of money,' she says, immediately stepping in. 'Matt lives at the Montserrat mansion. Some of the new recruits are allergic. You have to take him.'

'So give him to Arzo,' I snap. Then I pause. 'What do you mean,' I ask slowly, 'new recruits?' It's too soon for Montserrat to be looking for newbies. A few of the older vampires have passed away but not enough to begin the whole process of recruiting again.

Beth frowns. 'I thought you knew.'

'Obviously I don't. What's going on?'

She exchanges looks with Matt. 'It's because of Medici.'

'What is?'

Her eyes drop to the pavement. 'It's the only way.'

A tendril of unease snakes through me. 'Go on.'

'Maybe I've said enough. If Lord Montserrat didn't say anything...'

'Screw Lord Montserrat. What the hell is going on?'

'Ask him.'

I look at Matt. 'Tell me,' I order.

He glances helplessly at Beth. She gives a minute shake of her head.

'What?' I scoff. 'You think I'm going to run to Medici and

give away all your secrets? It can't be that big a deal. Tell me, Matt.'

'It doesn't work any more, Bo,' Beth interjects.

I stare at Matt's face. 'O'Shea's spell? It really has worn off after all?'

They both nod. I sigh. I should be happy. We'd been told that there was no hope for Matt. The enhancement spell which O'Shea created, and which Nicky stole to manipulate all the male vampires into doing her bidding, had messed with his mind, leaving him unable to refuse any direct order. He also seemed to have lost a ton of IQ points in the process although, admittedly, he wasn't the sharpest tool in the box beforehand. He's obviously still doing whatever Beth tells him to do, bespelled or not.

'The others? The other vampires who were affected?'

'We don't know. They're all in other Families.'

'So? I assume that Montserrat is still working with Gully, Stuart and Bancroft. Just get Michael to bloody ask them.' She looks at me. I blow air out through my cheeks. 'He doesn't know, does he? Your Lord Montserrat doesn't know that Matt has beaten the spell. Well, well, well. You're breaking ranks.'

Matt steps forward. 'No, we're not. We just want to keep it quiet for a while. We thought it might help you.'

I shake my head. 'I don't see how.'

'Bo...'

'You're supposed to tell him, that's how the Family hier-archy works. I'm not in the Family. You need to leave me out of it.'

Matt tries again. 'Bo, everything's going to shit. We really do need you.'

'Find another sucker.'

'What about Kimchi?'

The dog takes that moment to whine. They must have stood

on his tail or something. I look at him. His previous owners all but abandoned him and I hated them for it – but I'm no longer that person. I don't have room in my life for a pet.

Kimchi whines again. Fucking hell. I pat my thigh. 'Come here, boy.'

He requires nothing more. Beth drops the lead and Kimchi bounds towards me again. I receive another lathering from his tongue. I stand up while he paws me for more. 'What is that?' I ask, pointing downwards.

Matt shifts his feet. 'It's, um, a washing line. I lost his lead and the pet shop was closed.'

The Montserrat Family outsources all its laundry so Matt must have stolen it from someone's garden. I roll my eyes and pick it up. It's a good job I'm not worried about my street cred.

I jab a finger at them both. 'Stay the hell away from me. I like you both and you've done nothing wrong, but I don't need or want any friends.' I force a smile. 'It's me, not you. Got it?'

'Okay, Bo,' Matt says.

'Beth?'

'Whatever you say.'

I glare at her suspiciously. Short of tying the pair of them to the nearest lamp post, there's not much else I can do. I sniff loudly and, with an ecstatic Kimchi in tow, march off.

CHAPTER 4
LEGAL EASE

I mutter loudly to Kimchi all the way down the street. He swings his head up at me from time to time as if he's listening. I tell myself that he is.

'You're going to do what I say,' I order. 'There's going to be no chewing of X's pretty furnishings, no waking me up in the middle of the day because you want something to eat, no getting in my way when I'm working.'

Kimchi pants, tongue lolling.

'And,' I continue, 'you're going on a diet. It's embarrassing to be with a dog with a belly as round as yours.'

His head dives in for another lick. I only just manage to pull away in time. 'No licking either,' I tell him. 'Got all that?'

Kimchi halts next to a car and lifts his leg. Apparently that's all the answer I'm going to get. I wait for him to finish, double-checking that neither Beth nor Matt are continuing to follow me, then tug on the silly washing line tied to his collar.

'I'm a vigilante, Kimchi. I stalk the dark streets of London, ridding the city of evil and preventing crime. What I really need is a vicious attack dog. At least act like a Rottweiler even if you can't be one.'

An old woman passes by us. She sees me chatting away and gives us a wide berth.

'Maybe you're good for something,' I grunt, turning up the path towards the address I have for Lisa's ex. There's no doorbell this time so I rap loudly. I wait for a few minutes but there's no answer. I knock again.

The net curtains to the house next door twitch but, other than that, there's no response. I gnaw on the inside of my cheek and hop over the small fence. Adrian might not be home but his neighbour may be able to help me track him down. I have no desire to spend any more time in suburbia than is absolutely necessary.

I knock with a polite rat-a-tat. Nobody answers. I try again, a little more insistently. When there's still no sound of someone coming to answer, my eyes narrow. Alison Johnson was keen enough to speak to me; maybe it's just the residents of this street who are shy of visitors.

I flip open the letterbox. 'Hello! Can I speak to you for a moment? I won't take up much of your time.'

Silence answers me. I wasn't imagining the movement; someone is definitely home. Kimchi waits patiently, the washing line trailing behind him. He may be able to pull off restraint but I can't be arsed. I step back and launch a kick, slamming my foot into the centre of the door. I don't use enough strength to break it down; it wouldn't do me any good if I did as I can't enter a residence without being given permission first. The loud noise and vibrations across the door frame will make sure I'm not ignored, though.

'What do you want?' a female voice calls out.

I bend down and open the letterbox, peering through. A woman is standing in the hallway. I squint to get a better look. She's well dressed and pretty, although her shoulders are hunched. I'd put that down to my implied threat of violence if it weren't for the harsh bruise across her cheek-bone. When she sees me looking, she draws back so she's out of sight.

'I'm looking for your neighbour,' I shout. 'Adrian Leeman. It's urgent that I speak to him. It's about the disappearance of his ex-girlfriend.'

'He's not in.'

Which is why I'm thumping on your door, love, I think. I manage to bite my tongue. 'Do you know where he is?'

'Out of town at some arts festival in the country. He'll be back tomorrow. Now please go away or I'll call the police.'

I stand up. I got the answer I wanted. I look over at Kimchi and he wags his tail. 'Let's hang around here for a little longer,' I say to him. 'Just in case someone else decides to show up.'

I pull back from the doorway and return to Leeman's door. I sit down on the front step and wait. I'll give it an hour.

In the end, it's less than half that time. A gleaming car pulls up outside and a middle-aged man walks out, car keys still in his hand. I get to my feet and wave to him. 'Excuse me?'

He glances over. 'Yes?'

I smile prettily and get closer. 'I'm looking for Adrian. Have you seen him?'

'He's away for the next few days.' The man might be well dressed but there's a strong whiff of alcohol. I tut to myself. Drinking and driving. He peers at me. 'You're that vampire. The famous one.'

I give him a curtsey. 'At your service.'

He grunts. 'It's about time someone did something about all the crime in this city.' He jerks his head at Adrian's door. 'I'm not surprised he's mixed up in something dodgy. I always had my suspicions about him.'

My eyes drift down. His knuckles are slightly bruised. 'You've hurt yourself,' I comment.

He moves his hands behind his back. 'It's nothing. I tripped and fell the other day.'

I cock my head. 'If you tripped and fell then your palms would be bruised, not your knuckles.'

His face takes on an ugly cast. 'What are you suggesting?' I look over at his house then back at him. He snarls. 'Whatever she told you, she's lying.'

I lick my lips. 'Is she now?'

'She's depressed,' he starts to blunder. 'She makes up stuff.'

I'm tired of his talking. I grab him by the lapels and heft him up into the air. He's heavier than he looks so I let go. He flies into Adrian Leeman's door, his head crashing against it with what sounds like a painful thump.

'Oops.' I step over to him and bend down. 'I'm so sorry. Did that hurt?'

He groans. 'What the fuck are you doing?'

I sidle backwards and kick him in the groin, not hard enough to maim him but enough to make sure he's limping for a good few days. He doubles up. I sidle round once more and grab the tuft of hair at his forehead.

'Eww. This is pretty greasy. You should wash your hair more often,' I tell him. Then I slam the base of my palm into his cheek, at the exact spot where he hit his own wife. 'You know what I'm going to say, right?'

'Fuck off.'

I roll my eyes. This guy just doesn't know when to quit. I lean down further until my breath is against his jugular. My fangs scrape his skin, nipping until there's a bead of blood. I flick out my tongue and lick. Ugh. Too much alcohol in his bloodstream and it's not even good alcohol. If I were guessing, I'd say he's been chugging down cheap rum. Perhaps nasty pirate brew is the preferred tipple of wife beaters these days. Who am I to know?

'Okay, okay! I won't touch her again!' he wheezes.

I lick again. 'The trouble is,' I say, 'I'm not sure I believe you.'

'I'm not lying.'

The door flies open. His wife is standing there. She actually has a rolling pin in one hand and a garlic bulb in the other. 'Leave him alone!'

I straighten up. 'You don't mind that he beats you up?' I enquire. 'Punches your face because you burnt his dinner?'

'He's not doing that! He's not doing anything wrong. He's not a bad person! Unlike you.' There's an unmistakable sneer. 'You're a freak who should be put down!'

I raise my eyebrows. That's rather melodramatic. Kimchi, still hanging at one side, starts to growl. I hush him and clutch my heart. 'Words can hurt, you know. You've wounded me to my soul.' My lips curve upwards.

She blanches but still holds her ground. If she weren't defending her domestic abuser I'd be impressed. Whatever. I glance down at her husband. 'Hit her again,' I say very clearly, 'and I'll drain every last drop of blood you have.' I look back at her. 'And if you try to stop me, I'll do the same to you just for getting in my way.'

I call Kimchi to my side. His body is still rigid with tension but at least the growling has subsided. The wife beater's car keys are lying on the pavement where he dropped them. I pick them up. 'You can collect your car from Brewer Street police station tomorrow,' I tell him.

It's close to where my new flat is without being so near it'll raise suspicion about my address. Not to mention that an awkward conversation with the police about why it's illegally parked in front of their station in the first place will do him good. More than anything though, 'borrowing' his car will save me a heap of time.

IF I'D THOUGHT that there would be some lingering trace of X which would make Kimchi nervous about entering new territory, I was sorely mistaken. He rushes into the apartment with a delighted yip before I even step across the threshold. There is a loud screech of fear. Either he's located the pizza or Maria doesn't like dogs.

I pad in, trying not to look too amused when I see her on top of the kitchen table. Kimchi is circling round it in delight. He thinks he's made a new friend who's playing a fun game. She thinks she's about to be eaten. I'm tempted to leave them to it – until I spot the dribble of urine. Shit. She really is terrified.

'Kimchi!' I say sharply.

He turns and bounds towards me. I motion him in my direction, dancing away until he follows me into the main bedroom. With one twist, I get him behind me so I can get out and shut him in. He barks delightedly three times before realising this isn't hide and seek after all. Then he starts to paw at the door and whine. Sorry, mate.

Maria is still on top of the kitchen table. It's as if she's frozen in place. 'It's alright,' I say softly. 'He won't come near you now.'

She doesn't move an inch. I get closer and, ignoring her flinch, take hold of both her hands. Bit by bit, I coax her down. She's shaking violently. When her feet are finally on the floor again and she looks at the table and the stain on its top, she cowers as if I'm about to strike her.

'Don't worry about it.' Her expression doesn't change. 'Seriously, Maria. That's why some clever person with too much time on their hands invented cleaning products.' She still remains terrified and I sigh. 'You don't understand me and I'm being too smart-arsed.' I look into her eyes. 'The dog is Kimchi. He is friendly. He will not hurt you.'

She starts unconsciously rubbing her arm. My eyes follow the movement, noting the thick, ropy scars etched into her skin there. The ones that don't look dissimilar to dog bites. I bite my lip. 'Those bastards really did a number on you, didn't they? I should have snapped Malpeter's neck when I had the chance.'

Her teeth clench. 'Not him. Not Malpeter.'

I watch her. 'Someone else then. Someone worse.' Maria nods imperceptibly. 'Can you tell me who?'

She shuts down. I'm not likely to get anything else out of her tonight. I pat her arm and lead her into the bathroom, all but throwing her underneath the shower. Once she's clean and returned to the apparent safety of the spare bedroom, I release Kimchi from his temporary incarceration and go in search of a bad lawyer.

HARRY D'ARGNEAU IS in his usual spot in his usual bar. He doesn't see me approach but the bartender certainly does. While Kimchi settles down in the corner, I hop up onto the nearest stool and a martini is immediately pushed in my direction.

'On the house.'

I raise my eyebrows but don't comment. Once upon a time being a vampire was enough to get me thrown out of here. Now it seems I'm back in favour.

'You're doing good things,' the barman says unnecessarily, as D'Argneau finally registers my presence. 'My cousin's car was nicked last week and the police did nothing.' He gestures in frustration. 'Just signed his insurance report and said they'd look into it.'

'I don't have time to investigate carjackings.'

'I'm not asking you to. I know there are other crimes that you can stop.' He meets my gaze. 'We need someone like you.'

I keep my body still, forcing myself not to shift around in discomfort. It's not the first time in the last couple of months that someone has stated their approval of my actions. I've also had just as many hissed comments of disapproval, although those people think they're being smart by not confronting me directly. It doesn't sit well with me, though. I'm not responsible for the entire damn city.

The barman takes the hint and moves away. D'Argneau eyes me with something akin to glee. 'The Red Angel,' he breathes. 'Good to see you.'

'Don't call me that,' I snap.

He shrugs. 'As you wish. I wouldn't want to piss you off.'

I suck in air through my teeth in an obvious sign of irritation. D'Argneau is unconcerned. He takes out his phone and holds it up. I waste no time in sliding it out of his grasp before he can do anything with it.

'No,' I say clearly. 'No photos. I'm not the poster child for your law firm.'

He folds his arms. 'So why are you here then? Old times' sake?'

I slide over a single golden pound coin. 'I need a lawyer.' I try to ignore the delight that flashes across his face.

'You want confidentiality.'

I nod. 'I do.'

'You realise it only goes so far? Legal privilege only occurs in professional conversations and it's nullified if those conversations are for the purpose of committing a crime.' His expression turns serious. 'That includes someone planning to commit a crime to stop a crime.'

I just look at him. I'm not stupid. D'Argneau purses his lips and pockets the money. 'Very well. You are now my client.'

I tilt up my chin. 'Don't tell anyone.'

'Of course not,' he replies smoothly.

I harden my voice. 'I mean it. I realise you may want to use this as an advertising opportunity, or to bolster your own reputation, but it'll cause more problems for you than it's worth.'

'I represent one of the vampire Families, Bo. I don't think Lord Stuart would be impressed to know that the most famous bloodguzzling rogue since Jack the Ripper is on my books as well.' He smiles. 'My witch clients wouldn't be very happy either.'

I study him, eventually deciding that he's on the level. For once. I jerk my head over to a small table in the corner. The music in here might be loud but that doesn't mean we might not be overhead by anyone hovering nearby or wandering up for a drink. D'Argneau bobs his head in agreement.

'Why do you keep coming here?' I ask. 'The floor's sticky, the drinks are expensive and the music is bad.' I glance over at the empty dance floor. 'Unless you enjoy a bit of a boogie, that is.'

'You didn't come here to ask me about my social prefer-ences,' D'Argneau says, settling down into his new chair and neatly side-stepping my question. 'What do you want?'

'I think *all* the Families are changing their own rules.'

He leans back. 'In what respect?'

'Recruitment. They know that with Medici's new vamps, they're outnumbered. In order to keep the playing field even, they're going to match him, bloodguzzler for bloodguzzler.'

'Interesting theory.'

'I need it confirmed.'

'Then ask your little love bunny. You don't need me.'

I glare at him. 'If you're referring to Michael, our relation-ship is not like that. Not any longer. Increasing the vampire population is a big deal and I need to know whether the rest of the legal system will permit it.'

'You mean the human legal system. The vampiric legal system doesn't.'

I don't bother answering. We both already know that the most basic of vampire law is being run through with a bloody scythe. It's been that way since Medici decided to fling open his doors to all and sundry and ignore centuries of tradition. In the past, the other Families would just have assassinated him and moved on. Up till now Medici has been too canny to allow that – and he's also becoming too strong. Admittedly, the vast majority of his Family are now weak recruits so the other four Families could probably destroy them but Medici's strong numbers mean the cost in lives would be high. For Gully, Stuart, Montserrat and Bancroft to match Medici in recruitment would make a kind of sense to solve the immediate issues but there would be far-reaching – and potentially devastating – consequences.

D'Argneau runs a hand through his hair. 'You vampires don't answer to human law, Bo, you know that.'

'But there must be a breaking point. Otherwise, the Families could decide to recruit the whole damn country and no one would lift a finger. There must be something written down somewhere, even if it's centuries old.'

He sighs. 'There might be something.' The cautious note in his voice suggests he already knows of it. For whatever reason, he doesn't seem to want to tell me. That can only mean he's already been commissioned to search for the answer by someone else, probably the Stuart Family.

I drum my fingers on the table top. 'Medici managed to circumnavigate a lot of complaints when he opened up recruitment by stating that all his guzzlers would accede to human law. I doubt things will remain as calm when the rest of the Families get in on the act.'

D'Argneau laughs harshly. 'No matter what Medici has said, people are still unhappy.'

'Public opinion matters hugely to the Families,' I agree. 'But three months ago the anti-vamp camp was close to rioting. Now there are virtually no objections, other than tabloid grumbles. I can't believe that all those humans who were so keen to leave burning crosses on Family doorsteps and march in the streets are now going to sit back while the vampire population quadruples. It's like the entire country is holding its breath and waiting for something else to happen.'

'Some say that it's because everyone really wants to be recruited, no matter what they state to the contrary.'

It's certainly a workable theory. Until very recently, vampires were glamourised to the point of ridiculousness. People up and down the country clamoured to be recruited. Plenty still possess that desire – the ease with which Medici expanded his numbers proves that – but I'm not buying it. I saw with my own eyes how people were and how venomous they'd grown towards the Families. For all that antipathy to have melted away doesn't make sense.

'Has Stuart said anything to you?'

D'Argneau frowns at me. 'I represent Stuart and I represent you. You wouldn't want me to go running to him and blabbing all your secrets.'

'You made it pretty clear last time we spoke that you represented Stuart in name only.'

He stands up. 'Let's just say he's starting to trust me.'

I narrow my eyes. What does that mean? Before I can ask him more, however, he wanders back to his original seat by the bar. I curse under my breath and follow him. 'What are you doing?' I ask. 'I'm not finished.'

'Bo, this is my time. I'm enjoying my drink. I love my job but even I need a break.' He gives me a meaningful look. 'I'm going to be here until three.' He lifts up his phone from where I'd dropped it and makes a show of turning it off. 'I don't want to be bothered by anything. I'm also too drunk to drive, so take my car keys for me.' He reaches into his pocket and dangles them in my direction. Slowly, I take hold of the key ring and frown at him. He takes another sip. 'Don't lose them. My office keys are on there too. It'll be a pain in the arse if I have to get another set cut.' I look at him. He smiles. 'How is your grandfather doing now?'

'Same,' I mutter.

'I thought I might go and visit him. I know he's in Brighton Hospital but which ward is he in?'

I don't answer. D'Argneau flashes me another smile. I pocket the keys, grab Kimchi and leave.

CHAPTER 5

LEGAL ACTION

D'Argneau's office sits in a large gleaming building that's all style and no substance. Unfortunately the same can't be said for the tired-looking doorman who immediately recognises both Kimchi and me. Not because of my fame as the Red Angel but because last time I was here I set Kimchi on him in order to gain access to the upper floors. As soon as I push open the glass door, his eyes widen and he comes out from behind the desk.

'We meet again,' I call out, plastering a cheesy grin on my face.

'You can't be here.'

I lift my eyebrows. 'Why ever not?'

'I got into a lot of trouble when I let you in last time. Why do you think I'm working the graveyard shift now?' His expression is taut.

'You didn't exactly let me in. I didn't give you much choice in the matter.'

'It doesn't matter.' He holds up his palms as if to ward me off. 'You can't come any closer.'

I take a deliberate step forward. 'Can't I?'

'I mean it,' he babbles. 'If you do...'

His protest is interrupted by the squeal of an alarm. I cock my head. 'Your company has upgraded their security.'

His shoulders sag. 'I tried to tell you.'

Kimchi pants in excitement. Apparently my dog remembers our last encounter as well as the doorman does. I lay a hand on his coat and his quivering energy subsides slightly but his ears still remain pricked and alert.

I wander up to the doorman. His nostrils flare in obvious fear but he doesn't move. At the last second I veer off and hop onto the desk, perching myself on the edge with my legs dangling. He exhales loudly. I reach into my jacket and take out another lollipop. This one is blue.

'What do you think?' I ask, waving it in his direction. 'Blueberry?'

He stares at me like I'm a mad woman. I unwrap it and take an experimental lick. Then I shake my head. 'Raspberry. That's ridiculous. I mean, when have you ever actually seen a blue raspberry?' He whispers something to himself. I cup a hand to my ear. 'I didn't catch that. Speak up.'

'Rubus leucodermis,' he says. 'White-bark raspberry. It's where the colour comes from. The fruit is more black than blue, and blue dye is still added to things like that, but it helps to differentiate from strawberry-flavoured sweets.'

I stare at him. 'No shit.'

He looks away, uncomfortable under my gaze. 'I read a lot.'

A van pulls up outside and four men jump out wearing army-style camouflage. They appear to be carrying some kind of silvered weaponry. As all four turn in my direction, I frown. 'Do you think they're carrying silver because they believe I'm a werewolf in disguise?'

'They're specially adapted tasers,' the doorman informs me, backing away. 'They've been developed by...'

'Let me guess,' I say drily, 'by Magix.' The vast magical store possesses little love for vampires. They were never very keen on us but after I put their CEO behind bars they seemed to become even less enamoured. In reality it's all about their bottom line; if there's a market for something, they'll manufacture and sell it. I'm not exactly surprised that people are on the lookout for anything that'll stop a vampire. Even if the protests have subsided, we're still considered dangerous. 'Why won't they just give you one? You could have zapped me the moment I opened the door.'

He doesn't answer, just scoots further back against the wall.

I nod to myself. 'They don't trust you.' Idiots. I flick a look at Kimchi. His hackles are raised and he's growling at the men. He's smarter than he looks.

Two of the men hang back while another two stride in, the vampire tasers pointed in my direction. They take up position on either side of the door. I pop the lollipop into my mouth and watch.

'Leave,' the one to the left growls. I smile sweetly at them. 'We're not going to ask you twice.'

I take the lollipop back out and wave it in their direction. 'You know,' I tell them, 'chocolate used to be my teeth-rotting food of choice. Now I'm trying out new things. It's never a good idea to get stuck in a rut. This is raspberry flavour.' I glance back at the doorman. 'What did you say it's called? Rubus something?'

They raise their weapons; apparently they're not very chatty. I keep an eye on their hands. The moment I see their tendons tighten, I push myself up on my hands and somersault into the air. Two sizzling bolts of electricity smack into the wall behind me. I land back down on my feet. 'That wasn't very polite.'

The door opens again and the other two goons rush in. Four

against one. They're all burly, all armed, and all over six feet tall. I like those odds.

Kimchi's quivering focus remains pinpointed on the doorman. Make that four against two. I whistle and jerk my head in the direction of the nearest taser-holding man. For once, Kimchi understands, wheeling round and leaping towards him with his teeth flashing. He latches onto his arm and the man squeals like a girl at a Justin Bieber concert. The taser clatters to the ground. Kimchi growls and digs in harder, causing the man's blood to splatter round the pair of them in an arc. The dog has got this one. That just leaves three.

Another bolt of light zaps towards me. I throw myself down into a roll to avoid it but it nicks the edge of my shoulder and I feel a shot of stunning pain that sets my senses on fire. I jump back to my feet and crick my neck with a smile.

When I first moved into X's apartment and I was waiting for him to give me an assignment, I had little to do but cool my heels. I freely admit I spent two entire nights wedged on the sofa watching crappy television – including an old Steven Seagal movie where he managed to take out six assailants with some impressive hand-to-hand skills. Ever since I saw it, I've been wanting to try it out myself to see if it was mere Hollywood artifice or actually possible. As the man on the right rushes me, I prepare myself.

Using the balls of my feet, I feint left when he's barely inches from me. The floor is shiny so, when he doesn't slam into me as expected, his shoes skid and he goes flying. I spin round and vault forward, grabbing his collar and heaving him round in the air. The initial grab is difficult – I'm fighting against the laws of physics after all – but with a few hefty swings, I gain the momentum I require. A second later, I'm tossing him headfirst into his nearest companion, ten-pin bowling style. Strike!

The sound they make when they crash to the ground is

quite extraordinary. I waste no time in flinging myself at the pair of them and wresting their weapons from them. I point both tasers at them and fire. There's a slight groan from the man who is pinned down but nothing else happens. The remaining goon laughs coldly. I wrinkle my nose. I guess the damned things only work on vampires. Magix knows their stuff. Unfortunately.

As the weapons are useless to me but could still do me some damage, I quickly bend both barrels to render them fully incapacitated. While I'm doing that, idiot number four takes his next shot. I duck just in time. The electricity – or whatever the hell it is – only just misses me. I'm almost disappointed but it's probably just as well. Even though it only just skimmed my flesh, the shot that hit my shoulder is causing me considerable difficulties. The longer this fight goes on, the more numb my arm grows. I quite like pain but numbness isn't something that helps.

He resets the weapon and points it towards me once more. I get ready to dodge the shot but there's nothing more than a hollow click. Ha. Now it's my turn to laugh. The man recovers quickly, throwing the taser aside in favour of attacking me with his fists.

'Give it up,' he snarls, spittle flying into my face as he lands a hefty right hook. 'You can't win.'

'On the contrary,' I tell him, drawing back my head then slamming it forward into the bridge of his nose. 'I think I already have.'

He staggers backwards, falling against a door which swings open. I move over to finish the job but he's not done yet. From his sprawled position, he grabs the edge of the door and hurls it in my direction. This time I'm not quick enough and it smashes into my side.

'Ouch, that hurt.' I grin broadly. I'm rewarded with the first flicker of fear from my target. I leap forward, pinning him to the ground with my legs. His arms flail upwards, his fists clenched, but I dodge them easily. As delighted goosebumps rise up across my skin, his fear turns to pure terror.

I permit my fangs to grow then curve my head down to take a good long sip. The two men on the floor behind me have managed to get up and each of them grabs one of my arms from behind, hauling me off their buddy. I kick my legs upwards, wrenching my body away. This is becoming like whack-a-mole and, like all overplayed games, it's starting to lose its appeal.

I jump over the man who's fallen in the doorway. Lurking in the darkness behind him is a huge industrial floor-polisher. No wonder the floor is so shiny. I pluck the plug from where it's neatly coiled, pivot and run forward, holding the wire tightly in one hand. While the three men gape at me, I loop it round them and yank.

'Kimchi!' There's another muffled growl. I pat my thigh. 'Bring him here. Good boy!'

Kimchi's eyes are large and his tail is wagging as if he's having the time of his life. He has absolutely no desire to do as I ask. He simply shakes his head as his captive continues valiantly to try to free himself. He's not going to manage it. Those jaws are pretty damn powerful.

With an exasperated sigh, I circle my three goons one more time to ensure that the wire is tight round them. Then I drag them towards Kimchi and their companion. If the mountain won't come to Mahomet...

They try to dig in, first with their hands and then their feet, but the cleaners of this place have done far too good a job of the floor. The men slide easily towards where I want them to go.

'Kimchi,' I say, in my sternest dog-handler voice, 'drop.' His ears prick and he looks at me. 'You heard me. Drop the nasty man.'

His mouth opens revealing a frankly disgusting mixture of dog saliva and goon blood. I look at the damage he's caused and raise my eyebrows. I'm not sure there's a surgeon in the world who'll be able to repair that.

I pull hard on the large polisher, giving myself more wire to work with. Once I have what I need, I throw it around the blooded mess of a man, attaching him to his three other friends. I think he's actually relieved; he doesn't try to struggle or protest, he just watches me with pain-filled eyes.

I secure the four of them together in the centre of the floor, double-checking that my knotting is good enough to keep them in place, and then I fold my arms and admire my handiwork. Four doleful faces stare up at me just as the phone on the doorman's desk starts to ring. Leaving Kimchi to drool threateningly over my captives, I crane my head round and give the doorman a pointed look. He reluctantly gets up from the floor and slides over, picking up the receiver and listening before holding it out to me.

'It's for you.'

I jog over and take it. 'Shiny office block,' I say in my best receptionist voice. 'How may we be of assistance?'

Harry D'Argneau's voice fills the line, barely audible above the thump of familiar, ear-wrenching music. 'I should mention that my building has changed its security measures recently. Just in case you were thinking about dropping by.'

'How kind of you to mention it,' I drawl.

'No problem.'

I roll my eyes. 'One would think that with a large law firm whose clients include an entire bloodguzzling Family, your landlord would be friendlier towards vampires.'

'I go to the Stuart Family, Bo. They don't come to me. There are strict stipulations against tribers wandering in unannounced. But I can't help it if a nasty vampire steals my keys and uses them to gain access.'

'If I didn't know better, I'd say you were trying to set me up.'

'Bo,' he chides, 'we're friends. I wouldn't do that.'

Yeah, right. 'I'm not sure "friends" is an appropriate term to describe our relationship.'

'Would-be lovers then.'

'Don't push your luck.'

He laughs. 'I have no doubt that you'll be able to circumnavigate the new system. Besides, I'm trying to expand onto another floor and the landlord is being … difficult. It wouldn't hurt for him to realise I have friends in high places.'

'You're using that word again. I'm your client, not your bestie.'

'Sorry,' he says, although he sounds anything but.

I sigh and hang up. I glance back over at the trussed-up goons. 'Who owns this building?' I ask.

Nobody answers. I tut and stroll over, grabbing the nose of the nearest one and pulling him up. 'Politeness costs nothing.' I twist and he yelps in pain. 'Now,' I say, repeating myself, 'who owns this building?'

'Barry Moran.'

'Moron?'

'Moran.'

I shrug. 'Daft name.' I release him and he drops back to the floor with a grunt. I head back to the desk and locate a small black book in a drawer. Barry Moran's name, address and phone number are listed first. How handy. I dial quickly.

'This had better be good,' a gruff voice answers, after several rings. 'It's the middle of the fucking night.'

'Mr Moron, how lovely to talk to you.'

'Who is this?'

'Bo. Bo Blackman. You've probably heard of me.' I look up,

spotting the CCTV camera in the corner. I walk over and wave at it. I'm betting that Mr Moron is the kind of guy who has a bank of live feeds sent to his own home. The moment he saw the caller ID, he'll have checked the video. No doubt he's watching right now. For good measure, I point in the direction of the huddled security team and grin.

There's a moment of silence. Then he speaks. 'You're on my property, Ms Blackman.'

'That's true. But I have permission from one of the lease-holders.' I reach into my pockets and pull out D'Argneau's keys, jangling them so he can hear. 'Setting up an anti-vampire security system smacks of racism, Mr Moron.'

'It's Moran,' he snaps. 'And I'm not racist.'

I drum my fingers against my leg. This is taking more time than it should. 'Let me guess. Some of your best friends are vampires.'

'No, they're not. I'm not racist because bloodguzzlers aren't a race. You're not born, you're made. Now get the hell out of my building.'

'I will when I've done what I need to do. But I wanted to talk to you first. You know, you should look into your security team. They're not very good at what they do. And I've not done anything wrong. They attacked me without provocation. I'm not sure that would go down too well with all my vampire buddies.' Not that I have any but he doesn't need to know that.

At least Moron catches on quickly. 'What do you want?'

'I want you to call off your dogs. The next batch of idiots you send won't get off so easily and you'll end up with a lot of blood on your hands. In return I will stay no longer than...' I check the clock on the wall '...an hour.'

'Fine.'

'There's no need to be so curt,' I purr. I glance over and check the doorman's name tag. 'I also want Joe Timmons to have his choice of shifts. Let him out of the doghouse. If he wants to work days, he can. You will not punish him for events outside his control. I won't like it if I come back and find out differently.'

'Very well,' Moron snaps.

That was remarkably easy. 'You're not just telling me what I want to hear, are you? You know, it's incredibly unwise to leave your personal details lying around where anyone can see them. Especially when you live in such a nice neighbourhood as Westminster. Princess Road, isn't it?'

He sucks in a breath. 'Timmons will get what he wants.'

I smile. 'Good.' I pause then shrug to myself. Whatever. 'You should probably seriously consider Harry D'Argneau's application to rent out more space, too,' I tell him. I don't really care. 'Anyway, lovely talking to you.' I blow the camera a kiss and hang up.

The doorman, Joe Timmons, stares at me. 'I'm sorry you ended up with shitty shifts because of my actions.' I jerk my head at the bank of lifts. 'I'm going upstairs now. I won't be long.'

He nods weakly. I pat his arm and walk off, gesturing to Kimchi to join me.

'Wait,' he says.

I half turn. 'Yes?'

He swallows. 'Thank you.'

I bestow another smile on him. 'You're much nicer than your boss,' I tell him. 'It really does pay to be polite – especially to people who have sharper teeth than you.' And with that I leave him in peace.

The truth is that, if I'd really wanted to, I could have found a way to sneak inside and break into D'Argneau's office but there's something far more satisfying about strolling in through the front door. Though I have to admit that using his keys to open the inner entrance doors once I've reached his floor does leave less of a mess.

I wander in, taking a free sweet from a crystal bowl on the receptionist's desk and making a mental note to tell D'Argneau to get in some blue raspberry. I ignore all the other closed doors and head straight for the back where I know D'Argneau's own office is housed. Kimchi decides to investigate the small galley kitchen. I let him; he deserves it.

In less than a minute, I'm sitting in D'Argneau's swivel chair, staring irritably at the photos on the wall. He's always been a glory hound and has never attempted to make a secret of that fact. Seeing my own face beaming at me from a framed photo in pride of place doesn't sit well with me. Eventually I rip my eyes away. I'm here to do a job after all.

I take a bit of time to open up various drawers and peer inside. Other than an array of legal pads and different coloured pens, there's not much of interest. After a few minutes rummaging, I stand up and head for the row of filing cabinets instead.

There are three large cabinets dedicated solely to the Stuart Family. Considering it's been less than six months since he took them on as clients, D'Argneau has done well to have garnered this much information on them. I flick through various reports of dull accounts and outside interests. I also look for any mention of the Montserrat Family, my curiosity about Michael still lingering despite everything that's occurred between us. There's not much worth reading but I am fascinated that D'Argneau is so old school and chooses to keep his records in paper form rather than locked into a computer. He does have some inkling of what hackers like Rogu3 are capable of; maybe he thinks his files are more secure like this. I shrug and finally pull out what I'm looking for. Recruitment files.

Unsurprisingly, the folder is very slim. There certainly aren't any Stuart names here. Each vampire Family makes a big deal out of keeping their recruits' identities secret. I suspect it's more from tradition than out of any real need – not to mention that they enjoy being shrouded in mystery because they seem to think that being enigmatic adds to their power. Whatever the reason, there's no way they'd hand over any such lists to D'Argneau, no matter what else he does for them. When it comes to human law, though, they appear to be less circumspect. There's a copy of a report they commissioned D'Argneau to write. Unfortunately it confirms all of my suspicions: they wanted to know how far they could push their own recruitment before the human government would act.

D'Argneau has certainly done his due diligence. He estimated that, in terms of longevity, each vampire life is worth 3.4 times that of a human life. With each Family's numbers previously capped at five hundred, their population is a drop in the ocean when compared to the daemons, the witches or the humans. Using various mathematical formulae, along with what appears to be the greasing of several pairs of hands belonging to members of Parliament, D'Argneau recommended that numbers could be pushed up to eleven thousand per Family before legal action was taken against them. It'll still mean that the vampires are a tiny percentage of the UK population. I scowl.

Five hundred is a small, manageable number. It means the Families are close-knit and their feelings of loyalty are incredibly strong, even if most of those feelings are engendered as a result of the initial turning process. Everyone has a voice and everyone has a place. To expand the population further – and especially to eleven thousand – would destroy all that. There will be more in-fighting. The need for fresh human blood will grow.

D'Argneau mentions that in his report and suggests that a

fund be started to cover any necessary costs. Humans on the poverty line can be encouraged to sell their blood. He's even built in a potential insurance policy for when accidents happen. *When*; not *if*. Further risk analysis includes dissension from the witches and the Agathos daemons. D'Argneau points out that their numbers are far greater, so the Families already have a ready-made counter argument.

Kakos daemons like X are an unknown quantity. At least D'Argneau encourages caution in that area, suggesting that the Families stop blaming Kakos daemons for unsanctioned kills. Provoking them in that manner would not be intelligent, not when the vampires are potentially seeking to grow their own strength.

I flick through to the back of the report. There's an appendix on the state of the human protestors. D'Argneau notes, as I have, that they have been quiet recently, and concludes that the most vociferous anti-vampire voices have realised they're fighting a losing battle. His reasoning is sketchy; I can't help wondering if it's because he thinks the Families themselves are responsible. A year ago I'd have said no way. But then a year ago, I'd have said the Families would never look to recruit in such large numbers.

The only truly helpful information is a list of around three hundred names, apparently of the protestors who've mysteriously disappeared. I hadn't realised there were so many of them. I scan down it, my heart in my mouth. I've hurt a lot of humans and tribers recently but I can honestly say that each one deserved it. To kill off someone just because they are exercising their right to free speech is a completely different matter. I don't want to believe it. I've made the mistake in the past of jumping to conclusions. These days I can't afford to do that and I'm much more circumspect and diligent before I make up my mind – but I can't escape the gnawing worry.

Using my phone, I take a photo of each page and carefully return the report to where I found it. I wrap my arms around myself. I understand that Medici is forcing the Families' hands in terms of recruitment but surely their combined might could help them to find an alternative route? I can't believe this is the only way out.

I'm going to have to confront Michael. The other Family heads look up to him. If I can change Michael Montserrat's mind about expanding his numbers, then I can change the others' minds too. I tighten my jaw. And until I have absolute proof that he and the others have something to do with the protestors' disappearances, I'll keep quiet, no matter how hard it might be. I owe him that, if nothing else.

CHAPTER 6

DIVING FOR DETAILS

I'm halfway down the corridor, looking for Kimchi, when I feel a change in the atmosphere. I'm no longer completely alone. I wrinkle my nose. X is checking up on me a hell of a lot lately. I wonder if it's because he's pissed off that I'm focusing a lot of my efforts on Medici rather than cleaning up the streets of petty criminals. He can go and screw himself, I decide.

I round the corner, finally spotting him in the reception area. Kimchi is on his back, presenting his smooth belly to X like a true submissive.

'What are you doing here?'

X throws out his arms in an expansive gesture. 'I thought I'd see how you were getting on.'

'As we've already discussed, I'm not your pet.' I eye Kimchi as if he's a traitor. 'Neither is my dog.'

'Bo, you're far too sensitive. I just wanted to make sure that you weren't going to waste this opportunity.'

I narrow my eyes. I may be working for X right now but it doesn't change the fact that he's a Kakos daemon and I can't trust him. He could end my life with one crook of his pinky, after all. Admittedly, that might be a good reason to stay on his good side but I'm not sure I care that much any more. Life is cheap. Even mine. 'What opportunity?'

He shakes his head and tuts. 'Your little human lawyer has a lot of tribers on his books. And a lot of humans who partake in, shall we say, less than savoury activities.'

I just stare at him. He rolls his eyes. 'Do I have to spell it out? You work for me. Your role is to put a halt to the criminal activity that's happening on the streets of London. Here's your chance to get a long list of many of the perps instigating those activities.'

'I understood what you meant,' I sniff. 'I can't do that though.'

He raises his eyebrows. 'Why ever not?'

'The files are private. I can't break that privilege. It wouldn't be proper.'

X laughs, the sound echoing down the empty corridor. His amusement rankles but he's right. Damn him. 'Maybe I was wrong. Maybe you're not the best choice for a vigilante.'

I tilt up my chin. 'You can always find someone else.' Other than the fact that I'll need to move home yet again, it doesn't bother me. I don't need X. Without his intervention, I'll be freer to focus on the witches. The thought is incredibly satisfying. I fold my arms and smile.

'Enough of that. You need me.' His tone of voice hasn't altered but I'm pretty certain I'm not imagining the tightness around his mouth.

Actually, I think, it seems like you *need me more.* X's mouth thins further. Now it's my turn to laugh. 'Chillax,' I tell him. 'You know I'm going to do what you've suggested.'

'Chillax? What kind of language is that?'

I smirk. 'Sometimes you remind me of my grandfather.' A

cold smile spreads across his face, making me instantly regret my words. I hold up a single finger. 'Don't. He is off limits.'

X gives me a tiny bow but he still looks amused. I grit my teeth. Unwilling to continue this conversation, I spin on my heel and return to the filing cabinets.

Although I'm not in the slightest bit afraid of what a two-bit loser like Barry Moran might do if I overstay my so-called welcome, I did promise I wouldn't be any longer than an hour – and I'm a woman of my word. I scan several files and jot down details of the worst offenders, stuffing the notes into my back pocket. With less than five minutes left on the clock, I return to Kimchi. The dog is now alone, staring mournfully at the lift as if he misses X's presence. There's also a rather sizeable splodge of drool on D'Argneau's expensive carpet. I grin.

'Good work, Kimchi.' His tail thumps and he gets up to his feet, eyeing me hopefully. I nod. 'Yup. We are out of here.'

Foxworthy is standing with his shoulders hunched, gazing out over the glittering expanse of the Thames. There are several other police officers nearby, all busying themselves with sifting through the area. A van with ominous lettering on the side advertising the city coroner sits several metres back with its doors flung open.

I peer inside as I wander past. Kimchi gets overly excited and tries to clamber in but the stench of old blood and bleach makes me yank him back. There's no body yet; maybe this is just a false alarm.

I pick my way down to the water's edge. Once or twice, uniformed officers step towards me to halt my progress but every time I turn my face in their direction, recognition of both who and what I am stops them in their tracks.

Foxworthy doesn't turn. 'I might have known you'd show up sooner or later,' he grunts.

'Like a bad penny,' I tell him cheerfully. I give him the once over. 'Trench coat? Really? Are you angling for a part on a cop show?'

His shoulders tighten and his brows snap together into a glower. He's obviously not very happy to see me. That's a shame. We worked together to bring down a pair of serial killers stalking the city and, throughout the course of the investigation, his natural mistrust of me melted into a grudging respect. Any ground I may have made appears to have disappeared now I have my new role as X's stooge. I shouldn't be surprised but that doesn't mean it doesn't rankle.

I step round until I'm facing Foxworthy and stretch out my arms. Then I envelop him in a tight, enthusiastic embrace, burying my face in his chest. 'It's so good to see you!' I burble. 'I've missed you!'

Kimchi is thrilled by the display of positive energy and gets in on the action, leaping up and placing his paws on Foxworthy's back. Other than a faint stiffening, the good inspector doesn't move.

'We should meet more often, you know. Take in a film. Discuss procedure over cupcakes. That kind of thing.'

'Bo,' he says, sounding strained, 'get off me.'

I take pity on him and let go. He folds his arms across his chest. It doesn't stop Kimchi.

'And the dog?'

I whistle. Kimchi ignores me. A line of spittle has dropped from his mouth and is now smearing Foxworthy's coat. It's for the best. Unless you're the kind of person who enjoys exposing their genitals in public, a trench coat is never a good idea. I arch an eyebrow in Foxworthy's direction and shrug. 'I guess he really likes you.'

He scowls. 'What do you want?'

I give up on the melodramatics and get down to business. I tell him the name of the officer in charge of Lisa's case. He squints at me.

'Do you know him?' I ask.

'He's a stickler for the rules.' His eyes flicker to me. 'And he doesn't like bloodguzzlers.'

'Not many people do. The trouble is, he has a few things I want. He's in charge of a missing person's case. Lisa Johnson. I want everything he took from her house and all the file notes.'

'And you think he'll just hand it over?'

I bestow my most patient smile on Foxworthy. 'I think you'll encourage him to do so.'

'Why would I do that?'

'Because we're buddies. Partners. Comrades in arms. Team mates. Associates.' I lean in a bit closer and whisper, 'Friends.'

He inhales deeply, drawing air into his lungs. 'Bo, I like you. You have a good heart for a triber, and we have a history together. But I can't condone what you do. And neither does anyone else in the police. The laws exist for a reason.'

'I'm a vampire. I'm above the law.'

'You know fine well what I mean,' he snaps. He's much angrier than he's letting on.

I study him for a moment, vaguely curious. 'Your knickers really are in a twist,' I comment. 'Why do my activities bother you so much?'

He shoves his hands into his pockets. Kimchi eventually gives up on licking his coat and drops down to examine a leaf, pawing and sniffing it with extraordinary dedication. 'You're not a hero, Bo. You think you're helping by running down perps? All you're really doing is driving the real criminals deeper underground. You're making people more afraid, not less afraid. And what happens when you make a mistake? When you slit the throat of someone who you think deserves it but who simply happens to be in the wrong place at the wrong time?'

I raise my eyebrows, choosing to ignore the fact that I used to believe all that bumph myself. 'Like the police never make mistakes,' I scoff.

He turns away. 'That's why we have due process. What you're doing is wrong. It makes you as much of a criminal as everyone else.'

'There are at least four humans who are alive tonight because of my actions over the last month. I saved their lives. I didn't see any boys in blue on any of those occasions.' A muscle jerks in his cheek. He doesn't answer. 'I don't see you or any of your mates rushing to arrest me either.'

'You know we can't.' He glances back at me. 'That might change though. Even those idiots in power aren't going to let you run amok on the streets doing whatever you want forever.'

I push back my hair. 'Don't you see that's what I want? Vampires shouldn't be above the law. If they weren't, someone would have done something about Medici by now.'

'The way I see it,' he says heavily, 'between Lord Medici and you, you are by far the more dangerous.'

I pat him on the arm. 'Thank you.'

If anything, Foxworthy's demeanour grows even colder. 'You think this is all just a game.'

'No, I don't.' I roll my tongue over my teeth. 'Anyway, you were going to help me get the files on Lisa Johnson.'

'I'm not.'

I smile and pull out the crumpled paper from my back pocket, smoothing it out. I read the first of my hastily made notes. 'How long exactly have the police been looking for David Hellstrom?' I ask.

Foxworthy freezes. 'The Baudelaire Butcher?'

My smile grows. 'I think that's what he's called. How many murders is he responsible for? Eleven?'

'That we know of,' Foxworthy growls.

'What if I could tell you where he is right now?'

'If you knew where he was, you'd go after him yourself. You wouldn't be able to resist.'

I have to admit it's tempting. But I need information and I have to barter for it with something. Besides, what little I know about Hellstrom suggests that he'll never let himself get caught. He'd rather go down in a blaze of bullets than end up inside. Whether I go after him or the police do, the end result will be the same.

'I have every faith that you'll be able to deal with him yourselves. Get me what I need on Lisa Johnson and I'll give you Hellstrom's address.'

Foxworthy desperately wants to tell me to go to hell but he wants Hellstrom more. I'm sure there's a pun in there somewhere. 'Fine,' he snaps, holding out his hand.

I shake my head and laugh. 'Nuh uh. I wasn't born yesterday,' I chide. 'Get me what I need first. Then you get Hellstrom.' My eyes twinkle. 'There's more where he came from too, if you play your cards right.'

Foxworthy balls up his fists for a brief moment before relaxing with what appears to be considerable effort. 'Where can I find you?'

'I'll drop by tomorrow night. I trust twenty-four hours will be long enough for you to get what I need. I assume you won't be hanging around here by then, though.' I look out across the river. The water breaks and a diver's head bobs up, gesturing at something. 'Anyway, why are you here in the middle of the night?'

'A witness saw a body being dumped over the bridge a few hours ago. CCTV confirmed it.'

I frown. 'If it's true, then they're already dead. Why the rush? It'd be much easier to conduct your search in daytime.'

Foxworthy's expression turns to granite. 'Because the description matches Alan Campbell.'

I sift through my memory. That name rings a bell; I snap my fingers as it comes to me. 'The police commissioner's kid? The one who went missing last year?'

'That's right,' Foxworthy says shortly.

'Shit. I'm sorry. I can help...'

'No.'

I can understand that; this is about looking after one of their own. Unless Foxworthy – or the police commissioner himself – asks for my help, I'll keep out of it. 'At least his family will finally get some peace,' I say. Not knowing can be the hardest thing.

Foxworthy throws me a doleful look. 'You don't get it,' he says finally. 'I'd keep it secret, especially from you, but someone's already leaked it to the press so by tomorrow morning the whole world will know.'

'Know what?'

'Alan Campbell doesn't match the victim's description. He matches the perp's.'

My eyes widen. 'Shit.'

'Yeah.'

Another diver appears. From the far bank a motorised boat starts up, searchlights flickering across the river in their direction. 'I guess they've found the body.'

'Yeah,' Foxworthy replies, his mouth set in a grim line. 'I guess so.'

~

I ROUND off my night as I always do, sitting in plain sight right across from the Medici stronghold. For once, I'm less concerned about what Medici is doing than about crossing my fingers that Michael will show up again so I can ask him about recruitment. Unfortunately for me, the street remains silent. I'm not even offered any drinks or nibbles. Poor showing.

Kimchi is beginning to show signs of fatigue, flopping down at my feet and sighing heavily as if he has the weight of the world on his broad doggy shoulders. Feeling sorry for him, I reach down to ruffle his fur. 'It's you and me against the world, buster.' I smile. 'It helps that we both have super powers, though. I'm a vampire with speed, strength and my own natural cunning and you're a world leader in drooling. With that combination, we can't fail.'

He licks my hand. The wind picks up, causing several leaves and a discarded leaflet to skitter past me; the paper has a toothsome, smarmy human politician gazing out from the front page. I recognise his mug from Jonesy's newspaper: Hale something.

I shrug and cast a trained eye across the long shadows where Medici is hiding himself. There's not even a glimmer of light from inside but I know the place is jam-packed with newbie vampires. I stretch out a hand and point towards it, unblinkingly. It's like I'm Babe Ruth. And if anyone inside is watching, it might just make them feel ever so slightly nervous. Right now, I can't ask for much more.

CHAPTER 7

BLAZING SADDLES

I know something is wrong before my eyes open. Kimchi's heavy lump of a body, which had been draped across most of my huge bed while I was squeezed into a tiny corner, has vanished. I can hear him pawing and scraping at the bedroom door, every so often emitting a tiny whine. Even if it weren't for his actions, there's a change to the atmosphere. I can't exactly put my finger on it but it's clear that something is different. It can only be because of Maria.

I rub my eyes and get out of bed, worried that she might have harmed herself. When I catch the low murmur of voices, I stop in my tracks and my eyes narrow. That's not the television. Someone else is here.

My mind whirrs through the possibilities. I know next to nothing about her. She may well have invited someone round. It can't be one of her fellow strippers or prostitutes. The police aren't entirely incompetent; they'll have ensured that all those girls are being well looked after. If there was shouting, I'd assume it was her former boss, the one more evil than Malpeter, who is now after her in revenge. Despite the tingle in the air, there's not enough sense of danger for that.

It could, I suppose, be X. It wouldn't surprise me considering how often he's popping up these days. But I doubt X would take the time to chat to her. As far as I'm aware, he doesn't chat to anyone who's not a fellow Kakos daemon – apart from yours truly – and he was unhappy that I'd brought her back in the first place.

The only other person I can think of who would show up here unannounced is Michael. The thought that he might have tracked me down fills me with wariness. As much as I want to talk to him, I need this safe sanctuary. I don't need him tempting me back round to his side.

I pad silently towards the door, nudging Kimchi out of the way. I press my ear against the wood and listen. I have particularly good hearing – all vampires do – but whoever is out there is well aware of that fact. Both the intruder and Maria are speaking in hushed whispers so I can't tell who it is.

I glance down. Kimchi's ears are pricked and alert and his tail is wagging. I raise my eyebrows at him. 'Can I trust you?' I ask softly. 'Is this really a friend?'

His eagerness doesn't dissipate.

'Michael is not a friend, you know.' I ignore the faint wrench I feel at those words. 'And you should stay away from X.'

Kimchi whines again.

'Fat lot of good you are,' I tell him. I place my hand on the doorknob and carefully ease it open half an inch.

'I like it with the fruit,' Maria says. 'The ... what do you call it? Pie Apple?'

'Ewww! No! Pizza should not have pineapple on it. No way. It's wrong.'

I clench my teeth together so tightly it almost hurts. Unbelievable. Of all the people who should stay away... I fling the door wide open and march out.

Maria scrambles to her feet and backs away, her eyes wide

and her face suddenly pale. Kimchi rushes out from behind me, bowling into Rogu3 and smothering him in an exuberant display of licking. I put my hands on my hips.

'What the hell are you doing here?'

Pinned down as he is, all I can hear is Rogu3's muffled protests. 'Kimchi!' I yell. 'Leave him alone and get back over here!'

Naturally Kimchi completely ignores me. I can only presume it's because the teen hacker tastes good; it's certainly not because any of us should be pleased to see him. I spin round, heading to the kitchen to find some kibble to distract the dog with, just as Maria flees back to the sanctuary of her own room. I curse under my breath.

It only takes the opening of one cupboard for Kimchi to abandon Rogu3 and bound back to me. Before I can also be assaulted by his tongue, I throw the food into a bowl and stalk back out again.

'Let's start that again,' I say, anger rippling down my spine. 'What the hell are you doing here?'

Rogu3 grins and stretches his arms behind his head, propping up his feet on the coffee table. Just because it's the same position I adopted when I was waiting for Jonesy doesn't make it any less irritating. 'Duh. You invited me.'

'No.' I enunciate every word very clearly. 'I did not.'

'You asked me to find out who Maria was. I didn't find anything by the way. You should just ask her.'

Irritation boils through me. 'You were only to contact me through email or text. You cannot be here!'

'Why not?'

I count slowly to ten in my head. 'For one thing it's not safe. For another your parents will go crazy. You're also supposed to be in school.' I throw my hands up in the air. 'You're complicating everything!'

'If you were going to eat me, Bo, you would have done so already. And I don't think Maria is going to hurt me.'

Somehow I think that once she recovers, she's going to be a force to be reckoned with. 'Don't underestimate her,' I say. 'Besides, my landlord is the touchy kind.'

'What's he going to do?' Rogu3 asks. 'Chop off my head for popping round to say hello?'

And eat your heart, I think. 'Rogu3…'

'Hey,' he says, holding up his palms. 'Don't worry about it, Bo. I know you've gone all Grizzly Adams but I'm one of the good guys. I'm your friend.'

I cross my arms. 'You shouldn't be here,' I repeat. 'Working for me almost got you killed.'

'My parents know where I am,' he says quietly.

'Bullshit.'

Rogu3 stands up, his expression earnest. 'It's true.'

'They would as soon drive a wooden stake dipped in holy water through my heart and then serve me up on a bed of roasted garlic as let you come here.'

He frowns. 'Garlic and holy water don't hurt bloodguzzlers.'

'I was making a point,' I mutter.

He meets my eyes. 'You don't have to worry about them.'

'It's not them I'm worried about. It's you.'

Rogu3 steps closer until I'm forced to crane my neck to look at him properly. It's galling that he's so damn tall when he's not even reached the age of consent yet. 'After what happened, there was something inside me.' His hand reaches up to his chest in what I'm almost certain is an unconscious movement. 'I knew it, you knew it and my parents knew it. It was like a darkness.'

I swallow. I know that darkness. 'And you were working on getting it out of your system. You're young, Rogu3.' Painfully so. 'You'll get over it.'

'I know.' His voice is clear and confident. 'But I'm not going to get over it by turning up to French or maths lessons or by sitting in the school cafeteria and eyeing up the girls. I know what's going on in the world. For fuck's sake, Bo, you're all over the news!'

'Don't swear.'

He smiles. 'I know what's going on with Medici as well. He has to be stopped.'

'You're preaching to the converted on that one,' I snort.

'I can help, Bo.' He says the words quietly but he draws himself up. He's changed. I suppose we all have.

'Your parents…'

'They know I'm here. It's not exactly with their blessing but they understand.'

'I don't believe it.'

He shrugs. 'Call them. They came around a bit after you found those men. The ones who hurt me. Even my dad is more … sympathetic towards you.'

Probably because I summarily executed the men who tried to hurt his son. I run a hand through my hair and try a different tack. 'You used to take your education seriously. You're fifteen years old. You can't just drop out of school.'

'I'm still going to take my exams. I'm still planning to go to university. But there are other things I want to do first.'

'No.'

'You said that if I needed anything I was to call you. You made it clear that if I needed help, you would come running.' He tilts up his chin. 'Well, I need help. I need to help you. I need to know I'm doing some good. I need to battle this thing inside me. Make the world a better place and all that jazz.' The corner of his mouth quirks up. 'I know it's all a great big cliché but I want to do this. I *choose* to do this.'

'No.'

'I'm not a child, Bo.'

'Yes, you are.'

He scowls. 'That's exactly what my dad says. Word for word.' He turns on his heel and paces away for several steps. I can hear his quickened, frustrated breath with the sound of Kimchi's chomping in the background. 'I've been approached by someone else,' he says finally.

What the hell? My eyes narrow. 'Who?'

'MI7.' His head drops slightly. 'It's probably against the spy code to tell you but I figure with your grandfather and all, they might give me a bit of a break.'

'MI7 came to you?' My voice is rising. 'To work for them?'

He spins back round to face me, wincing. 'You're shrieking, Bo Peep.'

'I. Am. Not. Shrieking.'

'You kind of are.'

I slam my fist into the wall, ignoring the crack that immediately appears. 'They had no right. You're too young.'

'I'd rather work for you than them.' He smiles. 'I'm not very good with rules and you'll let me do what I want.' When he sees the look on my face, he abruptly backtracks. 'I mean, up to a point. You won't mind if I break a few laws if it's in the name of the greater good.'

'Neither will they. That doesn't mean you should work for them,' I add quickly. I close my eyes briefly. 'Rogu3, you're a genius. You can do whatever you want. Just don't do this.'

'I have to do this. Don't you see that?'

'I'm not part of New Order now, Rogu3. I have no authority. Everything I do is against human law. Sooner or later someone's going to realise that and do something about it. You don't even have vampiric status to protect you. You'll end up behind bars.'

'I know how to cover my tracks. Honestly, I've been doing

this sort of stuff for years. You're not my only client. You are, however, the only one I trust.'

X will hit the roof. First Maria and now Rogu3. He's a Kakos daemon, not the saviour of waifs and strays. As it is, when he finds out that Rogu3 tracked me here, he might make a move against him. I sit down heavily.

'How did you find me?'

'It was pretty hard actually. Why do you think it took me so long to get here? Forty-eight hours to find one damn address! I'm normally much better than that.' He shrugs. 'I must be rusty. I know that Streets of Fire has something to do with it though,' he says, naming the internet company of which X is the head, although not openly. 'Their fingerprints were all over your system and your name. It's lucky you emailed otherwise I'd never have found you.'

I throw him a look. 'Lucky?' He smirks. I take a deep breath. 'Look, I'm not the lone wolf everyone thinks I am. I have a … benefactor who is helping me out.'

Rogu3 rolls his eyes. 'No shit. Unless you won the lottery, you'd never be able to afford this pad. I know your bank balance.'

I shake my head in disbelief. 'Anyway, he might not be very happy that you're along for the ride as well. I'll have to check.'

'That's okay. I can wait. I'm sure when your mysterious benefactor realises who I am, he'll be happy for me to stick around. Go and ask him. It'll give me a chance to get to know Maria better.'

'You should leave her alone. She's been through a lot.'

The smile disappears from his face. 'I know. I can tell.'

I pinch the bridge of my nose. I can't begin to imagine how this conversation with X is going to go. There will be numerous threats of violence and I'm certain he'll tell me to throw Rogu3 out on his ear by the end of it. At least then my conscience will be clear, I suppose. But throw Maria into the mix ... I shake my head again.

I pull out my phone and wave it in Rogu3's direction. 'I'll go and talk to him now,' I say. 'If you get a missed call from me, then you have to take Maria and run. Don't go back to your parents. Don't go back to school. Don't ever try to contact me again. If you do, you'll be dead.' I pause. 'And look after Kimchi. Please.'

'Jeez, Bo. Who exactly do you work for?'

I jab my thumb at him. 'You really don't want to know.' I fix him with a hard look. 'You can still back out.'

He grins. 'No chance.'

I WAIT until I'm back in Lisa Johnson's neighbourhood before I take out my phone to call X. My hands are trembling. This is reckless and stupid but I saw the expression in Rogu3's eyes and I recognise that stubborn streak. He's not going to walk away unless I give him a good reason to. A Kakos daemon strikes me as a pretty good reason. I'm sure will X help me out on this much.

He picks up on the second ring. 'Bo,' he purrs. 'And I thought you wanted me to stay away. Are you missing me already?'

I suck in a breath. 'I have a tiny problem.'

'Problems, I think. The hacker and the whore.' I stiffen at his words. Of course he already knows all about them both. I shouldn't be surprised. 'You know,' he adds conversationally, 'that would make a great film title.'

'I understand you don't want either of them there. Maria will be fine, I'm sure I can find a women's shelter for her if she won't tell me who her family is. Rogu3 won't give up easily though. If you could just scare him off then…'

'Hold your horses. Who says I don't want them around?'

I blink. Er…

'Maybe I've changed my mind. At least as far as those two are concerned anyway. An IT expert of that quality should be working for me. He's grown up a lot since last year. In fact, if you don't want him, I'm certain I can find him a very well-paid position at Streets of Fire. We need more humans of his calibre. And don't forget, it's my blood which is running through his veins.' He chuckles, referring to the fact that I used X's blood to change Rogu3 from his temporary turn as a vampire in order to save his life. 'We're practically family.'

'He's fifteen.'

'So? By the time I was fifteen I had already killed more than…'

'I don't want to know. He's annoying though. And far too curious. He'll seek you out and then you'll be forced to kill him and eat his heart. Then because I'm a vigilante seeking justice for all, I'll have to go after you. In return you'll kill me and you'll be left without a single stooge to do your dirty work for you.'

X laughs. 'That's a lot of assumptions. Keep the kid. In fact, let's do dinner tomorrow night. You, me and him.'

Oh fuck. 'B-but you don't want anyone to know about you.'

'Thanks to you, he already has enough suspicions to fill a cruise ship. Besides, I'll need a back-up plan for when you mess up.'

'No. Absolutely not. You are not using him. It's not fair.'

'You're not six years old, Bo. Fairness as a concept is for fairy tales. Tomorrow night. La Bohème. And bring the girl too. She could probably do with some fattening up. You have my word I won't hurt them – as long as no one else finds out where you live or who I am. If that happens I may just change my mind.'

I choose not to focus on the explicit threat. 'X, wait.' It's too late though; I'm already speaking to dead air. I curse loudly. That was not how I expected things to go. I punch a nearby lamppost. It doesn't hurt enough, so I punch it again. And again and again.

It's some time before I regain my composure. X is too much of an enigma. It's irresponsible of me to draw anyone else into this relationship with him. I know his word counts for a lot; he's a lot like my grandfather in that respect, despite his daemonic nature. But that doesn't mean I want either Rogu3 or Maria to get involved in his machinations.

I tell myself that neither of them has given me a choice. If Maria had any sense, she'd have left by now. If Rogu3 had any sense, he'd have stayed far away. They have their own free will just like anyone else. I drop my hand, ignoring the blood now dripping from my fingers. Lisa Johnson deserves my concentration for the next few hours at least.

I start with the doctor. It's a small surgery so its hours are limited. Thankfully, on Tuesday nights there's an after-hours drop-in session for women to encourage open discussion on sexual health. Perfect.

I stroll in, much to the dismay of the apple-cheeked receptionist.

'You ... you can't go in there!' she blurts out, before immediately clapping a hand over her mouth. Her other hand tightens around a clipboard until her knuckles are pure white. Perhaps she's afraid that I'll bite off her head for daring to confront me. I admit I briefly consider it but it'll cause a lot of mess and she seems like a decent sort.

'This is for women, isn't it?' I enquire. I cup both my breasts in an open gesture to prove that I am indeed of the female sex. The woman's ruddy cheeks turn scarlet.

'Humans,' she says. 'Vampires don't get STDs.'

I waggle my eyebrows at her. 'They can be carriers though.' I lean in closer and lick my lips. 'They can transmit them.'

She blinks rapidly. 'Er … er…'

A white-coated woman appears behind her. 'It's alright, Joy. She can come in.'

'But…'

'I'm expecting her.'

'Dr Bryant, I presume?' I ask, pleased that Lisa's mother has done as I requested and phoned ahead.

'That's correct.' She looks me up and down.

I smile. 'I know, I know. You thought I'd be taller, right?'

'No. Your height makes sense; short people often act bullish. There have been several studies on the matter, in fact. I believe it's related to self-esteem.' There's the faintest hint of challenge in her eyes. Go the good doctor.

I make a show of looking around. 'You don't have any china around, do you? Bullish is my middle name.'

She snorts. 'Bo Bullish Blackman?'

'BBB for short.'

'I wonder if you'd be as famous if your name weren't quite so catchy,' she muses.

I gaze at her impassively. 'Are you deliberately trying to rile me?'

'Would it work if I did?'

'That depends. Are you a witch?' She shakes her head. 'A criminal?'

'No.'

I shrug. 'Then probably not. It might depend on whether I'd had breakfast or not though.' I permit my fangs to elongate; Dr Bryant doesn't so much as flinch.

'You're not wrong about the STDs. There have been numerous cases where humans have become infected after relations with vampires.'

I smirk. 'Relations?'

Her eyes remain cool. 'Sexual relations. You can't embarrass me, Ms Blackman. I'm not afraid of you either.'

I sense she wants to say something else but before she can, a petite mousy-looking woman pops out from a nearby doorway and asks in a trembling voice, 'Are we going to start soon?'

Dr Bryant gives her a brisk nod. 'Right now.'

'I'd like to talk to you first,' I interrupt.

'You'll have to wait until the session is over.'

I cross my arms. 'It's important. Lisa Johnson's life might just hang in the balance.'

'Just because I can't do karate or kung fu or sink my teeth into someone's jugular, doesn't mean what I do isn't important.' She points towards the waiting room. 'There are eight women in there whose lives are also important.'

'They're not currently in mortal danger.'

'You don't know that. What happens in this room in the next hour may very well save their lives.'

'In the long run.'

'Is there any other kind?' She points again. 'Go in, sit at the back and don't say a word. When we are finished, I will talk to you.'

'You're wrong, you know,' I inform her.

'In what way?'

'There are seven women, not eight.' For the first time she looks surprised. I grin. 'I can hear their heartbeats.'

Dr Bryant swallows. Of course, that's absolute bullshit. The clipboard which Joy, the plump receptionist, was holding had seven names ticked off. But making Dr Bryant a little more wary of my abilities is more fun than telling her the mundane truth. For some reason she wants me in this meeting. My curiosity is piqued enough that right now I'll oblige.

As amusing as it might be to brazen it out with the other waiting women in the same manner, I decide to take the quieter approach. I slip in behind the doctor and take a seat towards the back. If one of them has something to say that I'm going to find interesting, coming across as a predator won't encourage them to speak up. All the same, two or three of them turn to me. When the rest spot the movement, they also crane their necks round to gawp. I provide them all with a meek smile.

Dr Bryant's wariness is replaced by a flicker of amusement. She quickly masks it under her façade of professionalism though. 'Ladies, thank you for coming. I'm sure you recognise Bo Blackman. I have asked her to join us. I think she'll find our meeting illuminating.'

'She's a vampire.'

I have to sit on my hands to prevent myself from giving the woman who spoke a slow round of applause.

Another older woman looks at me. 'Thank you,' she says quietly.

Okay, I wasn't expecting that. 'For what?'

'Isabel is my friend. What you did for her was a good thing.'

I don't have the faintest idea who Isabel is. I simply gesture with my hand to indicate that, whatever I did, it was nothing.

'What did she do?' someone else asks in an overly loud stage whisper that makes me roll my eyes.

'Hit that prick husband of hers where it hurts.'

Realisation dawns on me. Isabel must be Adrian Leeman's next-door neighbour. Interesting. This must be a tight-knit community. Perhaps this will be a very useful hour after all. One good turn does deserve another.

Ignoring the gasps, Dr Bryant speaks up. 'Let's pick up where we left off last time, shall we? We were discussing alternatives to condoms for those of you who have partners who dislike using them.'

I lean back in my chair. Really?

Less than five minutes later, I'm so bored that I find myself entertained solely by the fluttering pulses at the base of each woman's neck. I'm like a small child pressing her face up against the window of a sweet shop. The dark-haired girl in the far corner is wearing a scarf so I rock to one side in an attempt to see better. If I can just inch a little bit further to the right then...

I go too far and end up crashing to the floor in an ungainly heap. Everyone turns to look at me. Dr Bryant's brows snap together in an irritated glower. I mutter a vague apology and get to my feet, pulling the chair upright. I've got better things to do than this; I'll catch the doctor some other time.

She clears her throat as I start to turn. 'That's exactly the kind of thing Lisa would have done.'

There's a murmur of amused agreement from the others. I freeze. Lisa Johnson came to this group? She would have been the youngest by far but it's certainly possible. Slowly, I return to my seat as they change the subject.

'I've not seen her since last month,' Mrs Mousy says. 'I hope she's not gotten herself mixed up with anything stupid.'

Bryant rubs her chin with the base of her thumb and nods. 'Indeed.'

I grip the edges of the chair. Come on. Give me something to work with.

'I mean,' someone else continues, 'everyone's entitled to live their own life but it sounded like she was planning to sleep with multiple partners.'

'Well,' Bryant says cautiously, with a fleeting glance in my direction, 'that's not *exactly* what she said.'

It occurs to me that this is why she made me come to this meeting. There are strict limits about what she can reveal to me.

Doctor–patient confidentiality covers all that. But if someone else other than her were to repeat her words…

'What exactly did she say?' I ask suddenly, causing all the others to jump.

There's a long moment of drawn-out silence and I think I've made a mistake by speaking up. Then the dark-haired girl speaks up. 'She wanted to know how likely a person who had sex with several people would be to pass on a venereal disease.'

Someone else snorts. 'Those weren't her exact words. What she said was, "If you fuck more than one person, how much more likely are you to pass on blazing saddles to someone else?"'

The others wince at the language. Considering this is an STD meeting, you'd think they'd be less sensitive – although as a euphemism, blazing saddles is rather, er, graphic. It's also a pretty stupid question.

Lisa Johnson may not have been setting the academic world alight but there's nothing I've come across that suggests she's a total idiot. In fact it's more likely that she brought it up because she was looking for someone to talk her out of whatever course of action she was planning. There's little doubt that it's related to her disappearance.

Now that I'm sitting up and taking note, the group appears keen to help me. It's certainly not because I'm a vampire and I doubt it's down to my fame either; I reckon it's a result of taking Isabel's wanker of a husband in hand. I wonder whether they'd feel the same if they knew how upset Isabel herself was with me.

'She wanted to know if there was a way to stop her periods as well,' Mrs Mousy interjects.

'I don't blame her. I hate it when my Paul still wants sex and I'm all, you know, icky down there.'

Icky? She has to be kidding, right?

Dr Bryant interrupts. 'Now, ladies, you know there's nothing wrong with having intercourse when you are menstruating. It's down to personal choice. You should speak to your boyfriend if you don't like it though, Tabitha.'

'Like that will do any good.'

I raise my eyebrows. 'I can have a word with him, if you like.'

The group stills. Tabitha coughs awkwardly. 'No. That's alright.' She coughs again. 'Thank you.'

One of the quieter women wrings her hands nervously, casting me a shy look. 'Ms Blackman, um...'

'Call me Bo.' It's the least I can do, considering all the information they've given me so far.

She blushes and smiles. 'Bo. Do you ... do you, um, menstruate?'

I try not to look too amused at her formality. 'No.'

'Ha!' says the dark-haired girl. 'There's a reason to be recruited if ever I heard one.'

My expression turns stony. 'I will never have children. I'm hated by 99.9% of the population. I can't go out in sunlight.'

'Not yet,' she interrupts. 'But you also have super powers.'

I grit my teeth. 'They're not super powers. I can't turn invisible or fly or anything like that. I'm just a bit stronger and faster, that's all.'

Someone else opens her mouth with what can only be another question. I intercept her. 'You don't want to be a vampire,' I say flatly, my tone brooking no further discussion on the matter. 'Now, did Lisa say anything last time she was here? Give any other hints about someone she was seeing? Or somewhere she might be going?'

The women exchange looks. 'No,' Tabitha finally answers. 'She did give me a really big hug at the end of the session though. She wasn't usually so touchy-feely and I was a bit taken aback. It was like she was saying goodbye or something.'

My suspicions that Lisa left of her own volition are growing stronger by the minute. I don't imagine her parents will take the news well. I mull over everything while Bryant steers the conversation back to other matters. With my own thoughts swirling round my head, the rest of the time passes quickly and I'm surprised when everyone stands up to leave.

'Thank you for coming, Ms Blackman. I mean, Bo.'

I shake the woman's hand. Others come up and murmur similar platitudes. 'Will you come again next time?' asks Tabitha.

'I doubt it. But if I have any more questions about Lisa…?'

They all nod vigorously.

'And if Isabel has any further trouble, don't hesitate to get in touch.' I jerk my head towards Bryant. 'I'll leave my number with the doctor.'

Their gratitude is almost embarrassing. They file out one by one, until only Dr Bryant and I remain. She looks me over with a cool, appraising gaze. 'I trust you found that helpful.'

'I did, actually. Thank you.' I incline my head. 'I have just a few more questions.'

'I cannot discuss any of Lisa's medical history.'

I chew the inside of my cheek. As I suspected. 'Can you tell me at least if she was having normal periods?'

'No, I can't tell you.'

'Or whether you gave her anything to stop her periods as she requested?' I know there are some contraceptive pills on the market that are capable of doing that. Obviously, Lisa wasn't already on them or she wouldn't have asked the question in the first place.

'No, I can't tell you that either. The rules on what I can and can't say are very clear cut, Ms Blackman. And anyway, I have not seen Lisa since that last session.'

Meaning that if she did change her usual prescription, it wasn't with Bryant. The good doctor has done a remarkable job of getting around the patient confidentiality laws. I tilt my chin and meet her eyes. 'You've been very helpful,' I say honestly. 'But why do you trust me? I get as much bad press these days as good.'

She considers the question. 'Lisa is a good girl. She's naïve and often far too headstrong and passionate for her own good but her heart is in the right place. It's not like her to just get up and go without saying a word to her parents. The others were right. She was asking some very strange questions in our last session.'

'Then why didn't you do something?'

She lifts up an eyebrow. 'What would you have had me do? Tie her down to stop her from seeking out as many men as possible to sleep with? She was an adult, Ms Blackman, and entirely capable of making her own choices.'

I stare at her. 'She *is* an adult.' Why do so many people seem so convinced that she's already dead?

Bryant colours. 'You're right. She is an adult. Not was. I just...' She shakes her head. 'It's not like her. That's all. I didn't mean anything by it.'

I study her carefully. She appears genuinely contrite but there's still more to this than meets the eye. 'What aren't you telling me?' She drops her gaze. 'Dr Bryant?' I prod.

She sighs. 'I didn't always work at this clinic. I moved here six months ago from the other side of the city. I had a patient there, a young woman called Melissa Greek. She was very much like Lisa – high ideals and a determination to change the world.'

'What happened to her?'

'She walked out one day and never returned.' She shrugs,

attempting to appear nonchalant and failing miserably. 'Some people thought she'd been recruited by your kind. Others thought she might have run into a Kakos daemon. The truth is, nobody knows.'

I purse my lips. 'People disappear every day. What makes you think there was a connection between her and Lisa?'

'Melissa used to wear a necklace. A small gold pendant with what looked like a tree on it.'

I frown. 'So?'

Bryant leads me out to the front reception area. Joy, the joyless receptionist, has disappeared thankfully. She points over at the corked notice board. There's a poster of Lisa on it, beaming out at the camera. 'Look,' she says softly.

I lean in. Lisa Johnson is wearing a delicate gold necklace; hanging from it is what looks like a little tree. I rock back on my heels. 'Did you tell the police about this?'

'Yes.'

'And?'

'They said they'd look into it. That's the last I heard.'

Interesting. It looks like Foxworthy and I are going to be negotiating again sooner rather than later. He'll love that.

CHAPTER 8
SWEETHEARTS

There's a definite chill in the air when I step out from Bryant's little surgery. I check my watch. Although I spent far longer with the doctor than I'd intended, there is still time to get to the café which Lisa recently visited. It's not likely that I'll find anything but right now I'm short on clues so I need to use every little morsel of information that I can dredge up. It helps that it's on the way to Adrian Leeman's house.

When I reach the café, I'm rather underwhelmed by its appearance. I can't see much from outside as the windows are steamed up. There is old paint peeling off around the window sill and a rusted metal grille covering the door. A faded sign warns that hawkers, vagrants and vampires aren't welcome. I grin. This might be fun.

There's a jarring tinkle as I push the door open and step inside. Despite their anti-bloodguzzler approach, there's no spell or warning alarm to prevent or signal my entrance. Commercial properties are different to residential ones: I can enter any shop, restaurant or public venue when I wish but homes are slightly different. That doesn't mean business owners can't find their own methods of preventing vampiric entry – Magix does a booming line in vampire-prevention products – but judging by the poor upkeep of this place, I'm guessing they can't afford anything that would work.

The place provides a different angle on Lisa Johnson's personality. Did she choose to come here or did someone bring her? It certainly doesn't tally with the 'nicer than nice, save the world' personality that she advertised.

There's one customer in the corner with a dog-eared copy of *Mein Kampf* and what looks like a cold cup of insipid tea, the sort that's had a tea bag waved at it in vague disdain. A man wearing a stained apron appears from the back room, wiping his hands on its front. His face is lined and heavy, with flabby jowls and pores which look wide enough to drive a truck through.

The second he catches sight of me, his face twists into a snarl. 'We don't like your sort in here.'

The customer carefully lays down his book and pushes his chair back. I smile disarmingly at them both. 'What?' I coo. 'Don't you know who I am?' I give myself a mental high-five. I've always wanted to say that.

'There's the door,' the owner grunts. 'Now fuck off. I don't care if you're Lord Medici himself. You're not welcome. Geddit?'

I look from him to the customer. I could try talking them round. I could even leave. But after the eager friendliness of the women at Bryant's clinic, these guys make a refreshing change and I'm ready for some fun.

I leap backwards, scooping up the cup of tea and throwing it at the customer. It drenches him, the table and the book. He splutters and advances towards me then, when he catches sight of the expression on my face, he thinks better of it and spins round, virtually sprinting out of the door.

I smile nastily. 'One down. One to go.'

The owner pulls out a phone and jabs in a number, pressing send before I can lunge towards him. 'Not for long,' he grunts. 'I heard you were hanging around here yesterday. I have a few friends who will be happy to make your acquaintance.'

I clap my hands together. 'Oh goody. Are they as handsome and charming as you?'

He snarls but, instead of attempting to fight me, he turns. Rather than running out of the shop, he vanishes into the room behind the counter, slamming the door shut. There's a click as the lock is turned. Idiot. Does he really think a flimsy lock like that will stop me?

I vault over the counter and past the grubby till. With one swift kick, I splinter the door and it bounces open. I just have time to see the barrel of a gun pointing in my direction before there's a deafening bang. At first I think he's missed but the pain sets in a second later, spreading across my side and into my gullet. He raises the gun to take another shot.

He's already gotten lucky once; I'm not going to let it happen again. Gritting my teeth against the searing agony of the wound, I lunge forward and yank the gun out of his hands. I turn it on him and he blanches.

'And to think,' I say in a strained voice, 'all I wanted was to ask a few questions. Now if I'm going to get out of here alive, I need to drain you of all that blood.' I make a face. 'I bet you don't even taste good.'

'I won't let you near me, you devil spawn,' he hisses. 'I'd rather die.'

I shrug then regret it as the pain only increases. 'That can be arranged.' I pull the trigger, aiming for his thigh. He collapses with a scream, clutching his leg and contorting his face. He starts writhing and moaning. Curious, I step closer. Those are remarkable histrionics for what is really only a flesh wound.

'It hurts,' he screeches. 'It hurts.'

Little lights start dancing in front of my eyes. 'Goes to show you're not dead yet,' I manage, then grab him by the scruff of the neck and haul him upwards so I can reach his jugular.

Without a moment to spare, I sink my fangs into his neck and drink. The blood won't heal me instantly but it will stop me passing out. The strength it gives me will keep me going for now – even if his little friends do decide to show up. He actually tastes surprisingly good. If it weren't for the fact that I need to ask him some questions, I think I would drain him dry. Instead I force myself to stop while he's still conscious, though his pupils are dilated and glassy.

I wipe my mouth with the back of my hand and stare hard, giving him every ounce of badass attitude I can muster. 'Do you have CCTV?'

He doesn't respond. I glance round the small room. It doesn't appear so and I didn't spot any cameras in the café. That's annoying. I pull out the photo I have in my pocket of Lisa and wave it in front of his eyes. 'Recognise her?'

He seems unable to focus. I grip his shoulder and he yelps, some measure of clarity returning. 'I said,' I repeat, 'do you recognise her?'

His eyes fix on the photo. He blinks twice but remains silent. Yep, he knows exactly who she is. I tighten my grip and lower my head so that our noses are almost touching. 'Tell me about her.'

He gasps. 'Screw you.'

'Come on,' I purr. 'Play nice and I may even change my mind about killing you.'

He opens his mouth to speak but, before he can, his face twists. I frown and peer at him. He can't be in that much pain, surely? When I see the sweat across his brow, feel the dampness even through his clothes and hear his short gasps of breath, I snarl out a curse. Heart attack. Brilliant.

I let him go and he drops heavily onto the floor, his legs twitching. His hands reach up and clutch at his chest. I shake my head in irritation and start looking round the room. There is a small desk covered in paper, most of which seem to be old invoices and food orders. I flick through the piles. There's next to nothing of interest. Well, this is irritating.

I glance down at the café owner. His face is turning an extraordinary shade of purple. I wonder whether his impending heart attack was the reason why his blood tasted so good. After a moment, I bend down and take his phone from his pocket. I memorise the last number he called, just in case the details about his 'friends' may be useful. Then I helpfully punch in 999 for him.

'You see,' I tell him softly, as his eyes bulge at me, 'I'm not *all* bad.' I drop the phone and stroll out. This was a total waste of time.

The cold air outside has given way to a light drizzle. You certainly can't beat England for miserable weather, I think as I cross the road. I turn up the collar of my leather jacket not because I feel the cold – I don't – but the sensation of dripping water down my neck is not pleasant.

I feel for the bullet hole. I'm pretty sure the damn piece of metal is still rattling around somewhere in there. At least the agony has given way to a dull, throbbing ache, even if my blouse is now soaked in my blood. I prod around experimentally. I'd really like to go three for three and get hold of Adrian Leeman before I head home but the last thing I want is to collapse along the way. I'm pretty certain I'll be alright. That café owner's blood helped a hell of a lot.

I'm just about to start walking again when a car screeches down the quiet street and comes to a badly parked halt in front of the café. Aha. This must be the aforementioned friends. I watch with interest as a couple jump out and run in. They are clutching shotguns – the sort that could do considerably more damage than the peashooter the owner directed at me. Whoever they are, they definitely mean business.

Unfortunately for them, they are followed less than a minute later by a racing ambulance. Its red and blue flashing lights illuminate the street so I draw further back into the shadows. I congratulate myself on being kind enough to call for it in the first place. Its appearance may just help me get an ID on the two 'friends'. It never hurts to know who your potential enemies are. I'm not really in much shape to confront the pair of them right now but I will be once I've gotten this damn bullet out and a few stitches.

It doesn't take long for the paramedics to emerge with the café owner on a stretcher. The 'friends', apparently having realised that I've gone, follow behind. There's a lot of gesticulating and raised voices. Apparently spotting the gun, which I left behind, has encouraged the paramedics to call the police. I smile. That's nice.

The angry pair head for their car, unwilling to hang around and see if their pal is going to be alright. That tells me a great deal: either they're not as close as he'd like to think, or the last thing they want is a confrontation and awkward questions from the strong arm of the law. Maybe they're already wanted criminals. My smile grows. That'll mean I'm justified in tracking them down again later.

As the one nearest me ducks down to get into the driver's seat, the flashing light from the ambulance throws his entire body into stark relief. I ignore the ridiculous army camouflage get-up that he's wearing and focus on the tattoo on his neck. It's not a magical one and it doesn't signify any allegiance to the witches. It is an odd symbol that looks remarkably like a tree.

I pull back further and wrinkle my nose. Despite the café's less than welcoming atmosphere and the evidence I have of

Lisa's visit, I hadn't thought this place was linked directly to her disappearance. I was very, very wrong. Lisa certainly isn't the goody-two-shoes her mother and Dr Bryant made out. Whoever these people are, they mean serious business. A visible tattoo etched into someone's neck also suggests both dedication and longevity. I wonder why I've never heard of this lot before.

I slide out my phone and send a quick text to Rogu3, telling him that my 'benefactor' would like to meet him and Maria tomorrow night and asking him to run down the number plate of the car. I suppose it's just as well that he showed up at my place after all.

I watch as the paramedics continue to protest at the tattooed-tree people's departure but, to be fair, they have their hands full with the heart attack. The car screeches off in much the same manner that it arrived and I'm left pondering over the thickening plot.

As the ambulance departs, I leave too. I feel like I'm in much better shape than I was last night – in terms of information if not health. No doubt Adrian Leeman will have a wealth of enlightening information on his less-than-perfect ex-girlfriend.

ALTHOUGH THE CURTAINS ARE DRAWN, there is a light on in Isabel's house. I pause for a moment to listen. Her husband's heap of a car is parked outside so he must be inside as well. I can't hear anything so I guess that, for once, all is quiet with their lives. I certainly hope so.

Satisfyingly, this time there is also a light on inside Adrian's house. I ring the doorbell and wait for him to answer, smoothing my features into my best, polite, unvampiric expression.

When he opens the door, he doesn't seem surprised to see me. 'You're Bo Blackman. I heard you might be coming round to talk to me.'

I waggle my fingers. 'Great. You're Adrian then?'

He nods. 'You're not coming in though. It's not that I don't trust you,' he adds hastily, 'but...'

'But I'm a vampire.' I try to reassure him. 'It's a sensible decision, Mr Leeman. Is this a good time to ask you a few questions about Lisa?' I don't really care whether it is a good time or not, I'm going to ask the questions regardless, but it sounds better than launching straight into my interrogation. It's the kind of thing my grandfather would want me to say.

'Sure.' He tugs at his collar as if he's nervous. 'We broke up quite a while ago. I'm not sure how much I can help you.'

I smile. 'You'd be surprised at how much is locked away in your head and how useful it might be.'

He swallows. 'Uh, okay.' I take a step back to avoid crowding him. I need him to feel like he has both space and time to consider his answers. As I do, a wave of dizziness abruptly overtakes me. Damn it. I blink rapidly and try to focus. I can't feel any pain now; unfortunately that's probably not a very good sign. Pain reminds me that I'm still alive. In a manner of speaking.

Adrian Leeman looks alarmed. 'Are you alright?'

'I'm fine.' I dismiss his concern. 'Now, can you tell me how long you and Lisa went out together and why you broke up?'

'We got together in Year 11.' He scratches his neck. 'Well, she was in Year 11,' he amends. 'I was in Year 13.'

Aw, high-school sweethearts. Bless. She must have been quite something for a student on the edge of graduating to get involved with. I'm well aware that girls mature faster than boys but street cred is important at that age.

'And you split up when?' I enquire.

'Five months ago. Give or take.'

Judging from the pained expression on his face, he could tell me the exact day. Probably even the exact hour. He may have been older than her but Adrian Leeman is definitely still head over heels in love with her. That means she's the one who instigated the break up.

'Why did she do it, Adrian? Why did she break up with you?'

His eyes fly to mine. For a moment I think he's going to try and suggest that he's the one who broke things off. He seems to realise it's futile and sighs, pushing back his light-brown hair. 'She said she wanted more space.'

Oh, that old classic. Sensing there's more, I remain silent. The best way to get people to open up is to keep your mouth shut and encourage them to fill the void themselves. Adrian Leeman doesn't disappoint.

'I didn't believe her,' he says finally. 'I thought maybe there was someone else. When I pressed her, she said that I didn't have enough ambition.' He throws an arm behind him. 'I've got my own place though, and my own job.' His mouth takes on a bitter twist. 'She said it wasn't enough. That I didn't see the world in the same way that she did. The guzzlers...' his cheeks colour '...I mean the vampires, were trying to take things over and run everything themselves. Her words, not mine.'

I raise my eyebrows. 'Really.' Certainly Medici has been like that of late but five months ago there was little evidence of his plans. Unnecessary bloodshed and violence maybe, but not power seeking.

'Those were her words,' he says hastily, as if he's afraid I'm going to hurt him for repeating what she said. 'I don't think that.'

'Maybe you should,' I murmur, then shake my head and re-focus. 'So she wanted to stop the Families?'

'Not just the Families. She thought the government was

weak. She was always going on marches and protests and trying to get me to join her. Environmental stuff, better wages. She jumped around from cause to cause like she had ADD.' He bites his lip. 'It wasn't that I didn't agree with her but I have a job. I can't just drop everything to stamp around the streets for a few hours holding a sign.'

I nod. 'Of course.'

'Her parents supported her in everything. Gave her money, a roof over her head, cooked her meals. I don't have that, I have to support myself. Lisa didn't understand that. She told me we were responsible for everything that happened in the world but she didn't even know how to take responsibility for herself.'

I'm betting that poor Adrian said just that to her. I'm also betting she didn't take it well at all.

'Do you think someone's hurt her?' he asks anxiously. 'If I'd gone along with all of her plans then maybe...'

It's not my place to reassure him or make him feel better. All the same, I have more questions and the last thing I need is for him to collapse in a puddle of guilt at what might have been. 'We can spend our lives wondering what if, Mr Leeman. I doubt there's anything you could have done.'

He doesn't appear mollified. The anguish in his expression increases and I get the feeling I'm about to be subjected to a tirade of self-hatred. Neither of us really wants that.

'Tell me about your sex life,' I say, pre-empting any further angst.

He blinks, taken aback. 'We didn't do anything kinky, if that's what you mean.'

'I'm not interested in your positions or proclivities. How often did you have sex?'

'How is that relevant?' His square jaw hardens and I see a flicker of what Lisa might have found attractive in him.

'You don't know what's relevant,' I say coolly. 'How often?'

He really doesn't want to tell me. He struggles with the question for another moment before his shoulders droop in resigned acceptance. 'Three or four times a week.'

Probably once or twice a week then. 'Contraception?'

He looks stung. 'Lisa was on the pill. She got really bad periods and it helped regulate them. But I always used a johnny too.' He coughs. 'A condom.'

I keep my expression deadpan. 'I know what a johnny is, Mr Leeman.' I wonder how old he thinks I am. It does clear up one thing: the strange questions Lisa was asking at Dr Bryant's sexual health clinic had nothing to do with Adrian Leeman.

'Did you have sex when she was having her period?'

'I thought you didn't want to know about that kind of stuff,' he mutters, his cheeks staining scarlet.

'Adrian.' I sigh, going for the friendlier approach. 'Please just answer the question.'

He looks away. 'Sometimes.'

'Thank you.'

'Was she seeing someone else? Is that why you're asking all these questions?'

'I have no idea. I'm simply trying to get a clear picture of the sort of person she was.'

'By wanting to know when we had sex?'

'Like I already said, you don't know what might be relevant.' I tap the corner of my mouth thoughtfully. 'Now, all these demonstrations she was participating in. Do you know whether she ever took part in anything illegal?'

This time his answer is immediate. 'No! Lisa was a good person. She wouldn't break the law!' He scowls at me as if I just accused her of eating babies. 'Look, are you going to ask much else? I've got things to do. I'm only talking to you because her parents asked me to.'

I look past him. The flickering light of a television is just visible from the open hallway. He's not as busy as he'd like me to think. I'm pushing things as far as I can though. 'One last thing, Mr Leeman.'

He's surly now. 'What?'

'Do you have a pen and a piece of paper I can borrow?'

He stares at me. 'Wait here,' he says finally. He turns and disappears back into his house then returns with a tattered sheet torn from a notepad and a pink pen with some strange fluffy attachment at the end of it. When he spots my raised eyebrows, he explains in a gruff voice that it belonged to Lisa.

'Do you have anything else that belonged to her?'

He shakes his head. 'No, she took everything when we split up. I found that underneath the sofa.'

I take the pen and paper from him. 'Did she have a gold necklace with a little symbol of a tree on it?'

'No.'

'Are you sure?'

'Lisa didn't like gold. She said there was no way to be sure that it was ethically sourced or something. I tried to give her some earrings on her eighteenth birthday.' His mouth twists. 'She virtually threw them back in my face.'

I nod and scribble the words 'I'm watching you' on the paper and fold it up. Then I pass him back the pen. 'Well, thank you for your time. I might return with more questions later.'

As I turn to go he reaches out and grabs my arm. I look down, my gaze turning icy. He abruptly drops his hand. 'You will find her, won't you?' he still asks. 'You will promise to bring her back?'

I'm not promising a damn thing. 'I'm going to look for her,' I tell him. It's the best I can do. Then I hop over the adjoining fence and drop the note into his neighbour's letterbox while he looks on, the very picture of a dejected and rejected man. Life's a bitch. And then one shows up and stamps on your heart.

CHAPTER 9
CHINKS IN ARMOUR

By now I'm starting to feel incredibly woozy. The sensible thing would be to go home and lie down but I promised Foxworthy I'd go and see him and I still want to confront Michael about his stupid recruitment plans. Unfortunately, I don't think either of them can wait. Eeeny meeny miny mo...

I'm at the end of the road when my mind is made up for me. Apparently returning Kimchi wasn't enough for Beth or Matt; their familiar figures are silhouetted against the orange lamppost on the far corner. Both of them have stiff, wary postures as if they're afraid of what I'll do when I see them following me. I roll my eyes in their direction and stomp over.

'Still tailing me?' I enquire. 'Don't you have anything better to do?'

Matt's bottom lip juts out. 'Bo, what's wrong with you?'

I ignore my sudden flare of guilt. I don't owe him anything; if anything, he owes me. Other vampires affected by the enhancement spell ended up in padded cells. I like to think that my involvement with Matt saved him from that kind of fate, whether he's better now or not.

'You mean aside from the fact that the pair of you can't take a simple hint and leave me the fuck alone?' I snap.

Beth peers at me. 'Don't be such a cow, Bo. Matt's right. You look really pale.'

I realise I completely misunderstood Matt's intention. He isn't upset at my words; he's just concerned about my wellbeing. I open my mouth to answer just as my vision starts to cloud. Damn it.

'Bo?' he asks in alarm.

I raise a hand as if to ward him off. 'I'm fine,' I mutter.

'I think she's going to faint,' Beth says, as if from a long distance away.

I scowl. I'm not some soppy eighteenth-century maiden. And I'm not about to faint. Unfortunately that's the exact moment that the ground rushes up to meet me.

When I come to, the first thing I notice is the unmistakable smell of new leather. The faint sound of an expensive engine meets my ears and I sigh. This can only be some stupidly over-priced Montserrat car. That means they're taking me back to the Montserrat mansion. Yes, it's where I intended to go anyway but I wanted to walk through the door with all my abilities intact, not arrive like some forlorn female in need of Lord Michael Montserrat's heroic assistance.

I force my eyes open. I'm plonked between Beth and Matt, as if they're afraid I'll make a rush for the door and barrel out of the moving vehicle just to get away from their well-meaning intentions.

'Relax, Bo,' Beth murmurs. 'We're just taking you to get some help. You've been shot.'

No shit. Does she really think I hadn't noticed? I pull myself up and stare stiffly at her. 'I'm fine.'

She snorts. 'Yeah, right. That's what you said right before you keeled over on the pavement like a sack of potatoes.'

'Why are you alone, Bo?' Matt asks. 'Where's Kimchi?'

'Relax.' I struggle to sit up straight. 'I've not munched on him or anything like that. He's with Rogu3.'

'The kid?' Matt's face is the very picture of hurt dismay. 'You've let him back into your life but you won't let me?'

I frown at him. 'I thought you were better. What's with all the "woe is me" crap?'

A flash of anger lights his eyes. Good. He really *is* better. 'That's not fair.'

'No,' I sigh as the car pulls up to a halt. 'But then life isn't fair, is it?'

'You're not going to do anything stupid are you?' Beth asks.

'Like what? Run away from a thousand do-gooder vampires?'

'There's only five hundred of us. You know that.' I give her an irritated look. She subsides. 'Okay. Maybe now there are more.'

'How many more?'

Beth doesn't answer. Instead the door opens smoothly and Matt climbs out, before reaching in for me. I succumb to his help only because it'll make him feel better. From what I remember of pre-spell Matt, his ego was all important to him.

Once I'm outside, I see both Ursus and Ria waiting on the steps. Michael looms behind them, all dark frowns.

'Hey,' I say, with as much weak cheeriness as I can muster. 'The old gang's all here.'

Michael marches towards me, taking my arm as Matt releases me. 'You're an idiot,' he informs me.

I shrug. 'Takes one to know one.'

He rolls his eyes. Fair enough, I would too at such a crappy rejoinder. I need to work on my snappy comebacks – at least where he's concerned.

'Have you stopped drinking blood again?' he demands. 'Is that why you're like this?'

I stumble, falling against him and cursing. His jaw tightens and he helps me get back upright again. I suppose I should be thankful that he's not trying to carry me. There are limits. 'No. In fact, I had a great meal just a few hours ago.' I bare my fangs at him and pat my stomach. 'I like blood now. The more the better.'

His face leans in towards me. It's almost like he's sniffing me. His closeness is unsettling and it's making it difficult to think. I'd put it down to the wound in my gut if I didn't already know better. I can only fool myself so far.

'Hmm,' he says, eventually pulling back. Thank goodness. I allow myself to breathe again. 'At least that part's true.'

'You think I'd lie to you? You're the one who's been hiding behind untruths. What the fuck are you doing recruiting more vampires?'

He draws me closer, his hand like a steel clamp round my shoulders. 'This is neither the time nor the place, Bo,' he says through gritted teeth. 'Shut the hell up and let me help you.'

I stop speaking. It's not out of any desire to do as he wants, it's just that the effort required to form words is simply too much. I let him guide me indoors, ignoring the wide-eyed looks from the Montserrat vampires milling around at the front. Back here again. Just brilliant.

~

AN UNNAMED MONTSERRAT VAMPIRE, whose face I vaguely recognise, bends over my torso with a pair of lethal-looking tweezers while Michael glowers at me from the doorway.

'You know,' I tell him, 'I don't need you to rescue me. Or to send the troops out after me. I was doing alright.'

His eyebrows shoot up. 'Is that what you call it? You passed out in the middle of the street. What if a Medici minion wandered by? What would have happened to you then?'

Pain lances through me as the tweezers dig into the bloody mess, searching for the bullet. I squeeze my eyes shut momentarily. Mind over matter: it doesn't hurt, it doesn't hurt, it doesn't hurt...

I let out a small moan. 'I was in suburbia,' I gasp. 'I hardly think Medici guzzlers would be likely to stroll past. Not unless they are in the market for a cute little starter home with floral curtains.'

The other vampire shoves something into my mouth. 'Bite down,' he instructs. 'This is going to hurt.'

Like it isn't hurting already? I do as he says, my hands gripping onto the sides of the narrow bed.

'You're not invincible, Bo,' Michael says, crossing his arms. 'You're still a newbie. We've had disappearances lately.' He takes out his phone and holds it towards me, flipping through a gallery of photos. 'All strong vampires, all missing presumed dead. I know you're stronger than most because you took so long to complete the turning process, but you're still vulnerable. You can still be killed. I bet you can't even go out in daylight yet.'

Thankfully I'm saved from responding because of the thing in my mouth. I groan loudly. How long is this going to take? Surely it can't be that hard to find one bullet. Agony sears through me; it feels as if he's pulling out my intestines, inch by slow inch. Tears spring to my eyes. *Bloody* hell.

'You seem determined,' Michael continues, 'to act as if you're always on your own. This isn't the first time you've done a runner. Come back. We can help you get through this. How are you surviving? Do you even have a roof over your head?'

There's a grunt from the other vampire, followed by the

ding of metal hitting metal. 'Got it,' he says. 'She's lucky it didn't hit any major organs.'

Yeah, yeah. Michael murmurs a thank you as the medic quickly sews me up. I prop myself up on my elbows to watch; I want to make sure he doesn't fuck it up. Fortunately this obviously isn't his first time at such manoeuvres because the stitches are small, neat and even. Less than five minutes later, I'm good to go.

The makeshift doctor departs, leaving Michael and me alone. I swing my legs round and sit up. I still feel a bit dizzy but normal service is definitely resuming. Thank goodness.

'First of all, the last time I did a "runner", as you call it, you manipulated me into it. Second, I'm coping perfectly well.' I'm ridiculously glad that he still doesn't know where I'm living – or that X is helping me out. Even though the Kakos daemon has said he wants to meet Rogu3 and Maria, he has warned me like a damned stuck record that if anyone else finds out about his existence he'll be forced to destroy them. Michael is very strong and very powerful but he'll never be a match for someone like X. No one is.

'You've still not been to see O'Shea or your grandfather,' Michael points out.

'We had this discussion two nights ago. I don't see why we need to have it again.' I sigh. I'm not trying to come across like a petulant child and I know he's only acting like this because he's worried about me but I don't need or want his concern. 'Please, Michael,' I say, dropping my defences. 'Just leave me in peace.'

His face shutters. 'It seemed like you needed me the other night.' He throws a pointed look at my wound. 'You needed me tonight as well.'

I take a deep breath. I can be gracious. 'Thank you for your help.' I stand up, wobbling ever so slightly. My eyes harden as I meet his. 'Now tell me what the fuck is going on with recruitment.'

'It's none of your concern.' He leans down towards me. I pretend not to notice his taut muscles or the whiff of spicy aftershave. 'Not unless you want to return to the Montserrat Family, that is.'

He knows I don't; he's just trying to goad me into another argument so he can avoid the question. 'It's every bit my concern,' I tell him. 'Do you really think that flinging open your doors and getting more vampires is the answer? The numbers have been capped for centuries! You can't change all that in a blink of an eye!'

'I told you that we had a plan for getting rid of Medici.'

I put my hands on my hips. 'And this is it?' I demand. 'Making the rest of the world hate you even more than they already do?'

'Sacrifices are necessary. We can work on our PR once Medici is out of the way.'

'Remember what happened with Nicky. If you rush the recruitment process, you have no idea what manner of criminals you might end up with.'

'I'm not an idiot, Bo. Every precaution is being taken.'

'Really,' I say flatly. He's lying and we both know it. I ball up my fists and resist the urge to grab him and shake him very hard. Then maybe kiss him. No, wait. Not that.

He drops his voice. 'You're never even here. How would you know?'

'How many more are you bringing in?'

'Enough.'

'Enough for what? To storm Medici's citadel and kill most of them in the process? Do they know that you're recruiting them as nothing more than cannon fodder?'

'It's not going to be like that.'

'You hope!'

'What else would you have us do? He has superior numbers. Until the remaining four Familes can match him vampire for vampire, we can't make a move.'

'You should have done something the first time he stepped out of line,' I growl.

He reaches out, taking my hands in his and squeezing them gently. 'You know we couldn't.' A muscle jerks in his cheek. 'But we should have. Hindsight is a wonderful thing.'

My shoulders drop. 'Have you tried contacting him? He never wanted to change the old traditions. That's how all this started in the first place. If you talk things out with him then maybe...'

'We've tried.' His voice is grim. 'Believe me, we've tried.'

'He's one damn vampire. Take him out. I'm sure the other Medici bloodguzzlers will fall into place once he's gone.'

He releases my hands. 'We've tried that too. Why do you think he's now locked up inside, refusing to come out? We even sent in a human, under guise of recruitment, hoping they could take a shot. Someone who owed us a lot of favours.'

Considering that would be a suicide mission whether it succeeded or not, that would have to be a hell of a lot of a favour. 'What happened?'

His expression is pained. 'His dismembered head was sent to us by special delivery.'

I wince. 'Michael, he must know what you're doing. He'll have some kind of plan. He's not going to let you recruit enough numbers to beat him, he'll make a move against you long before then.'

'We've been trying to keep it quiet.'

I snort. 'Not quiet enough.'

'How did you find out?'

I shrug awkwardly, not willing to drop Matt or Beth in the

shit. 'I heard a few whispers. D'Argneau confirmed them for me.'

'The lawyer?' Michael's eyes glitter angrily.

'There's still nothing going on between us,' I tell him. 'Not that it's any of your business if there is.'

'Of course it's my business.' He moves even closer. 'No matter how hard you try to fight it, you know we have a very special connection.' He places husky emphasis on the word 'special'. I swallow. 'It's not just because I turned you. It's not just because you seem to want to fight me every time I make a simple request. You might think you're too screwed up for a relationship with me, but you don't understand that you can't run from me. You can't run from this. Every time you do, you'll just end up coming back. We're meant to be together, Bo. It's as basic as that. I want you. You want me. What else is there to worry about?'

Warring emotion surges through me. 'I'm not the same person I used to be. I've changed.'

'I don't care.' He lifts up his index finger and trails it down my cheek. 'Besides, I don't think you've changed as much as you pretend. I see the hardness in you that wasn't there before but I also still see Bo. You're still you.'

Goddamnit. Why is he the only person who can pierce my self-protective armour? I scowl. Then I step up on my tiptoes and do exactly what I promised myself I wouldn't. I kiss him.

For a horrifying moment, he doesn't react and I think I've made a terrible mistake. Then he returns the kiss and pulls me towards him. The heat between our two bodies is searing. I moan involuntarily and he jerks back.

'Did I hurt you?'

I smile. There's definitely a wicked tinge to it. 'No. But I might like it if you did.' He frowns at me in astonishment. I quickly backtrack to avoid awkward questions and tug at his shirt, pulling it upwards from his waistband to distract him. When I rip it open, revealing his taut stomach and the line of dark hair leading downwards, I think I'm the one who's distracted. 'Just don't stop, Michael, that's all,' I breathe. 'Don't stop.'

He leans forward and kisses me again. My senses swim. His fingers deftly reach for my own clothes, pulling them off me until I'm completely bared to his hot gaze.

He reaches out and gently touches the lace of my panties. 'I like these,' he says with a wicked smile of his own.

'Get naked,' I growl.

Michael bows. He steps back, slowly taking off his shirt. His body is exactly the same as I remember it. I take in the well-defined muscles and the edges of the vast angel wings tattoo which curves round from the edge of his shoulders all the way across his broad, rippling back.

He holds the shirt up in the air on one finger and twirls it once before tossing it aside. Tease.

'Faster.'

He laughs at me. 'No.'

I hiss through my teeth and snap towards him but he holds me at bay with a single wag of his head. He licks his lips and I forget to breathe.

'Pleasure is found in anticipation. Be patient, Bo.'

I only just manage to keep myself in check. My heart is thudding rapidly to the tune of the throbbing ache in my loins. Michael undoes the button on his trousers so slowly that it's painful. I clench my teeth. This is becoming unbearable.

He starts to inch the material down over his narrow hips. I catch a glimpse of silk boxer shorts – in the Montserrat House colour of midnight blue, naturally. I'm not entirely convinced that's what the founders had in mind when they designated that colour. He reveals a little bit more skin. His erection is breathtakingly obvious.

I've had enough of the teasing. Deciding to get my own back, I hook my fingers round the lace of my own underwear and match him, slowly sliding them downwards. I'm rewarded with a sharp intake of breath and his eyes darken with undisguised lust.

'Bo,' he groans.

'What?' I ask innocently. 'I thought you wanted to play.' I push them down an inch further.

A guttural sound emits from deep within his chest and he pounces. At last. He pushes me down on the narrow bed. 'Are you sure about this?' he asks, raising his head. A lock of hair falls across his forehead in the sexiest little curl I've ever seen.

I answer him by reaching round his waist and wriggling into position. He groans again and, with one swift movement that has me clutching at his sweat-covered back and screaming, plunges inside me.

This is no gentle coupling. I think there's an animalistic part of both of us that's begging to be fulfilled. My hips rise to meet his and I moan loudly, not caring who in the Montserrat household might hear me.

'You were wrong,' I tell him, taking short gasps as my entire body quivers under his.

He bites my ear sharply. 'Explain,' he orders and he thrusts once more.

I smile, knowing I'm reaching the crescendo. 'Pleasure isn't found in anticipation. It's in release.'

He bares his fangs in agreement vant and slams into me with a hoarse cry. Our bodies shudder in a simultaneous, earth-shattering orgasm that goes on and on and on. When it's finally over and he relaxes, I feel a deep satisfaction of the sort I'm not sure I've ever experienced before.

Michael shifts his weight. 'Am I too heavy?'

'You're perfect.'

There's a moment of silence. 'Bo,' he says, 'listen, I...'

'No.' My voice is too sharp. 'Don't. Let's just enjoy this moment.'

He sighs. I know he's struggling and I know he wants to talk. I can't though – not right now. Right now this has to be enough. The rest can come later.

CHAPTER 10

THEM'S FIGHTING WORDS

He sees me out. The vast lobby is conspicuously absent of other vampires; it's good to be Lord Montserrat. I stretch up on my tiptoes and kiss his cheek. The stubble along his jawline is rough and I have to force myself not to rub my cheek against his like a cat would.

'Do you know anything about a group that uses a tree as their logo?' I ask, dropping back down and sketching it out in the air.

He frowns at me. 'No. I can ask around though.'

I shake my head. 'Don't worry about it. You've got bigger things to worry about. I'll figure it out.'

'We could figure it out together.'

I meet his eyes. 'Will you let me help you figure out Medici?'

He tenses. 'I can't. The other Families...'

I roll my eyes. 'I know, I know.' I look away. 'I have to go.'

'Bo,' he says, his voice low.

I press my lips together. 'Mm?'

The expression in his eyes is dark and serious. 'Don't be a stranger. I once promised to lock you up and I'm not averse to doing it. Not if it's for your own good.'

I laugh. 'I'd like to see you try.' With an impish grin I head off, trying to ignore him standing there, watching me go.

I've got less than an hour before dawn and I shouldn't have spent all that time with him, whether I'm walking on air right now or not. I'm on a damn clock. I dash down the street at a sprint. I've gone less than fifty metres when I halt in my tracks. This is stupid; even with my increased vampiric speed, I can't run across the city before the sun rises. I could go back and ask Michael for help. Or I could do things my way.

I twist left and head for the first parked car. 'Sorry,' I tell it. 'It's an emergency.'

The car doesn't bother answering back until I put my elbow through the driver window. The alarm peals out, echoing across the street and causing a nearby urban fox on its way home to flee for safety. Nobody else stirs. That's the trouble with car alarms: people hear too many of them. No one is going to get out of their warm bed to investigate.

I clear away the worst of the glass then loop my hand round to unlock it from the inside. It's an older model, not yet computerised, so it's simple to hotwire. Less than three minutes later, I'm at the traffic lights.

Foxworthy finished his shift a few hours ago. Taking a chance that he'll have gone home rather than see out the rest of the wee hours in one of the many twenty-four-hour pubs or clubs, I make another beeline for suburbia but this time towards a different district to Adrian Leeman and the Johnsons.

I park in Foxworthy's driveway, ignoring the security light that flashes on as I get out of the car. Then I stroll up to his door and thump on it loudly until I hear a noise from inside.

He opens up, bleary-eyed and not particularly pleased to see me. 'I just got to bed an hour ago,' he growls. 'Couldn't this have waited?'

'I told you I'd come and find you tonight and I'm a woman of my word.'

'Don't you know what time it is?'

I grimace. 'Actually, I do. That's why I was hoping I could take shelter in your place for the day. I can't risk getting caught in sunshine.'

He scratches the stubble on his skin. He's actually considering refusing me then he steps back and gestures. 'Fine.'

I don't move. 'You need to say the words.'

Sleep is still clouding his logic and for a moment he seems confused. It doesn't take long for his face to clear, though, and he gives me an irritated bow. 'You're invited.'

I smile and step over the threshold. 'Cheers.'

'If this reaches the Chief, I'll be suspended,' he warns.

I punch him lightly on the arm. 'Relax. I'm not going to blab.'

Foxworthy shakes his head. 'There's a line, Bo. You're treading dangerously close to it.'

To be honest, I think I crossed it some time ago. I decide it's probably better not to say that to him so I just smile some more. 'Got anything to drink?'

We sit down in his kitchen. I'm surprised to see photos of various kids on display on the fridge. He follows my gaze. 'My grandchildren,' he explains shortly, as if he's afraid that I'll track them down and try to drain them of their young, inexperienced blood.

'I didn't even know you had children,' I comment. 'Let alone grandchildren.' He must have started young; I'd say he's still a fair way off retirement age. I jerk my chin upwards to the first floor. 'Wife?'

'Don't worry, we divorced a long time ago. Married too young.' He flicks his fingers in a dismissive gesture, as if this is a story he's sick of telling. 'Same old mistakes as a million other people.' He takes a sip of his whisky. 'You don't look well, Bo. Been in a fight?' He asks the question in the same manner that you might enquire about the weather. Foxworthy may once have possessed genuine concern for my well-being but my vigilantism has knocked that out of him. I decide it's for the best. The last thing a steadfast, straightforward guy like him needs is to be worried about a bloody vampire.

'It wasn't a big deal,' I answer. 'Although I would like to ask you if you recognise this.' I stroll over to the kitchen window. It's cold enough outside that the warmth from the central heating, not to mention our own body heat, has made the windows steam up. Using the tip of my finger, I draw the shape of the tree emblem. It's not a perfect match but it's clear enough.

'What is this? Pictionary? It's a tree.'

I roll my eyes. 'It's used as a symbol for something, some kind of group as far as I can tell. Have you seen it before?'

He purses his lips. 'It's not ringing any bells.' His gaze is far more alert now. 'Witches?' he asks, reflecting his quick-witted intelligence. I should have known my focus on their kind wouldn't go unnoticed. X and Foxworthy actually have a lot in common – not that either of them would thank me for pointing that out. Kakos daemons and members of Her Majesty's constabulary don't tend to mix well. Although to be fair, Kakos daemons don't mix well with anyone.

'I'm staying away from the witches,' I answer coolly. 'And no, I'm pretty sure everyone involved is human.' It stands to reason. If they hate vampires, they probably hate witches and daemons too.

'If you want me to check out the database...'

'That would be helpful. There's another missing woman called Melissa Greek who might be linked to them too. That might provide more leads.' I wait for a beat. 'What would you like in return?'

'I think I've done enough deals with the devil for now. I'll look it up and let you know if I find anything. It won't take long.'

I fiddle with a strand of my hair. 'Thank you. I appreciate it.'

Foxworthy grunts. 'I won't be able to keep doing this, you know. Nicholls is already suspicious.'

I'm not surprised. If she found out the truth, she'd probably flip. Nicholls has never liked me. Even before I turned vigilante, I'm sure I was top of her hit list.

'I understand,' I tell him quietly. 'But I would like to get Lisa Johnson's file.'

Foxworthy's fingers tighten round his glass. Other than that, he gives no hint of his unhappiness at our deal. 'Hellstrom first.'

I arch a teasing eyebrow as if to joke that I'm not sure I trust him. Foxworthy is clearly not in the mood for jokes – at least, not from me. I sigh and give him the address.

'He won't be alone,' I warn. 'He's too canny for that.'

Foxworthy gives me a distracted nod. 'I don't suppose you're going to tell me how you came across this information?'

'I'll tell you if you want.' I mean it; I owe this gruff old policeman a great deal, even if relations between us are now at breaking point.

He shakes his head. 'Perhaps not.' He gets up and opens a drawer, passing over a manila envelope. It's on the slim side.

'Is this it?'

'It's all I could get at short notice.'

'I wanted to see the items taken from her room as well,' I remind him.

'Bo, you wouldn't believe the strings I had to pull just to get you that. Be satisfied because there's nothing else coming.'

I look into his eyes. He's telling the truth. So be it. I lay the file to one side; I'll look at it when I have peace and quiet and I'm in a position to give it all my attention.

The sky outside is already starting to lighten and my eyelids are growing very heavy. I expended a lot of energy getting shot tonight. I need my beauty sleep.

'There aren't any curtains in the spare room,' Foxworthy says. 'But I have a cupboard which has enough space.' He looks me over critically. 'It helps that you're the size of a thimble.'

The corner of my mouth quirks up. Was that a friendly overture? 'It's very kind of you,' I say. 'I won't disturb you any further.' I nibble on my lip. 'Apart from...'

He sighs. 'What? I can't help you with the Lisa Johnson case. It's not mine and I've stepped on too many toes as it is.'

'No, that's okay. The file should help. It's, um, the car outside. The one I came here in.'

His eyes narrow. 'What about it?'

I reach into my jacket and pull out a wad of banknotes. 'I need you to put this in the glove box and get a uniform to return it to Hyde Park.'

Foxworthy's mouth drops open. 'Did you steal it?'

'I borrowed it.'

'Well, so much for being all high and mighty and ridding London of its criminal elements,' he says with obvious anger. 'Last time I looked, stealing cars was a crime too.'

'I'm compensating the owner,' I point out. Very generously, as well.

'Is that supposed to make a difference?'

'Yes.' I sigh. 'Okay, it was wrong to take it but I had to get to see you and there was no other way to do it in time. You live too far away from the Underground train lines and I left my bike at home.'

Foxworthy shakes his head. 'What's happened to you?'

I don't answer him. 'Can you show me that cupboard?'

The anger drains out of him and he looks at me sadly. For some reason that's far worse. I avoid his eyes.

'Fine,' he says finally, 'follow me.'

IT'S NOT the most comfortable place I've ever slept but it's far from the worst. I spend most of the day curled up in a foetal position with some surprisingly soft towels. Foxworthy may be the archetypal grumpy divorced detective, but he knows how to use fabric softener.

When I finally wake up, my eyes snapping open and my body alert, it's clear that Foxworthy is long gone. I take the file and wander down to the kitchen. My stomach growls in irritation at the lack of blood but it's no matter. I can go hunting when I leave. It will take depressingly little time to find someone breaching the law; I can drink from them to show them the error of their ways. It's win-win.

The first few pages contain little more than Lisa's basic background information and notes from the initial interviews with her parents and neighbours. Everything confirms what I'd already discovered on my own: Lisa is a well-liked young woman who is passionate about any number of causes and has no problems voicing her opinions about them. Other than Adrian Leeman, the police found no evidence that she had any romantic entanglements. As far as the world is concerned, Lisa Johnson lived a blemish-free life.

It's only when I reach the fifth page that I come across new information. It's interesting information, as well. What her parents neglected to tell me — although it's no surprise that they kept it quiet — is that her latest venture involved joining the anti-vampire protests. Together with a bunch of others, she targeted a prosperous apartment building not far from Soho which is well known for housing vampettes for the Bancroft Family.

Vampettes are willing victims, happy to allow access to their jugulars in return for favours and compensation. Most of them, like poor Connor, aren't in it for the money; they enjoy the thrill of danger or being close to power. A good number hope that being a vampette first will make it easier to jump the queue when it comes to recruiting season. Unfortunately for them, the Families don't care about that kind of thing.

An alarming number of new bloodguzzler recruits are actually criminals. As Michael has explained many times, recruitment is meant to encourage them to move to the straight and narrow and turn over a new leaf. He believes it keeps crime numbers low. I think the real reason for the policy is something far less admirable: not only do criminals possess skill-sets which the rest of the law-abiding population rarely have, but they're also likely to be more loyal – and more dangerous. When the five Families capped their numbers at five hundred, the only way one Family could get ahead of the others was by making sure its vampires were the biggest, baddest and downright meanest. Most vampettes don't fit that bill. If I tried to suggest this to Michael, he'd tell me I was being unnecessarily cynical. I call it realistic.

The Soho protests didn't take long to turn nasty. Someone, whether it was Lisa or one of her best buds, used pig's blood to daub the front of the vampettes' building. The vampettes called out a few vampire protectors who, in turn, threatened the crowd. As far as I can tell from the report, none of the Bancroft guzzlers intended to do anything more than shake their fists and bare their fangs but the protestors didn't know that. Several of them rushed the vampires – never a smart move at the best of times – and while no one was seriously injured, many of the protestors spent the rest of the night in jail. Lisa was questioned but managed to escape incarceration.

Judging by events at the café last night, I wouldn't be surprised if the tree people's *raison d'être* is halting the vampires in their tracks. They might have approached her after seeing her at one of the rallies and she may have disappeared because she's run off to join them. What I still don't understand is if that theory is true, then why aren't the tree people better known? And why have the protests died down rather than getting worse? I nibble my bottom lip. There is a way to find out. Unfortunately, it's just not something I can do on my own.

I tuck the file inside my jacket and zip it up, making sure it's not going to fall out, then I let myself out of Foxworthy's house. The car has gone. If I'd been smart, I wouldn't have mentioned it at all and I could have taken it back myself. At least then I'd have had some form of transportation; now I have to use my own two feet. It's not that I'm lazy but time is constantly against me. That's what happens when you can only go outside when the sun is down. I could nick another car but I have a feeling that Foxworthy's patience won't extend to me stealing from his neighbours. The nearest train station is three miles away. I can cope.

I set off, winding my way out of the cul-de-sac and towards civilisation. Not only is my to-do list growing, but so are my hunger pangs. I need to find people. Tasty, juicy people.

WITH MY STOMACH full and the three hoodie-clad blokes who are old enough to know better trussed up on a rusting kids' roundabout, I get down to business. I'm in a position to kill several birds with one stone and I intend to take full advantage of the opportunity. Poor Medici will be feeling left out after I skipped last night's vigil as a result of getting shot, so I head out towards his stronghold first.

When I get there, I admit that I'm surprised. Instead of its usual 'shrouded in darkness because we're a lair of evil vampires' image, the Medici building is bathed in light. Not only have the curtains been thrown open so any passerby can peer inside, there are several large spotlights dotted around the front. For some reason, hundreds of candles are flickering in the gentle night breeze. Perhaps Medici is planning to break the record for the world's largest séance. Or, more worryingly, he's making his place look even more inviting and is literally lighting the way for more recruits to join him.

I take up my usual spot across the road. I'm not the only one; various members of the tabloid press are also there. I guess that news of Medici's illuminations has spread quickly. Unsurprisingly, several of them break away and barrel their way towards me.

'Bo!'

'Red Angel!'

I hold my palms up to ward off the flashing cameras. Bloody idiots. I open my mouth in a snarl but this lot are as bloodthirsty as I am. They're not going to be put off by a flash of white teeth.

'Why are you here, Bo?' a greasy-haired man asks.

'Are you planning to join Medici? Has he asked you to come?' babbles another.

I roll my eyes and mutter a curse under my breath. Fools. I fold my arms and drop the ferocious vampire façade. 'Why don't you tell me why you're here?' I ask coolly.

I receive several blinks in response. They're not used to being asked questions about themselves. A journalist for the *Evening Post* steps forward. I vaguely recognise him. In fact, there was a story less than a fortnight ago with his byline that questioned whether I'd gone off the rails or not. 'Tit for tat, Ms Blackman,' he simpers. 'Tell us why you're here first.'

I shrug and point at the mansion. 'I am doing what the police can't,' I say in a loud, clear voice. 'Lord Medici is breaking with hundreds of years of tradition. He's a power-hungry maniac who needs to be stopped.'

The delight on the journalists' faces reminds me of Kimchi when I open the fridge. 'Are you going to stop him, Bo? What are you going to do?'

I look directly in the cameras. 'I'm a vampire.' Duh. Obviously. 'Anyone would think that I would support the vampires' legal status. However, it's wrong. The UK government needs to wake up to what's happening and revoke the current laws allowing the Families to act as they wish. They are outdated and, worse, dangerous.'

'But you break the law every day, Ms Blackman,' the journalist persists. 'Do you think you should be punished for your actions?'

'If the law did its job,' I answer, 'then I wouldn't have to cross that line.'

'So are you going to stop Lord Medici from recruiting anyone else?'

I try to keep a straight face. Anyone with half an ounce of knowledge would know that I don't have enough power to stop Medici from doing a damn thing. I'm pretty certain this lot are aware of that fact; they just want to see blood – and they don't care who it belongs to.

'I would like Medici to come out from his hiding hole and talk to me. And the other Families.' I clear my throat. 'He's not going to do that though. He's too scared.' I inject just enough sneer into my voice to make my challenge clear. It would be extraordinarily nice for Medici to come out now because he wouldn't dare kill me in front of an audience. Despite my vigilante activities, I'm still the media's darling. I know it won't last; reputations turn on a dime as far as the gutter press is concerned. They might love me today but tomorrow I could be enemy numero uno. It doesn't matter. The publicity that such an act would generate would nail Medici's coffin shut. He's far too clever to let that happen.

The journalist raises his eyebrows. 'Them's fighting words.'

I turn to the flickering candles, making a show of sweeping my gaze across the entire Medici base. 'You betcha.' I return my attention back to him. Tit for tat. 'Why are you here?'

He laughs at me. 'Isn't it obvious?' He gestures at the lights. 'He's up to something. Whatever it is, we ain't gonna miss it.'

I frown at him in exasperation. 'You don't know what he's up to then?'

'Nah.'

Like I said – idiots. I move away from the cluster, presenting them with my back to make it obvious that the questioning session is over. A few still persist but when I continue to ignore them they give up, saving their ammo for another day. They know I'll be around again with a soundbite. As long as public opinion is against Medici and with me, then I have a chance. A slim chance, I admit, but still a chance. The paps know I need them more than they need me.

When I'm sure they're going to leave me in peace, I hop onto the roof of a nearby car and cross my legs, resting my chin on my hands as I stare at Medici's place. It's a deliberate move on my part and I'm rewarded by several more camera flashes. It'll make a nice story for tomorrow's papers – Bo Blackman staking out the Medici Family with a hard look in her eyes. Yadda yadda. If nothing else, it might piss Medici off.

'Good evening, Bo.'

I freeze. This is no journalist. I slowly look round, my eyes meeting those of Arzo's. Appearing out of nowhere is a nifty trick when you're in a wheelchair. A few of the paps turn but he's not interesting enough for them to bother lifting their cameras. They already have all the shots they need.

I press my lips together. He's acting casually enough, his hands on his knees and his posture relaxed. I know better.

'Lord Montserrat told me I might find you here,' he says, 'although I was expecting you to be later than this.'

'I have things to do later,' I mutter.

'You left without saying goodbye.'

'Yeah.' What of it?

'You're a founding member of New Order. You didn't have to run away.'

'Why does everyone think I did that? I wasn't running.' It's true. I strolled towards X after Connor and Dahlia died. I fold my arms. 'I didn't do anything wrong. I just needed a change of scenery. It was getting too crowded in those offices and I wanted a change of pace.'

'You've not been to the hospital to see your grandfather.'

I throw my hands up in the air and leap down from the car. This time the journalists do take notice but I ignore the whirrs and clicks from the cameras. 'For fuck's sake! He's in a coma! He's not going to know if I'm there or not!' How many times do I need to say the same damn thing? I jump down and stride towards him. Arzo doesn't flinch and the expression in his eyes doesn't change. 'Have *you* been to see him?' I demand. 'Because it was your insistence on keeping that bitch around that sent him into hospital. *She* poisoned him. *She's* responsible for this mess.'

He shakes his head. 'No. Medici is responsible.'

I snort. 'He just pointed the way. She pulled the damn trigger.'

His arms remain by his sides but all the same I'm wary. 'Did you kill her?' he asks quietly. 'Lord Montserrat said you didn't but...'

'You don't believe him,' I say flatly. 'Well, for your information no, I didn't kill her.' I pause for a beat then throw as much defiant menace into my tone as I can. 'But I should have. I wish I had.'

'She wasn't all bad, Bo. And neither are you.'

I tilt up my chin. 'Yes, I am.' Unwilling to continue the conversation, I spin round and return to my original spot on top of the car. A minute or two later, when I look back, Arzo has gone. Good.

RogU3 meets me a few streets away, far enough from the prying eyes of the journalists so that we can talk in private. Maria is with him but she hangs back, her shoulders hunched and her eyes on the pavement. If she's pretending to be invisible, she's not doing a very good job.

'Did you track the number plate I sent you?' I ask.

He beams at me cheerfully. 'Sure did. The plates are fake. The car must have been stolen.'

Just great. I curse under my breath. 'If I gave you an image, would you be able to track where it came from?'

He shrugs. 'Possibly. What is it?'

'A tree. One of the men who stole the car had it tattooed onto their skin and two missing girls were wearing it as jewellery before they disappeared. There's a whole group of people out there with it as their emblem and I can pretty much guarantee they're up to no good.'

'Images are harder than people,' Rogu3 tells me, 'but I can certainly try. Do you want me to do it now?'

'No. We've got a dinner date.'

Rogu3's eyes gleam. 'Ah ha. The mysterious benefactor. Is he of the sharp-fanged variety?'

'No. And you'll need to stop making cracks like that.'

'He doesn't have a sense of humour?'

Actually, X seems to find almost everything funny but it doesn't mean he won't eat Rogu3 if he feels like it. This will be a good test, I decide. If Rogu3 can cope with this, I reckon he'll cope with anything. If he's so determined to hang around then I'm going to make full use of him.

'Shall I drive?' he asks.

I stare at him. 'What do you mean? You're fifteen years old.'

He points across the street. There, propped haphazardly against a lamppost, is my motorbike.

My mouth drops open. 'Tell me you didn't.'

'I didn't.'

I have to curl my fingers into a fist to stop myself from slapping him. 'You can't drive!'

He grins at me, a self-satisfied flicker on his face of the sort that only a teenager can pull off.

'He very careful,' Maria says helpfully. When I look at her, she seems to regret speaking up and draws into herself. She's wearing a shapeless set of dungarees. They're about as far removed from fashion as a bin bag. I wince guiltily as I realise that I've been so wrapped up in other matters I've forgotten to get her something to wear. 'Where did the clothes come from?'

She wraps her arms around herself, clearly regretting speaking at all, even if it was in Rogu3's defence.

'Me,' he says casually.

'You bought her that?' I ask.

'She chose it.' He shrugs to himself as if the ways of women are a mystery to him. I'm well aware of what she's doing though; she thinks she can blend into the background. She wants to wear the unsexiest clothes it's possible to find so that no one ever thinks of her in that way again. Unfortunately the over-sized denim simply makes her look more fragile and pretty. I decide to keep my mouth shut on that matter and keep my attention on Rogu3 instead.

'Thank you for doing that.' He sweeps out a bow and I sigh in irritation. 'But you still shouldn't have driven here. Do you have a death wish or something? Because I didn't damn well save you from being a bloodguzzler for you to end up as roadkill under the wheels of some lorry.'

'Jeez, Bo, since when did you become such a buzz kill? And stop being so hypocritical. It's not like you care about the law.'

Actually, I do care, I care very much. I just ignore a lot of the current laws because they're not helping anyone. It's at times like these that I wish I still had Doctor Love, the shrink assigned to deal with my PTSD, on my speed dial.

Two months ago, Rogu3 reverted to being a kid, happy to stay at home and work through his nightmares on his own. Now he's completely reversed his position. Maybe it's like the seven stages of grief or something: denial, anger, acting like a complete lunatic...

'You can't ride around the streets of London on a motorbike.'

His bottom lip juts out. 'I wore a helmet. So did Maria. The law is arbitrary. I'm a much safer driver than lots of people who are older than me.'

'Have you even taken lessons?'

He scoffs. 'It's not that hard.'

I shake my head. 'This is a really stupid idea. You need to go home, Rogu3. To *your* home. You don't belong in my world.'

'We've been through this. I'm not going anywhere.'

'If I can't trust you to get yourself around town in one piece then...'

'Fine! I won't take your damn bike again!'

I shake my head. Taking the pair of them to meet X is such a bad idea. Maria is acting like prey and Rogu3 is acting like he's invincible. The pair of them are doomed.

Rogu3's petulance ebbs away. 'Listen, Bo, I know you're upset. I didn't think it would be such a big deal. I'm already in your world. Whether either of us like it or not, we've both been sucked in. I might not be a triber like you but for good or bad, this is who I am now.' He jerks his head towards Maria. 'She feels the darkness too.'

I sigh in exasperation. He already knows he's won. Whether he'll feel the same way after meeting X remains to be seen, but if this is what he really wants then this is what he'll get.

'I'll drive,' I say shortly. It's just as well it's a big bike and I'm petite. Fitting three people onto the back of it isn't going to be comfortable. I suppose I should be glad Rogu3 didn't bring Kimchi along as well.

He grins. 'Cheers Bo.' He drops his head. 'Guess what the word of the week is?'

I roll my eyes. A tiny smile still tugs at the corner of my mouth though I try to stop it. 'What?'

'Scofflaw. It means...'

'I can guess,' I interrupt drily. I check my watch and sigh. 'Come on, we'd better go. The last thing we want to be is late.' There's no telling what X is going to do this evening; antagonising him with unnecessary tardiness seems stupid.

CHAPTER II

DINNER

I'm relieved that we reach the restaurant first. All three of us have barely sat down, when I hear the familiar mellifluous murmur of X's voice. My stomach churns and I glance over. When I see he's in full glamour, with his tattoos masked and his 'human' face on display, I relax infinitesimally. That's something at least. There again, as he glides over to our table I can't believe that anyone could actually mistake him for human. No one who's not a Kakos daemon moves like that.

Maria, hunched into the corner and still trying to pretend that she's not here, doesn't see his approach. Rogu3 is a different matter. His eyes follow mine and when he catches sight of X, his jaw drops comically.

'I know him...' His face pales and he swallows hard. 'He works for Streets of Fire. You could have told me!' He jumps up, wiping his sweaty palms on his jeans. That's the precise moment when he realises that he is wearing jeans. He glances down at himself and looks embarrassed. 'I could have dressed up!' he hisses.

If there were not such potential for this dinner to go disastrously wrong, I'd be amused. I get to my feet, my entire body tense. Make a move against him, X, I project, and this restaurant will become a bloodbath. He glances at me, answering my thoughts with a wink. Then he turns to Rogu3.

'Alistair,' he says holding out his hand. 'I'm so pleased to finally make your acquaintance. Bo has told me a lot about you.'

Not voluntarily, I think, as Rogu3 reaches out and takes X's hand, pumping it furiously. 'I'm so thrilled to meet you,' he babbles. 'I had no idea you were Bo's benefactor.'

X's mouth curves into a smile. 'Believe me, the pleasure is all mine. And I find it hard to imagine that Bo hasn't spoken about me.'

I just manage to stifle a snort. X made it very clear that anyone I told about his existence would have their heart cut out of their chest and munched upon.

'Mm,' he continues fluidly, 'shall we sit down? I'm so hungry I think I could eat a heart.' I stiffen visibly. 'Perhaps even brains, intestines and an entire horse.'

Rogu3 beams in adoration. Maria jerks away. I realise too late that the one empty seat is right next to her. That was poor planning.

'Alistair,' X says, continuing to use his real name for some unfathomable reason that makes me wary, 'why don't you sit here next to Maria?'

I blink. That was ... nice of him. Rogu3 jumps to his request, quickly scoots round and we all sit down. I keep my hands under the table. I don't think either Rogu3 or Maria need to see how white my knuckles are.

The waiter wanders over, handing each of us a menu and reciting the specials in a vaguely bored tone. He doesn't recognise me, which is rather nice. Next to me, Rogu3 is bristling with excitement, sending repeated surreptitious glances in X's direction as if he can't quite believe he's really here.

'Thank you,' I say firmly, once the waiter has finished. He

nods, seeing me properly for the first time. There's a confused look in his eyes, as if he remembers me from somewhere but can't quite work out where. He leaves, giving us time to choose what we want.

I clear my throat and look at Rogu3. 'I'm surprised you've heard of my, um, benefactor here,' I say, testing the water. 'He tends to keep out of the limelight.' Very deliberately; that's why he's not named as the CEO. There's a human puppet in that role.

To my surprise, Rogu3 shoots me an annoyed look. 'I keep up with everyone important in the tech world,' he mutters. 'Anyone who works for Streets of Fire counts as important.'

X shakes out his napkin and places it in his lap. 'And anyone who has the wherewithal to hack past our impressive firewall also counts as important.'

Oh no. I stare at Rogu3, whose head droops. Shit, shit, shit. Is that why X has been so keen to meet him in person? Because he wants to hurt him for hacking into his company? Dread fingers its way through my veins. If only I'd known.

'I'm sorry.' Rogu3 almost whispers the words. 'I was a lot younger then. I didn't intend any harm.'

'I know,' X replies cheerfully. 'And no harm done.'

Is that it? I glare hard at X, waiting for him to say or do something else. He just smiles at all of us instead. 'Are we ready to order?'

The waiter materialises out of nowhere. Maria gives a minute shake of her head, unwilling to speak aloud with so many strangers around.

'How about the chicken Provençale, my dear?' X suggests.

Her eyes fly to his. Something flickers in her expression and, for once, I wish I were like X and knew what she was thinking. It's a fleeting desire; I have enough problems as it is without seeing inside everyone's souls.

Knowing what's going on in Maria's mind would probably turn me crazy. I don't require telepathy to know that she's experienced more horror in her young life than most people do in a lifetime. I'm not sure whether Maria is going to make a run for the door or swing a punch at X, but suddenly she nods. He smiles approvingly, and turns to the waiter, requesting a bloody steak for himself. Rogu3 opts for pasta. I bypass everything and choose three things from the dessert menu. I don't need human food to survive – in fact it does absolutely nothing for me – but I do have a sweet tooth. Besides, I assume that since X demanded our presence here, he's going to foot the bill. He doesn't appear murderous so far; if his mood changes, it'll be better if he takes it out on the manager for offering over-priced plates than on us.

Hearing my thoughts, X gives me a toothy smile. I smile back, baring my fangs.

Rogu3 leans forward eagerly. 'There have been lots of rumours about which new processor you're going to choose to promote. The XT3 is looking really good.'

X waves his hand in an airy, dismissive gesture. 'Its operating speed leaves a lot to be desired.'

Ten seconds of computer talk and I can feel my eyes glazing over. If this is why X wanted to meet Rogu3, it's going to be a bloody long evening.

X snaps his head towards me and, for a moment, familiar terror at being in the same room as a Kakos daemon attacks me. 'I already have everything I need,' he tells me with a sniff. Rogu3, unaware of what's really going on, looks surprised.

Then can we go? I ask, posing the question silently.

'We should get some wine,' he says aloud. 'Such a lovely occasion as this deserves a decent tipple.'

I scowl. 'Rogu3 and Maria are under age.'

He lifts his eyebrows, clearly amused at the idea that

someone would stop him from filling their glasses. He has a point, in a way. 'You really do have a strange relationship with the word of the law, Bo,' he comments.

Rogu3 laughs. 'That's what I've been telling her. A small glass won't do any harm.'

'Yes, it will.' I fold my arms and frown like a disapproving teacher.

'No wine,' Maria says suddenly in a clear voice. Both Rogu3 and I turn to her in astonishment. Her cheeks colour. She already seems to be regretting speaking up.

'Okay.' Rogu3's voice is quiet and my surprise only grows. Like all teenagers, he'll argue with me at every single turn and on every single matter – but two words from Maria and he's as docile as a lamb.

X's smile grows. 'Young love.'

Neither Rogu3 nor Maria look enamoured of X's observation. To mask his embarrassment, Rogu3 leans forward and starts peppering X with more computer-based questions. Maria looks relieved. I take advantage of the situation to relax back in my chair and let my mind drift. I mull over what I know of Lisa Johnson and what my next move should be. There's also Medici to consider – and Michael. He inadvertently pops into my head. I run my tongue across my lips. If I concentrate, I can still taste him, still feel what it was like to have his body against mine, with his dark eyes glittering down at me. Then I get a sharp kick in my shin from under the table. X. Shit. I should be far more guarded with my thoughts, even when he seems to be otherwise occupied.

I ignore the flare of heat in my cheeks. X is on a roll tonight in terms of making his dinner companions blush. Thankfully the waiter uses that moment to deliver our meals.

'So, Alistair,' X says, savouring a mouthful of meat, 'do you fully understand what it is that Bo is doing and why?'

I pause, my spoon halfway towards my mouth. Here we go. Rogu3 swallows. 'Yes. At least I think so.'

'She's dancing with legalities, you know. Even for a vampire, interfering with the rest of the legal system is dangerous. And she has immunity. If you agree to work with her – to work for me – you'll have no such guarantees.'

I stiffen. I don't want this.

Rogu3 responds calmly before I can butt in. 'As I think you know, I don't always stick to the right side of the law myself. This will be no different.' He holds up his hand and wiggles his fingers. 'If this really is a job interview, then I have a few caveats.'

X's mouth twitches. 'Big word for such a young boy.'

There's a flash of a scowl from Rogu3 and I shift uncomfortably in my seat. I don't like the way this conversation is going. X kicks me under the table again, although he doesn't look in my direction. I hiss under my breath.

'One,' Rogu3 says, holding up his index finger, 'I am not a field operative.' What is this? *Call of Duty*? 'My best work is done with a computer screen.' Not to mention he's no doubt wary after his past experiences out in the 'field'. 'Second,' he continues, 'I will require time off for my examinations.'

'Pff,' X dismisses. 'You don't need those things.'

'All the same,' Rogu3 says, with far more composure than I think I could manage, 'I want to sit them.'

'Very well.'

He holds up another finger. 'Three. When I'm twenty-one, should I so desire it, you will give me a management-entry position at Streets of Fire.'

I have to give it to Rogu3, he certainly thinks on his feet. Thirty minutes ago he had no idea that we were meeting someone with clout at the large internet company. I regard him with newfound respect. He knows what he wants and he's going after it.

'Very well,' X replies with a straight face. 'I can agree to those terms. However, I have a few caveats of my own. There is to be no further hacking of the Streets of Fire systems. Ever.' There's a sudden hard glint reflected in his eyes. X is more pissed off about that than he's letting on. 'Secondly, you answer to Bo. In everything. She answers to me and I trust her judgment.'

I try not to look too surprised. Although given that I know X's true nature, he probably has little fear that I'll step out of line.

'Done.' Rogu3 reaches across the table, his palm outstretched for the obligatory handshake.

I clear my throat. Everyone turns to look at me, even Maria. X's mouth twitches; he knows exactly what I'm about to say. 'About the field operative part. There is just one thing.' I meet Rogu3's eyes and lower my voice. 'You won't be in any danger. I promise you that.'

'One thing?'

I nod.

'Okay,' he agrees. The open trust in his expression gnaws at me. I want to scream that I'm not trustworthy at all. Neither is X.

X flicks a look at Maria. 'Everyone's happy,' he says softly. And that's when I know what this meeting was really about. He couldn't give a shit about Rogu3 – it is Maria he wanted to meet.

WE STAND on the pavement watching X climb into an expensive

looking sports car and drive off. As soon as he's gone, Rogu3 lets out a low whistle. 'That was intense.'

'Mm.' I bite my lip and look at Maria. She's staring at me with clear green eyes. I don't think I'd noticed until now what an unusual shade they are.

She takes a deep breath. 'What type vampire are you?' she asks in her usual stilted way. She's obviously been rehearsing this question in her head. 'What vampire is friends with Kakos daemon?'

I stiffen. Rogu3 simply looks confused. 'What do you mean, Maria?' he asks. 'He's human.'

She doesn't take her eyes off me. Damn it. 'Rogu3 is right,' I tell her, hoping the lie is smooth enough to fool him at least. 'He's just a human.' I laugh hollowly. 'If he were a Kakos daemon we'd all be dead and instead of rare steak, he'd have been munching on our hearts.'

'I do not understand what this munching is,' she says. 'But you lying.'

I can't think of any way to deny her claims other than by continuing to protest – and that will be a dead giveaway. Instead I do the only thing I can: I look at Rogu3 and swallow. 'About that field work. We need to go now while there's still an audience.'

He looks from me to Maria and back again. He must realise that I'm not going to say any more about the matter. Unfortunately this is obviously a conversation he's going to have with her later. I'll have to get her on her own before then and tell her to keep her mouth shut, for all our sakes. X chose to keep himself hidden from Rogu3 so our previous agreement still stands. If anyone finds out his true nature, then we're dead meat. Literally.

CHAPTER 12

THE REDEEMER

I put Maria in a taxi. Frankly, I wouldn't be surprised if she decides to leg it before she ever gets back to my place. That might not be a bad thing. Ignoring the curious looks I'm still receiving from Rogu3, I motion him towards the bike.

'Get on,' I say shortly. 'We're heading back to Medici.'

That puts paid to any further awkward moments. He swallows, his Adam's apple bobbing nervously in his throat. 'Okay.'

'I won't let anything happen to you.'

His face twists. 'Bloody hell, Bo! You're not my mum, alright? You're not responsible for me, so stop treating me like I'm a two year old. I'm not a complete idiot. I can look after myself. And I trust you. Stop second-guessing me.'

I ball up my fists. I'm not going to let him get hurt but that doesn't mean he should continue to blindly trust me. Rather than say anything, I climb on the bike and turn on the engine. We need to get there sooner rather than later. The last thing I need is for all those journalists to head home for the night.

When we pull up in front of Medici's place, there's still plenty of them milling around. I had briefly considered keeping myself out of sight but tabloid journalists are a canny lot.

They'd figure out I was involved, and staying hidden would only create more questions. I need them to focus on Rogu3. Fortunately, they all recognise him; his near-death experience at his school placed him front and centre of most newspapers. The fact that he's with me causes a rush of sudden excitement.

'Alistair Jones!'

Before I manage to turn off the engine, we are surrounded. I feel Rogu3 tense up at my back. 'I'm not sure about this,' he mutters in my ear.

'You can do it,' I soothe. 'It won't be that hard. I wouldn't ask if it wasn't important.'

He expels an irritated breath. 'I am not a child.' He jumps off the bike and faces me, his arms outstretched. 'I've had enough of you keeping me in the dark. You think you can order me around as you please. Who the hell was that guy we just had dinner with? You shut Maria up pretty fucking quickly when she asked.'

'Don't swear,' I say automatically.

'Fuck you.'

I wince. That was a bit uncalled for. The journalists stare at us, absolutely agog. For once they're more interested in watching our argument play itself out than asking any questions. Rogu3 registers their interest and gestures at the lot of them. 'Check it out, ladies and gentlemen,' he says with a sarcastic edge. 'Bo Blackman, the supposed saviour of the streets. You call her the Red Angel. Well, let me tell you, she's no angel. She saved my life but she's still a vampire. Still a freak.' He injects enough sneer into his voice to make me step backward.

I stare at him with a mixture of hurt and confusion. 'Rogu3…'

He ignores my plea. 'Do you want to know why she brought me here?' He throws out a hand towards Medici's mansion. 'To make it clear to you all what I think of him. Lord fucking Medici who thinks he can turn the whole of London into a city of bloodguzzling murderers. She's not wrong – he's a monster and everyone should wake up to that fact. But she's a monster too. All vampires are.' He gazes back at me with cold eyes. 'I should know. I almost became one.'

'If it wasn't for me, you'd be dead.'

He towers over me. 'And how many others *are* dead because of you? You make this big show of cleaning up the streets and solving crimes. Of getting rid of the shitheads who can afford good lawyers to beat the system.' He leans in towards me. 'But how many of those have you drunk blood from? Is your self-righteousness because you really care about what's happening to society, or are you just after your next meal?'

'There are plenty of vampettes...' I begin.

'Screw the vampettes. It's the chase you like. You enjoy it when humans act as prey. That's all we are to you.' His voice rises. 'Aren't we?' He starts shouting, spittle flying onto my face. 'Aren't we?'

One of the journalists gets too close, thrusting a camera so close to my face that the photo will probably pick up every damn pore. I snatch it out of her hands and smash it on the ground. She lets out an inarticulate howl, no doubt in direct proportion to just how expensive the stupid thing was. To shut her up, I let my fangs lengthen. I snarl at her and she backs off.

'You see?' Rogu3 yells. 'You see what she's capable of?' He jabs his thumb in my chest. 'Stay the fuck away from me.' He thrusts his hands into his pockets and spins round, marching off down the street. Several of the journalists follow him, throwing out questions which ricochet off his rigidly straight posture. The braver ones stick with me, although I notice that this time they keep their distance.

'Is he telling the truth, Bo?' one of them asks.

'How does it make you feel to have a teenager talk to you like that?' throws in another.

I let all their questions bounce off me. With a narrow-eyed look of hatred towards the Medici fortress, because there's no doubt Medici has been enjoying the show, I turn my back and get back on the bike. I gun the engine and the journalists scatter. Then I screech off into the distance, in the opposite direction to Rogu3.

I COME to a halt several streets away, sliding the bike into Mile Stop Alley. It's dark enough here that I finally feel safe. I tilt my head upwards towards the clouded sky. Even the moon is obscured from sight so there's no chance that I'll see any stars. All the same, the expanse helps calm me down, reminding me that I'm nothing more than a tiny speck in the universe. I inhale and exhale several times.

'Very Zen, Bo,' I mutter to myself.

'Talking to yourself? Are you going senile already?'

I drop my head and glance over. 'You got here quickly. Are you sure you weren't followed?'

Rogu3 grins at me. 'Duh. They gave up on me ages ago.' He gives me a huge, dramatic bow. 'I was pretty awesome, wasn't I?'

'You were alright,' I admit grudgingly.

'Alright? Even you half-believed me! I could see it in your eyes.'

'Okay,' I allow. 'You were pretty convincing.'

He beams. 'I knew it! I'm a far better actor than anyone ever gives me credit for. You know, when we did *West Side Story* last year, Mrs Thomson put Mike Allan in the lead role and I ended up in the chorus. She had no clue what she was doing. It serves her right that he got mono the night before the first performance and…'

'Rogu3.'

'Sorry.' He doesn't look contrite. 'That was just so much fun. Can we do it again?'

I frown at him. 'No. Besides now you have to go home.' I raise my eyebrows pointedly. '*Your* home.'

'Oh come on, Bo Peep…'

'It won't work unless you're with your parents. Do you really think none of those journos will attempt a follow-up? If anyone discovers you're staying with me, all this will have been a complete waste.'

'I'm a world-class hacker and I didn't find out where you were staying until you emailed me directly.'

'You still found me. And we have no idea what resources these tree people have at their disposal.'

'Fine,' he grumbles. 'You shouldn't call them tree people though. If they really are as bad as you think, making them sound like they belong with Greenpeace hardly fits.'

'Well,' I say firmly, taking him by the shoulders and propelling him back out of the alley, 'when they contact you and tell you who they are, I'll call them something else.' I flag down a passing taxi and virtually throw him inside.

'I'll phone you,' he promises.

Something prickles along the back of my neck. 'Good,' I tell him. 'Now go.' The door closes and the taxi speeds off. I cross my arms, ready to meet whatever fresh new hell is about to descend.

'Come on,' I whisper as Rogu3 disappears round the corner. 'Whoever you are, show your face.'

No one appears. I narrow my eyes. I wasn't imagining things – someone is definitely watching me. I lick my lips and bend down as if to tie my shoelace. As I do, I catch the flicker of movement up on the opposite rooftop. There you are.

I pretend to fiddle with my shoe then stand back up again, looking casual. I stroll across the street until the angle of the buildings above conceals me from sight. The moment I reach a shadowed spot, I leap upwards. I don't like being spied upon.

Whoever is up there is definitely a triber. No human would hang around on the top of such a high building at this time of night. I'm betting vampire. When I pop my head above the parapet, my arms barely straining against my own body weight, I know I'm right.

It's a woman, dressed in black and peering down to the street. Obviously she's still looking for me. Ha! I enjoy watching her scanning up and down, her brow furrowed in confusion. Let her take that back to Michael, I think dismissively. He can't send minions to follow me around and not expect me to notice. I'm not *that* green.

She turns away with a half shrug, apparently giving up. That's when I spot the flash of bright red round her wrist before it's swallowed up by the cuff of her jumpsuit. Not one of Michael's, then; Medici has sent her out. That causes problems.

Rogu3's little show wasn't for Medici's benefit; I needed him to publicly disavow vampires. It's the only way that the tree people will reveal themselves. It doesn't mean that openly berating Medici wasn't a benefit though. I know from past experience that he has a short temper. Pissing him off with so many people watching might encourage him to step out from his fortress – but he won't do that if he knows it was a trick. Worse, he might even tell them all that it was a trick and I can't let him do that.

I gnaw at my bottom lip. The only sensible recourse is to slice off the bloodguzzler's head and make sure she has no way of talking but that's a bloody course of action and she's not yet done me any wrong. Then I shrug to myself; what's one less Medici vampire in the world?

I pull myself up, standing spread-eagled on the rooftop just as she realises she's not alone. She turns to face me, her stance showing that she's preparing for attack.

'Oh happy days,' she sneers. 'It's the dwarf. I was just looking for you.'

Any trace of guilt I might have felt vanishes. Just because I'm short doesn't mean I'm going to let people push me around or use my height as a weapon against me – even a verbal one. I sweep a glance over her. She definitely exudes power. Outwardly she appears to be in her mid-twenties but I'd put her guzzler age at closer to fifty. That means she's got a lot more power at her fingertips than me but it doesn't mean I can't beat her. I just need to be smart about it.

She circles me. I keep my distance, matching her step for step.

'Come on,' she purrs, 'what are you afraid of? If you can beat a Kakos daemon, surely you'll find it easy to beat me.'

I sigh. She's referring to the little show X staged months ago when I supposedly killed him on live television. I'm starting to wonder whether anyone in the world was fooled by that. It certainly doesn't make my adversaries afraid of me.

I save my breath and don't answer, watching her carefully to make sure I avoid her first blow. We continue to edge round each other like feral cats in a staring contest. It's not going to last like this for long.

She's much taller than I am. That's no great surprise, most of the world is taller than me, but it puts me at a distinct disadvantage. I make sure I'm out of reach of her long arms so that when her fist flies towards me in a punch, I can duck and weave, shifting my feet to compensate. When she fails to hit me, she wobbles slightly and starts to lose her balance. I snap out a thrust towards her solar plexus and manage to achieve contact, but not hard enough. She gasps in pain but she's still upright. Bugger.

She recovers quickly. Rather than continue the standoff, she launches a flurry of punches. Although I do what I can to keep out of her reach, she manages to hit me several times. The pain doesn't make me to falter, it simply galvanises me into action.

Realising that my fists aren't going to do much damage, I vault upwards with a scissor kick, ready to smash the heel of my boot into her face. She's too fast for that and she grabs my ankle and twists. The only reason I avoid a broken bone is because I allow my body to move with her action but it hurts all the same. It really bloody hurts. I land back down onto the flat roof with an oomph. She laughs.

'Did that hurt?' she enquires, bending over me.

'On the contrary,' I snarl. 'I enjoyed it.'

Before I can scoot away, she lunges forward, taking hold of my ears and dragging my head upwards and then slamming it back down again. Pretty little lights dance in front of my eyes. Damn it. I roll to my right; I'm too vulnerable right now and I need to give myself some breathing space. Unfortunately little Miss Medici knows it. She's got her prey in her sights and victory on the horizon so she's not about to let me get away.

She snatches the back of my shirt and pulls me backwards, then hefts me into the air. For a brief half second, I feel a cooling breeze on my face, then I'm spinning out of control. I twist my body to halt the spin. There's not a lot of space on this roof and, if I go too far, I'm going to fall off the edge. I have excellent recovery skills but if I land badly, I might not get back up again.

My fingers scrabble as I start to fall downwards. I catch the edge of the roof while my legs crash into the side of the wall. I just need to pull myself up – ordinarily an easy feat – and then I can attack her properly. She's not stupid, though. I'm halfway up and about to prop my weight onto my elbows when she steps over and stands on my hands, one heavy foot on each. I collapse again. Her weight is crushing my fingers. The second she lets go, I'm not going to be able to hang on.

'You should go on a diet,' I gasp. 'You're heavier than you look.'

She laughs and crouches down. 'Say goodbye,' she smirks. She lifts up one foot. I try desperately to hang on but I don't have the strength; my hand is too bruised and broken. My arm drops, swinging uselessly in the air.

She starts to lift her second foot, amusement written all over her face. 'Medici wants you alive,' she says. 'I think he wants you to come to him. It'll be easier for all of us if that doesn't happen.' She moves her foot away.

I have one chance. Before I drop, I heave up one hand and then the other and grab both sides of her skull. I use her ears to gain purchase. Then I open my mouth.

It's a little-known fact that the masseter muscle, located in the jaw and used for biting, is the strongest one in the body. I have Kimchi to thank for giving me this knowledge. With one vicious move, I bite into her neck. This isn't the delicate nipping of a typical feeding, I'm ripping away her flesh. She screams, a sound that's abruptly cut off as I tear out her windpipe. I release my hands and use one to hold onto the edge of the roof and the other to yank the front of her shirt and pull. Her body sails over my head.

'Is it a bird?' I gasp as I hurriedly return my other hand to the safety of the roof and pull myself up. 'Is it a plane?' I roll over, bringing myself to safety. 'No. It's the incredible flying vampire.'

There's a loud thump as she hits the ground. Not so good at flying after all. I shrug and stand up, gently flexing my aching fingers. I snap three of the bones back into place with satisfying clicks, as easy as one, two, three.

My skin is tingling: I enjoyed that far more than I should have. Adjusting my ponytail, I smile slowly to myself. I'm not stupid enough to believe that I'm invincible – or that I'm strong enough to take on Medici himself yet. But that felt good. I stretch my arms out as if I'm Christ the Redeemer on top of Mount Corcovado. There's nothing redeeming about me, however.

I smile to myself then head for home.

CHAPTER 13
CRIME DOESN'T PAY

In my state of exultation, I forget that I still have to deal with Maria. I see her the second that I unlock the door to my apartment. She's curled up in a corner of the sofa in a tight ball. I can only imagine that Kimchi has been terrorising her with his unyielding desire to lick every inch of her body. It's difficult to know for sure because he's already bowling towards me with frenzied yips. He leaps up, placing his paws on my chest and assailing me with a cloud of doggy breath. Whatever good manners he learnt with Beth and Matt are quickly going out of the window. I tell him sternly to get down, which he takes as an invitation to jump upwards several times like a yo-yo.

'Sit,' I command.

Kimchi immediately turns and runs off, returning with the mangled remains of what I think was once a shoe. He deposits it at my feet, wagging his tail even more vigorously as if he's as proud of himself for killing it as I am for dispatching the Medici vampire.

I sigh irritably and pick it up. It's covered from head to toe in slobber. Thank goodness X gives me a large allowance; if

Kimchi's going to stick around, I'll need it to make sure I have something to wear.

Tossing the destroyed shoe in the bin, I walk towards Maria. Kimchi continues to bounce up and down by my side. The sensible thing would be to lock him away so he doesn't scare Maria but if she's going to hang around, she'll have to get used to him sooner or later.

Maria hugs her knees tighter.

'It's okay,' I tell her. 'He's just a dog. I know he's not exactly well trained but he wouldn't hurt you.' My feet crunch on something and I look down at a pile of large wooden splinters on the floor. What the hell? I glance at the ornate Chippendale table in the centre of the room. Oh no.

I glare at Kimchi. 'Was this you?' I bend down to inspect the table leg. There are definite teeth marks and I doubt it was Maria gnawing on a piece of priceless furniture.

Kimchi pants enthusiastically and sits down next to me. His tail thumps on the floor as if he's proud of his achievement. I roll my eyes. 'You killed the table. Excellent work,' I say drily. I suppose that'll teach me not to leave him at home when I go out.

I leave him to admire his handiwork and return to Maria. She's not moved an inch. 'You can sit down to dinner with a Kakos daemon,' I say softly, 'but you're scared of a fat dog who likes chomping on wood?'

Her wide eyes meet mine. They are no longer the bright green they were before; oddly, they've darkened to a murky, less arresting shade. Interesting. I sit down next to her. For a long time she doesn't say anything. Then she licks her lips and speaks.

'I understand daemon,' she says. 'Dog, I do not.' She throws Kimchi a baleful glance as if she's expecting him to launch himself at her at any second.

'How did you know?' I ask.

'About daemon?' she shrugs. 'I just know.'

'And he doesn't frighten you?' She just shrugs. Save me from teenagers. 'You can't tell Rogu3 about him.'

Her nose wrinkles. 'You mean Alistair?'

I nod. 'He isn't supposed to know.'

She absorbs this request. 'Okay.'

I pick at a hangnail. 'Maria, are you ready to talk about what happened to you?' She flinches. I hold up my palms. 'I won't make you. Don't worry.'

'I not worried.'

Maybe she should be. 'What are your plans?'

With an effort, she uncurls herself and stands up. 'You want me to go.' It's not a question.

'No.' I sigh. 'Sit down. You're welcome here for as long as you want.' At least, she is now that X has dropped his demands for her to leave. I look at her directly in the eyes and hope I'm telling the truth. 'It's safe here.'

She glances around, her gaze falling on Kimchi again.

'He's safe too. Honest.' I cross my heart. 'But maybe you want to contact your parents? You're still just a kid. What about school? Or...?'

She folds her arms and sits down, this time on the edge of the sofa as if she's ready to bolt at any moment. 'I do not want this talk.'

'Okay. What *do* you want?'

She considers this. 'I want to do same as you.'

I give her a careful look. 'What do you mean?'

'Hurt people. I want to hurt bad people.'

'That's not exactly what I...' I falter at her expression. 'It's dangerous,' I say weakly.

'I don't care.'

I study her. I can understand how she feels. Hell, it's how *I* feel. I nibble on my bottom lip. I'm probably going to regret this. 'Okay then.' I take out my phone and find X's number. He answers on the first ring.

'Bo,' he purrs, 'missing me already?'

'I need an assignment,' I tell him, all business. 'Do you have anything?'

He chuckles. 'What about the missing girl? Or Medici?' His voice drops. 'If you're bored, you can always call Michael again. Maybe this time you can return the favour and suck on his...'

'Lisa Johnson is in hand,' I interrupt. 'Medici is up to something but I don't know what and I'm not hanging around his place all night.' I don't mention Michael. 'Give me a crime to stop. Preferably something non-violent.'

There's a pause. 'Very well. I have the perfect thing. I do believe there's a break-in in progress. One daemon and he's a half-breed so you should have no problems.'

'Perfect. Where's it taking place?'

I can hear the smile in his voice. 'Magix.'

I clench my teeth. Just great. 'Isn't there anything else?'

'Of course. There are plenty of nasty criminal elements out and about. But you wouldn't want to confront anyone who might hurt little Maria, would you?'

I stiffen. He's not meant to be able to read minds from a distance. I pull the phone away from my ear and stare at it suspiciously.

X laughs. 'Relax. We've been through this. I'm just not stupid, that's all.'

I'm still not entirely mollified. I'm also not prepared to challenge him further. 'There's definitely nothing else?'

'There's a heist taking place on the other side of the city. But considering how long you have until dawn...'

'Fine,' I snap. 'Is there anything I need to know?'

'Not right now.' His lingering amusement makes me wary

but I don't think he'll put his pet in any danger. And if he wanted to hurt Maria, he'd have done so at the restaurant.

'Thank you,' I tell him, more out of habit than any genuine desire to show gratitude.

'Oh, little Bo,' X says, 'your grandfather taught you so well.'

I ignore his last comment and hang up. 'By the way,' I mutter at the phone, 'your expensive heirloom table has been half-eaten.'

I stand up and look at Maria. 'We have something. Let's go.'

'And dog?'

I look at Kimchi just as he cocks his leg against the table. Oh well. 'He's coming too.' I jerk my pinkie at her. 'You two need to learn to get along.'

THE THREE OF us stand across the road from Magix's flagship store. I've been here many times in the past and I know that I'm not welcome inside. The last time I ventured in, I wore a disguise. This time, not only did I not bring so much a hat to hide my hair, I'm not in the mood to hide my identity. Not from them and not when I'm here ostensibly helping them.

If it weren't for Maria, I'd let the damn robbery go ahead. Magix don't need saving from a burglar, they need saving from themselves. Even with their less than salubrious CEO long gone thanks to yours truly, they're still a vast conglomerate with fingers in many dodgy pies. All the same, I'm here now.

'I do not understand,' Maria says, puzzled. 'They are open. Time is late.'

I give her a distracted nod. 'Twenty-four hour shopping for all your magic needs,' I say, just as a shifty-looking black witch emerges. I bank down the temptation to jump him. 'Come on,' I tell her. 'We should probably head round the back. That'll be where the robbery is taking place.'

She frowns. 'How do you know?'

I point at the nearby traffic lights. 'Delivery van.' And not just any delivery van: it has darkened windows and the aura of magic around it. Whatever it contains, I'm betting it's dangerous. If it's dangerous, it's desirable.

We jog after it, rounding the corner and heading down the shadowy side street towards the back entrance of the store. With Maria in tow, I have to go more slowly than I normally would but it's no big deal. I'm not going to shed any tears if we don't stop the robbery in time.

By the time we get there, the van's doors are open and two tired-looking men are taking out boxes and depositing them by the back door. A stern woman, who is far too perfectly coiffed for this time of night, is ticking off each one on a clipboard. Her lips are tightly pressed together and she's not uttering a word to the poor delivery workers. The least she could do is offer them a drink of water.

I scan the street carefully in every direction. Kimchi helpfully does the same, his nose twitching; in fact, his whole body is quivering. I can't see a damn thing but something has set him off. I sniff the air but my nose isn't as well-developed as his.

'What is it, boy?' I ask, as if he can answer me. 'What can you smell?'

He jerks against his lead. Even with my vampiric strength, I can barely keep hold of him. He opens his mouth to bark but I nudge him with my knee in an urgent bid to keep him quiet. For once he obeys.

'Daemon,' Maria says, eyeing Kimchi with distaste. 'He smells daemon.'

Oh good. I look impressed and a tiny smile tugs at her

mouth, suggesting that she's more pleased by my admiration than she wants to let on. 'How do you know?'

She rolls her eyes, immediately reverting to type. 'Is obvious.' She points at the woman. 'She is daemon.'

I squint. Despite the dark sky, the light from Magix fully illuminates her. Everything about her screams human. I purse my lips. 'But…'

'Look.'

I try again, struggling to see what Maria does. Perfect hair, perfect skin. Human eyes. And she's not saying a word. Realisation dawns: she's not staying silent because of a pair of sleepy delivery guys. She's staying silent because she can't speak.

'Glamour,' I breathe. Whatever spell she's woven is good enough to mask her appearance but not to cover her voice at the same time.

Maria nods. 'Is good spell.' She shrugs. 'Not good enough.'

I grin. On the face of things, it's a pretty smart move. Magic yourself up to look like a bored Magix exec accepting a routine delivery. The delivery men will happily hand over whatever they're carrying and not think twice about it. Meanwhile, the real woman is probably tied up somewhere inside. Or worse.

I eye the woman up and down. Should I kill her or leave her for the police? I do have some sympathy for her situation; I'd be tempted to rip off the magic store too. The majority of daemons do little more than dabble in magic. The witches, whether black or white, tend to be far better at it. With a few helpful items, there's no telling what a daemon could do. I'll decide what to do with the glamorous thief once I find out exactly what she's trying to steal.

Kimchi's excitement is unabated. Deciding that the sensible thing would be to keep him out of the impending fight, I loop his lead round a nearby post. Maria smiles.

'It's for his own good,' I tell her with a frown.

Her smile grows. 'Of course.' I tut. 'So what is plan?' she asks.

'I'm going to get closer,' I say. 'You stay here until I tell you to move.'

Her lip curls. 'With dog?'

'Yes. With dog.' Before she can protest I cross the road, making sure my movements are low and swift so that I'm not noticed. Then I press myself against the wall and sidle along. I stop when I'm a few metres away and I can hear the puffed breaths of the two deliverymen. One of them is in dire need of a shower but, as that's not a good enough reason to put either of them in danger, I draw back into the shadows. The sensible thing to do is to wait until they leave.

'Don't you want us to bring these inside?' the burlier one asks.

From this angle, I can't see what the glamourised daemon is doing but I guess she shakes her head.

The men exchange glances then shrug. 'Suit yourself.' They remove the last of the boxes, close the van doors and get back in, ready to drive off.

The engine starts. I take a chance and sneak a glance. The woman is standing stock still but there's a definite smile playing around her mouth. She thinks she's almost home free. No such luck, darling. It's just not going to be your night.

The moment the van disappears, I make my move and spring out from round the corner. The woman's mouth drops into a perfect circle. She holds up her hands while I launch at her, grabbing her by the throat and smashing her into the door.

I raise her up, glaring into her face. 'Not having so much fun now, are you?'

She chokes. Beneath my fingers, her skin is heating up; she's removing the glamour. Her straight nose starts to melt, reshaping itself, and her smooth blonde hair starts to loosen. She croaks, trying to speak.

'Yeah, yeah,' I grunt. 'You're not really human. If you think I feel any kindred triber spirit, think again. I'm the Red Angel and I don't care who or what you are. If you're breaking the law then I'm going to hurt you.' I lick my lips and show her my fangs. 'I might even grab a bite to eat, whether your blood is daemon or not.'

There's an inarticulate yell from behind and the sound of pounding feet. Maria. Bloody hell. Why couldn't she just stay put? Kimchi also starts barking wildly, the sound filling the empty street.

Before I can say anything, Maria appears by my side, yanking the woman's fringe forward and then slamming it back so that her head cracks against the steel door. Her eyes flare in pain and she slumps; only my hand round her throat prevents her from collapsing completely. I loosen my hold and let her drop into a crumpled heap. Then I whirl round.

'What the fuck was that? I told you to stay on the other side of the road!'

'He is criminal,' Maria says simply.

So much for thinking the daemon is female. Changing gender as well as form is a particularly nifty feat. Right now, I'm more concerned with Maria's foolhardy attack. 'And,' I say through gritted teeth, 'thanks to your efforts, he's unconscious so I can't ask him any questions.'

She cocks her head, obviously puzzled. 'Why ask questions? He is stealing. We stop him.'

'We don't know what he's stealing or why. If he's unconscious, we can't find out if he's working for someone else,' I explain, beyond irritated. 'He might just be a foot soldier.'

Maria glares at me, stomps over to one of the boxes, flips it open and rummages around inside. 'Look,' she says shortly, pulling out a familiar looking silver weapon. 'This is not good thing to take.'

I reach for it but, the second I get close, pain surges through me and I draw back with a hiss. Maria blinks curiously.

'Tasers,' I say through gritted teeth. 'Specially adapted to work against vampires.'

Her face clears. 'Cool.'

I throw her an annoyed glance. 'This is why I need him awake. I need to know why he's stealing these. If he's making a move against the vampires then he won't be doing it alone. He'll...'

There's another loud bark from Kimchi. I look up just in time to see his lead fall loose. He barrels past me and leaps onto the fallen daemon. I lunge forward and grab his collar, yanking him back.

'For goodness' sake!' I yell. 'Why won't any of you do as you're told?'

Kimchi whines desperately. He's not interested in me or Maria, his focus is on the crumpled body at our feet. I turn round, confused. What's the big deal? It's just a damned daemon. Then I see what the problem is. Oh shit.

Whatever glamour the daemon had in place has completely vanished. No wonder X was so amused at sending me off to this crime. I should have known. What's left in front of me is the pale face of a very familiar triber: O'Shea. Goddamnit.

CHAPTER 14

DECLARATION OF TRUTH

It's not easy lugging O'Shea's inert body back to my apartment. Maria refuses to help and Kimchi seems determined to take every opportunity to leap up and lick the daemon as furiously as possible, as if canine saliva will bring him back to the land of the living. To add insult to injury, less than thirty seconds after I toss him down on my sofa, his eyelids flutter open.

I put my hands on my hips. 'You couldn't have done that twenty minutes ago?' I ask. 'Before I had to half-kill myself dragging your sorry arse up here?'

A weak smile flickers across face. 'Hi gorgeous,' he says. 'If you wanted me to make my own way here, you really shouldn't have knocked me out.'

My mouth twists. 'I didn't knock you out,' I say shortly. 'A fifteen-year-old human girl did.'

I point at Maria. He struggles up and gazes at her. She gives him a scowl then turns and walks into her bedroom, slamming the door shut.

'She's friendly,' he grunts.

'Can you blame her? We just caught you ripping off Magix.'

'Like you would care.'

I roll my eyes and pass him a glass of water. He sips at it delicately then gingerly touches the back of his head. 'That was a hell of a blow,' he complains.

I stare at him. He looks almost the same as he always did. Slightly more gaunt, perhaps, but he's still Devlin O'Shea, dodgy quarter-daemon. The one thing that's definitely changed is the hardness in his eyes. O'Shea always had a light, playful spirit which he managed to maintain even when his life was threatened. It's not there now. Admittedly, I've not seen him since before Connor died.

I sit down heavily next to him and run a hand through my hair. I'm not prepared for this meeting. To be honest, I'd not been sure that I'd ever see O'Shea again.

'You've been avoiding me,' he says.

'No. I just haven't been in your part of your town.'

'You've been avoiding New Order as well.'

'I *left* New Order.'

'Can you really tell me you've not been avoiding the hospital and your grandfather?'

I sigh, tugging at my ponytail. I knew bringing him back here was going to be a mistake.

'You didn't even come to Connor's funeral.'

I snap my head back towards him but he's not looking at me. He's staring directly ahead, unseeing.

'I couldn't,' I say finally. 'I just ... couldn't.'

O'Shea takes a deep breath. 'I needed you,' he says quietly. 'And you weren't there.'

I drop my head. I don't have an answer for that. I twist my fingers in my lap. 'It's my fault.' I swallow hard. 'It's my fault he's dead.'

'Did you kill him?' O'Shea demands. 'Did your fingers reach round and break his neck?'

My eyes narrow. 'No.'

He seems to regret his sudden surge of anger and sags back into the sofa. 'Then it wasn't your fault.'

I don't say anything. I know better.

'What the hell are you doing, Bo? You're running around the city like you're Batman. Is Foxworthy playing the role of Commissioner Gordon? Is that kid you've got in there Robin?'

'We're not in a comic book.'

'No, we're not. Don't you know that Michael has been going out of his mind? He almost charged over to Medici on a suicide mission because he thought it might bring you back.'

'I've seen Michael. He's fine.'

O'Shea snorts. 'He's far from fine. He's just like you – too damn stubborn to let the rest of the world see that you're hurting. Grief isn't a weakness, Bo. It's human.'

'I'm not human. I'm vampire.'

'You know what I mean. Humans and vampires are the same thing.'

'No,' I tell him flatly. 'They're not.'

O'Shea's spooky orange eyes stare at me unblinkingly. I try to meet his gaze but, after a second or two, I give up. 'You can take my room,' I say. 'I'll sleep out here on the couch.' I walk over to a cupboard to get out some spare bed linen.

'I wasn't nicking those tasers for me,' O'Shea half shouts. 'Michael asked me to get them. He thinks the humans have something planned. It doesn't make sense that all those protestors who were so loud and annoying have just dropped off the face of the earth.'

I think of Lisa and her delicate golden tree necklace. 'No. It doesn't.'

My sleep is restless. It doesn't help that Kimchi can't seem to make up his mind about where he'd rather be. He spends the day flitting from my room and O'Shea to the living room and me. That would be fine except that every time he comes back to me he launches himself, invariably landing on my stomach.

I don't sleep as well during the day as I used to. When I first turned, it was like I was dead; it's much more of a struggle now when I have a fat lump slamming all the air out of me every thirty minutes or so. Before the last of the sun goes down, I give in and get up. I take a glass of cold blood out of the fridge and drain it down. It's still fresh enough that it doesn't taste too bad and the act of drinking makes me feel better.

Once I've finished the first glass, I check my phone. Foxworthy has sent a text. He's uncovered about as much about Melissa Greek as Dr Bryant did. He does mention, however, that there are reports of new graffiti featuring trees springing up around the city – and they always seem to be close to religious buildings. That's interesting enough to give me pause.

Another thought strikes me and I flick to my photos, scanning through the images of disappeared protestors that I took from D'Argneau's office. Her name is right there in black and white on the third page. Well, well, well. The plot thickens.

With both O'Shea and Maria adapting to my way of life and staying in the bedrooms until they're sure night has fallen, the apartment is silent. I pour myself another glass of blood and wander to the window. Once again, I lift up the edge of the curtain and experiment with my little finger. The sunlight doesn't seem to be doing as much damage as it used to. Either that, or I'm getting more used to the pain.

My thoughts flit around like troubled butterflies and, much as I try to pretend otherwise, a great many of them feature Michael.

When I realise I've been holding my hand and half my arm

towards the sky and there's not a tingle of a burn across my skin, I know that dusk is finally here. I put down my glass carefully and check my appearance in the mirror. There are dark shadows under my eyes and I look tired. And old. Considering I'm a newbie vampire, there should be no reason for me to have started aging yet. I suppose the emotional trauma is getting to me more than I thought. I brush back my dark hair and dab on some foundation to hide the worst. Then I beckon Kimchi to my side and the pair of us leave.

I travel via the Underground, this time taking no pains to hide my existence. Several people come up to me, requesting help. Most of them have trivial problems: their neighbour is worshipping the devil (yeah, right), or an Agathos daemon family has moved in next door and they're definitely up to no good. A few are more insistent – and more tragic. Two people tell me that their loved ones have gone missing. I brush them all off as politely as I can; I can't bear to see the bleak desperation in their eyes.

My efforts are useless. As soon as I exit the train, I see Jonesy standing on the platform, his eyes darting anxiously. When he catches sight of me, his shoulders sag in relief.

'Ms Blackman!' he says, rushing forward in case I decide to spin round and sprint in the opposite direction. 'I've been trying to get in touch with you! Have you found anything?' He's breathless, even though he's been doing little more than standing around.

I reach out and place a calming hand on his arm. 'Relax,' I tell him. 'Have you been waiting around here just for me to show up?'

'It came down the line that you were on the train,' he explains. 'I hoped that you might get off here. It's the nearest stop to the Montserrat place.'

I raise my eyebrows. I had no idea that the network of

railway staff was so tight-knit – or so attentive. I'm not sure I like it. 'I'm still looking into things,' I say. 'There's no evidence that Lisa was kidnapped. It seems far more likely that she left of her own accord.'

His mouth droops. 'But she wouldn't do that. She wouldn't leave without saying goodbye. She's not that kind of person.'

'When we first met,' I say carefully, 'you wanted an autograph for both you and her.'

'Yes.' He bobs his head several times. 'Yes. We are both big fans.'

My gaze bores into him. 'That's not actually true, is it?'

'It is! You saved those people at the Agathos Court! You were so heroic!' He waves his arms around alarmingly as if to punctuate his earnestness.

'You might think that,' I say, 'but your daughter didn't.'

He falls silent, his eyes widening in what might be construed as alarm. 'She loved the vampire stories when she was a child. She always wanted to join the Bancroft Family because their leader was a woman.' Not any more, I think. Something else I could be considered responsible for. 'Of course,' Jonesy adds hastily, 'we'd never have let her be recruited. Not that vampires aren't amazing but there aren't very many of you and if she joined, she'd have to give up her family and…'

I save him from digging himself into an even deeper hole. 'I'm not interested in what she was like when she was five years old, Mr Johnson. I need to know what she was like when she disappeared.'

'She didn't hate you!' he bursts out. 'She didn't! She just thought that maybe the Families had a bit too much power. You left your Family. Obviously, you're different.'

Belatedly, I realise where his panic is coming from. I squeeze his arm gently. 'It doesn't bother me if she hates bloodguzzlers and wants to kill me. I'm not going to stop looking for her.'

He licks his lips nervously. A woman in ridiculously high stilettos appears by my side, thrusting a piece of paper in my direction. 'You're the Red Angel,' she bleats. 'Give me your autograph.'

I frown at her. 'Get lost.'

She pulls down the collar of her blouse. 'I'll let you feed from me.'

I gaze at her as if she's nuts. 'I already told you,' I say. 'Leave me alone. Can't you see I'm in the middle of something here?'

'I taste good.'

I push her away in irritation. It's little more than a gentle nudge but she goes flying backwards, knocking into another commuter who's carrying a cup of coffee. Inevitably, the hot liquid spills everywhere. Cue ensuing curses and yelps. Annoyed, I take Jonesy's arm and steer him into a quieter corner.

'You should have told me before how Lisa felt.'

He shakes his head. 'It doesn't make any difference.'

'Actually,' I say sternly, 'it does. I think she might have gotten mixed up with some anti-vampire protestors.'

'She wouldn't...' He stops when he sees the expression on my face. 'Okay,' he concedes. 'She might have done that. But she still would have spoken to us about it.'

'Did you know she was almost arrested for vandalism and inciting a riot against a group of vampettes?'

His cheeks redden. 'No.'

'She was probably mixed up in a lot of things you didn't know about,' I say. 'Don't feel bad about it. I bet you didn't tell your parents everything.'

'I thought...' he stammers, 'I thought we had a better relationship than that.'

'You did have a good relationship,' I soothe, wondering why the hell I'm wasting my time making him feel better instead of finding his damn daughter. 'Everyone keeps secrets. Do you know anything about the necklace she wore? A gold chain with a tree on it?'

'A friend gave it to her.'

'Do you know who?'

He looks defeated. 'No.'

I pat his shoulder. 'When I have something concrete, I will come and find you.' I gaze at him meaningfully. 'Notice I said *when*, not *if*. You just need to be patient.'

He clasps his hands and beams at me, hope emanating from every pore. 'Thank you, Ms Blackman. Thank you so much.'

I try to smile. 'No problem. I have to go.'

'You're looking for her right now?' His mouths opens wide in delight. 'You're going to get Lord Montserrat to help?' Er, not exactly. Jonesy isn't finished though. 'They say that he'll do anything for you.'

I blink, nonplussed, and step back. 'He has a lot on his plate right now.'

'Yes, yes.' Jonesy is so convinced that I'm going to find his daughter that he's making himself believe anything. He smiles at me in such a fatherly way that I take a step back.

'I have to go,' I repeat. Then, before he can say anything else, I twist away. It would have been a more effective exit if Kimchi had immediately come with me. As it is, I have to yank sharply on the lead to get him to follow.

When he does catch up, he licks my hand and lets out a faint whine. I cast him a look. 'Yeah, yeah,' I mutter. 'I'm going to find his daughter. Don't worry. There's just something else I have to do first.'

It's insanity but I've made up my mind.

IF I THOUGHT the Montserrat mansion was busy last time I was here, it's nothing compared to what it's like now. All manner of vampires rush past, each one clearly with an agenda. I spy several vampettes looking wan and tired. There are also far too many fresh faces, each with a look of wonder in their eyes. I guess the recruitment drive is already in full swing and curse to myself, even though nothing I could have done would have prevented it.

Despite the bustle, many stop and stare at me. It's even more annoying here than it is in the real world. I ignore all the wide eyes and stride forward. I'm on a mission.

A familiar voice cries out. 'Bo!' I glance over and see Nell rushing towards me. A lifetime ago, she was one of my fellow Montserrat recruits. 'It's been so long! How the bloody hell are you?'

'Great. Where's Michael?'

'Hey!' Matt beams, joining us. 'You brought Kimchi to say hello.' The dog leaps up, lathering Matt's face with spittle. Matt takes it in good spirit. 'This isn't the best time though. We're kind of busy.' He leans forward, dropping his voice to a whisper. 'All the rural vampires have been called in. We're preparing for war.'

I'm shocked. Already? The new recruits will still be in nappies, even if they've all woken up. The turning process isn't an easy one; I can attest to that. I shake my head. As curious as I am about what's going on, it's not the reason I'm here.

'Where's Michael?' I repeat.

There's a sudden lull in the crowd and I see several heads crane upwards. I follow their eyes, spotting the man himself at the top of the grand staircase. He's in deep conversation with

Ursus and completely oblivious to my presence. I clear my throat. It's now or never.

Passing Kimchi's lead to Matt, I jog up the stairs. I clear my throat. 'Lord Montserrat?'

He turns. The flicker of surprised warmth in his expression fills me with hope. Maybe this will go better than I hoped. 'Bo. What are you doing here?' His eyes scan me up and down. 'Are you okay? You've not been hurt again?'

I shake my head. 'No, I'm fine. I need to talk to you though.'

'My Lord...' Ursus begins, with a sympathetic look at me. 'We have to go.'

Michael sighs. 'I'm sorry. Unless this is urgent, I have to go.' He looks ruefully at the hive of activity below us. 'There's a lot I have to deal with.'

'So I hear. This won't take long.'

Ursus is insistent. 'Lord Montserrat, there's no time.'

Michael eyes me with regret. 'Can you come back later?'

I bite my lip. A vampire calls up from the bottom of the stairs, gesturing at a piece of paper. Michael curses under his breath and starts down.

Damn it, I'm not sure if I'll have time to come back later. Jonesy's plaintive expression is weighing heavily on my mind and if I don't do this now, I might lose my bottle. I take a deep breath.

'Lord Montserrat!' My voice rings out, loud above the buzz of conversation and running feet. Everyone stops to look at me. Shit. Michael also halts in his tracks. 'There's something you need to know.'

He slowly turns round. I see Beth appear in a doorway. She crosses her arms and stares at me; there's a hint of a smile on her face, as if she's fully aware of what I'm about to say. I cough and return my attention to the man himself.

'I'm in love with you,' I call out. 'I don't want to be, but I am.'

There's a dramatic gasp from the watching crowd, as if we're on the set of a dodgy soap opera. Given what I'm doing, we might as well be.

I pull my shoulders back. This is probably going to be really cheesy. 'I'm not a good person. Maybe I was once but not any longer. I don't regret the things that I've done or the things that I'm likely to keep on doing. This world is full of shit and I have to deal with it somehow. But,' I swallow, 'when I'm with you, I feel like there's hope. I feel like I can be better. I know you have high expectations of me and I want to meet them. I want to be the good person that you deserve. Because if I can't be with you then I'm not sure I want to be anywhere. You make...' I pause. I'm going to say it. I'm really going to say it. 'You make my heart sing,' I say simply. 'You make me want to be alive. When I'm around you, I can't think of anything else other than you.' I laugh sharply. 'Hell, even when I'm not around you it's difficult to focus on anything else. You consume me, heart, body and soul. There's probably a song in there somewhere. I could write a ballad. Some thumping power song with lots of high notes and a heavy piano chorus. The sort that I always thought was bullshit until I met you. Michael, I...'

'Shut up.'

I blink. 'What?'

'I said shut up. You're babbling, Bo Blackman.' He strides towards me. His face is set but there's a gentle warmth in his eyes that gives me hope. 'I know the feeling.' A smile tugs at his perfect, chiselled lips. 'I love you right back. I love your stubbornness and your hard-headedness and your determination to stay as free as you can. You know what, though?' He continues without giving me a chance to answer. 'You're not free. I'll never let you be free. You're *mine*.' His smile grows. 'Just because it's taken you longer to realise that than it took me doesn't change a damned thing. I'll just remind you about it when we're both old and hobbling around with our zimmer frames.'

He stops in front of me and cups my face. The other vampires around us blur into the background. I can still feel the darkness deep inside my heart but knowing I might be able to share that darkness with someone else gives me hope for the future. Lights dance across his eyes and he opens his mouth to speak.

'Lord Montserrat!' A panicked voice interrupts. 'You need to see this!'

His face twists into a fleeting snarl. 'Not now.'

'It's Lord Medici! He's outside. He's going to do something.'

I freeze. For a moment, Michael does the same. We share a look of mutual understanding. 'Let's go,' he growls.

I nod. Then the pair of us, followed by many others, run down the stairs and leave. This might be our chance to end Medici once and for all.

CHAPTER 15

THE AUDIENCE

We make it to Medici's stronghold in record time. We're also not the only ones. I spot clusters of bloodguzzlers from the other three Families – Bancroft, Gully and Stuart. That's not to mention the crowds of journalists, tribers and humans, all gawking at the Medici front door. A wave of satisfaction runs through me when some nearby witches spot me and hastily move away. Yeah, that's right. Don't get too close or you never know what'll happen.

Medici is standing out front, looking every inch the imperious vampire overlord. He's wearing a long sweeping cloak in bright scarlet Medici-Family red just in case anyone was under any illusions as to who he is. Beside him are three figures, hoods covering their bowed heads. A large ring of Medici vamps encircle them, no doubt as protection against the growing crowd. No one's made a move yet because no one knows what he's about to do.

'We can't wait,' I mutter to Michael. 'He's up to something. He's been waiting for all of us to appear. We have to pre-empt him if we're going to stay in control.'

'I agree,' he answers tightly. He bunches one hand into a fist and starts to raise it up in a call to action – but it's too late.

Medici steps forward and raises his chin. He flings his arms out, stretching them in an unpleasant facsimile of Christ on the cross. But Medici is no martyr; he's chosen others to play that role.

'I am surprised,' he intones, 'that we have such an audience. I was not expecting a crowd.'

I sniff. Yeah, right. That's why he's had his place bathed in bright lights for the last two nights and waited until every damn vampire Family showed up. Whatever he's planning, I'm betting it's not going to be good.

'I know that some of you are concerned that we are recruiting more people into the humble folds of our Family. I know you think that it's a reason to be wary of us. But we are not the enemy. These people came to us, not the other way around. They were on the periphery of society, poor humans destined to be always on the outside looking in. Yes, we have expanded our ranks but we've expanded them to give a home to people who otherwise would have no hope. People who were draining this city's resources, from its healthcare to social work to housing, and giving nothing back. We are giving them the opportunity they need for rehabilitation. We are providing a second chance.'

'He's trying to come off as some kind of benevolent charity worker,' Michael hisses.

'It won't work.'

'Look around you.' His voice is grim. 'It already is working.'

I sweep my gaze round the busy street. All the Families are stony-faced, arms folded and postures tense. The witches and the press look interested. The humans hanging to one side are positively agog.

Medici continues. 'My fellow Families will try to tell you

that I'm doing wrong, that I'm breaking with tradition.' He flicks his eyes from one group to another, eyeballing each Family Lord challengingly. 'But we have to move with the times. I am no monster, I only have the country's best interests at heart. The humans I brought into the Medici Family are being held to a very high standard. I will not brook anyone who dares to break human laws, whether we are subject to them or not. Rest assured, any wrongdoers will be punished.'

He drops his arms and moves over to the first hooded figure. With a flourish, he yanks off the hood. Everyone leans forward, curious to know who exactly he has there. I catch myself doing the same then, irritated that Medici has me eating out of the palm of his hand, I pull myself back. Just what is he planning?

The face that's revealed is hard and ugly. He might be a vampire but he's definitely a new recruit and whoever he was before he was turned, he led an uncompromising life. His face is pitted with acne scars and his nose is flat as if it's been broken one too many times. His brow is too large for his face and over-hangs his eyes like some creation from Dr Frankenstein. He is the stuff of nightmares.

'Go on,' Medici says. 'Introduce yourself to the crowd.'

Even from this distance, I can see the dullness in the new vampire's eyes. His pupils are enlarged and I realise he's been drugged. For what purpose remains to be seen.

He stumbles forward and opens his mouth. 'I have sinned,' he says in a choked whisper.

Medici nudges his back. 'Speak up.'

He clears his throat and tries again. 'I have sinned,' he repeats. 'I was a bad man when I was human. I raped three women. I hit my own son. Lord Medici tried to show me the error of my ways but I wasn't smart enough to listen. Two nights ago I ... I ...'

'Go on,' Medici says silkily. 'What did you do?'

'I left the Medici mansion. I was hungry and I needed blood.' His voice wavers. 'I came across a jogger in the street and I attacked her.' His head droops and he starts to mumble to himself. There's a flash of irritation in Medici's expression. His performing monkey isn't saying everything he should.

'Her name is Tara Wilkes,' Medici interrupts. 'She's in intensive care at Brighton Hospital.' He jabs a long white index finger at his captive. 'Because of him she almost died.' He inhales deeply, enjoying the rapt attention of several hundred people. 'We at the Medici Family will not permit this sort of activity. We will not allow vampires to hurt humans or tribers. We want to make this world a better place, one where everyone is free to walk the streets whenever they wish. We have everyone's best interests at heart.'

He whips off the hood from the second man and then the third. Both have equally unprepossessing features. Medici repeats the process with them, detailing their alleged crimes. Once he's done, he steps back and shakes his head.

'It gives me no pleasure to do this,' he says. 'But the public needs to be reassured that the Medici Family alone will act when one of our vampires steps out of line. We will take appropriate retribution against anyone who hurts another being.'

From behind, an older vampire steps forward and hands Medici a long gleaming sword. I stiffen. 'He's not going to...' I start to move forward. I'm not going to let him do this. Michael puts a hand on my arm.

'Don't,' he warns in an undertone. 'He's hoping for that.' He jerks his head to the right: five Medici vampires are watching me and me alone. They want me to act then Medici can dispatch me too and claim it was because I interfered in his sick show of justice.

I halt. Medici's eyes flicker once in my direction and I recognise triumph in their dark depths. He wins either way: if I act, he will denounce me as someone willing to let criminals get away with heinous actions; if I don't act, I'm not the brave vigilante that everyone holds me up as. I clench my jaw so hard that it hurts.

Medici addresses the waiting journalists once again. 'The Medici Family will ensure everyone's safety,' he says simply. He tests the blade once, swiping it cleanly through the air. He beckons the three to kneel and they do as he asks. As they close their eyes, he thrusts, lopping off all their heads in one single bloody strike. There are three nauseating thuds as each head falls onto the marble floor. Half the crowd turn away; the other half can't stop themselves from watching.

Medici bows once, passing the dripping sword back to his attentive minion. 'Let it be known that our retribution may be violent but it will ensure the safety of all. We only want what is best for England. We want this nation to be both great and glorious again.' And with that he turns and disappears back through the front doors of his fortress.

There's a moment of silence so studied that I think I can hear each racing heartbeat, then everyone explodes into a hubbub of disbelieving noise.

I glance up at Michael. His face is as pale as I imagine mine to be. Three or four journalists, recovering more quickly than the others, race in our direction. 'What do you think of Lord Medici's actions?' one of them shouts, tape recorder thrust out for a soundbite.

'We need to get out of here,' Michael murmurs, turning me away. 'They're going to do whatever they can to get a response from you.'

Because I go after criminals too. Sometimes I even kill them. I don't make a show out of it, though. Killing, whether it's justified or not, should not ever include an audience. Even I have limits.

I nod in distracted agreement and we leave as quickly as we arrived.

~

'THIS IS ALL HER FAULT,' Lord Bancroft rages, thrusting his face into mine and snarling. 'If she hadn't made a living out of killing anyone she comes across and getting good press out of it, Medici would never have done the same!'

I hold my ground, even though I have the very nasty feeling that he's correct. 'I'm right here, you know,' I tell him. 'You don't have to talk about me in the third person.'

'What's next?' he continues. 'Gunning down people in the street for petty crimes?'

Michael steps between us. 'You need to calm down.'

'Calm down?' Bancroft splutters. 'Calm down? Who the fuck are you to tell me to do that?' He throws up his arms. 'You're all maniacs!'

Michael turns to Lord Stuart, who is watching the byplay with narrowed eyes. Gully is in the corner, studying his phone. 'Do we have any word on the immediate reaction to Medici's little show?'

'It's the middle of the night. Most of the country is asleep,' he points out.

'Actually,' Gully interrupts, 'not everyone is in dream land.' He holds up his phone and we turn to look at the live stream he's displaying. He flicks up the sound.

'While I cannot completely condone Lord Medici's actions,' Vince Hale, the smarmy politician I read about when I was waiting for Jonesy, says, 'it is his prerogative to deal with his own vampires as he wishes. That is the way the laws of this land work and we must adhere to them. We should be grateful that he is taking matters so seriously. Perhaps if the other Families did the same, decent folk wouldn't be so afraid of the vampires in the first place.'

'Who the fuck is that?' Bancroft demands.

'He's a politician,' I tell him. 'Openly anti-vampire.'

'He's not that anti-vampire if he thinks that conducting open-air executions is a good thing.' Michael frowns. 'He's all but stating that Medici should be admired.'

'Medici's gone completely insane,' one of Lord Stuart's people says. 'There's no other explanation.'

There's a murmur of agreement. I shake my head. 'You're all idiots. This was planned, every single part of this was planned.' I point at the camera. 'Look at where Hale is.'

'The Houses of Parliament?' Bancroft gives a sneering shrug. 'You already said he was a politician. In case you hadn't realised, that's where they tend to be.'

I gaze at him in irritation. 'At four o'clock in the morning? Which politicians are so dedicated to their jobs that they hang around in the middle of the goddamn night? He knew this was going to happen. I bet he's working with Medici. All this is part of a larger plan.' I point at them all. 'A plan to discredit you.'

'Killing his own vampires isn't going to discredit us.'

'Yes, it is,' I say. 'Medici is acting when others won't, when you won't. Do you really think it's a coincidence that those three he killed are probably the ugliest-looking recruits he has? He wants the world to think that what he's done is right. Tara Wilkes, whoever she is, was probably paid off. Medici comes out looking like a hero.'

'Well, you'd know all about manipulating public opinion,' Bancroft sneers.

'I don't want a fan club,' I snap back. 'Everything Medici did was designed to attract as many eyes as possible. He's not crazy. He knows exactly what he's doing.'

'So what's next?' Michael asks. 'What's his next move?'

'I don't know.'

'You don't know anything. You're just a jumped-up little girl who...'

'That's enough.' Michael's tone brooks no argument. 'I think it's best if we discuss this alone.' He gestures to the other three Family heads. I know why he's doing it: he'll be able to control them more easily when it's just the four of them together. It still galls, though.

Everyone starts to file out. I wait until the end and then make to follow. Michael pulls me aside just outside the door. 'I'm sorry. They're old-school. They don't like the idea of a new vampire who's turned rogue telling them what they should have already worked out for themselves.'

'I get it.' I don't like it, but I get it.

He sighs. 'Thank you.' His eyes search my face. 'I'd really like it if you stuck around,' he says quietly. 'Medici notwithstanding, we have a lot to talk about.' There's a lot left unsaid in his expression. I reach up and gently brush my fingers across his cheek before glancing outside.

'Dawn is almost here,' I answer softly. 'I've got people waiting for me back at home. And Kimchi will need to be fed too.'

A muscle throbs in his jaw. 'And where is home?'

I stare at him. I really want to tell him but I'm still not sure what X will do if I give away my location. Medici is scary but X...

Michael's face closes off. 'You'll declare your love for me in front of a room full of vampires but you won't tell me where you live?'

'It's complicated.'

His face twists. 'I'll bet.' He turns to walk back into the room.

'Michael...'

He stops but he doesn't look back at me. 'I believe you when you say you love me, Bo. I have to. But I can't live like this. You need to make up your mind — either you're with me all the way or you're not. Anything else simply isn't going to work.'

I bite my lip, cursing to myself as he disappears and closes the door behind him. Why can't anything ever be easy?

CHAPTER 16

MULTI-TASKING

I've barely put a foot in the door when O'Shea leaps up off the sofa and starts babbling. 'Have you seen what Medici has done? It's all over the news!'

I sigh tiredly. 'I saw it. I was there.'

'It was a calculated move. It has to be.'

I look at him approvingly. He might be a petty criminal only just emerging from the strangling throes of grief but he's a hell of a lot smarter than most of those bloodguzzling idiots. 'I agree. I don't know what he's up to,' I say, 'but he's laying the foundations for something.' I pause. 'And whatever it is, it's not going to be good.'

'What are you going to do about it?'

Maria appears from around the corner. 'She can do nothing. He is Lord. She is nothing.'

O'Shea frowns. 'No, she's not,' he says loyally. 'You'd be surprised at what Bo is capable of. She's not called the Red Angel for nothing.'

'Maria's right.' I meet his eyes. 'I'm not sure what I can do. Michael has made it pretty clear that what happens with

Medici is for the other Families to sort out. I'm not part of the Families.'

'You're just going to let him publicly execute three people and get away with it?'

I sit down heavily. 'What can I do? I can't get inside the Medici house. Even if I could get Lord Medici face to face, he's so strong he'll make mincemeat out of me in seconds.'

O'Shea shakes his head. 'He's up to no good. You know it, I know it, hell, even Kimchi knows it.'

Hearing his name, Kimchi leaps up with unbridled enthusiasm. The tension of the night has even got to him.

'I can't take on two thousand damn vampires,' I growl.

'No.' Maria's voice rings out across the room. 'You can't. But the daemon can.'

O'Shea starts. 'Whoa! I'm no match for him.'

'I not mean you.'

'Then who?'

Maria raises her eyebrows meaningfully at me before turning away again.

'Who does she mean?' O'Shea persists. 'Bo, do you have other daemon mates that I don't know about? Because I think I should get to vet them first. I might only be a quarter Agathos but I have a great bullshit detector and I know a lot of the players. If you've been hiding away from me because you've found a stronger daemon as your sidekick, then you should be very careful and tell me who it is.'

'I was hiding away from you,' I say, with more honesty than I thought I was capable of, 'because it's my fault Connor is dead and your life has been ruined.' Before he can interrupt, I keep going. 'And I can't tell you about the other daemon because if I do he'll probably kill you.' I grab my phone and stalk away into the kitchen. If I'm going to do this, I'm going to need some peace.

It takes X a while to answer. When he does, he sounds as happy as he did last time. I try not to let it irk me.

'Hello, Bo. You'll have to excuse me. I've been having a rather wonderful night watching all the little bloodguzzlers run around in a panic.'

'I'm a little bloodguzzler,' I grind out.

'I suppose you are,' he says. 'I don't lump you in with the rest of them though. You're ... special.'

I'm not sure I enjoy X's brand of special. 'I want to talk to Michael,' I say.

'So talk to him. You don't need my permission for that.'

'You know what I mean.'

There's a pause. 'You want to tell him about me.'

'I don't want to keep secrets from him. I haven't even told him where I live because I'm so afraid of what you'll do! It's ridiculous.'

'You work for me, Bo. Romantic entanglements notwithstanding, you left the Montserrat Family.' There's a menacing undertone to X's words. 'Besides, tell him about me and he'll never trust you again. He'll always be wondering whether everything you do is because you're dancing to my tune. In any case,' he says, lightening up again, 'I think I've already made myself very clear. Tell anyone about my existence and I will kill them.' He trots out this last sentence without a trace of malice. He could be discussing the weather.

'You've broken that agreement,' I point out, 'by demanding to meet Rogu3 and Maria.'

'The boy has no idea who I am. He could hack every computer system from here to Timbuktu and he wouldn't discover my true identity. I don't exist virtually. Not in that sense anyway.'

I take a deep breath. 'And Maria?'

'She's different. Special.' He pauses. 'Like you. Anyway, you knew I was going to say that. Michael Montserrat is not the reason you're calling.'

X may as well be as psychic over the phone as he is face to face, considering how many times he knows what I'm thinking. 'Medici.'

He laughs. 'Yes. What about him? Because I assume you mean Lord Medici, not the entire Family.'

'As of this moment,' I growl, 'they're one and the same. He's the single biggest threat this city has seen. If I'm cleaning up the streets then I need to deal with him.'

'And?'

I grit my teeth. 'And I'm not strong enough. He's far older than I am and far more powerful.'

I can almost hear X shrug. 'So take him on and die, or leave him alone and live. It seems straightforward to me.'

'You're hell-bent on getting me to prevent crime. If you are really that bothered by it, then *you* should do something about Medici.'

'Is that an order?' His voice is silky smooth but I'm not stupid. I have to choose my next words very, very carefully.

'I wouldn't dream of such a thing. I'm just saying that he's up to something. The one triber in this city who is in a position to stop him in his tracks is you. I'm curious as to why you're leaving him alone.'

'I don't like to dirty my hands, Bo. You should know that by now. Why do you think I've hired you?' He exhales. 'Don't answer that. You should leave Medici to your pet Lord and his buddies. They'll deal with him in their own way. You need to concentrate on Lisa Johnson.'

'I'm working on her case,' I tell him flatly. 'Of course I am. But I can chew gum and walk at the same time. It is possible to do more than one thing at once. I'm a woman; multi-tasking comes naturally.'

'Multi-tasking is a myth. Lisa Johnson, Bo. Focus on her and everything will turn out alright in the end. Trust me.' And with that he hangs up.

I scowl at the phone. I don't understand why he's so concerned with one human girl. As he's pointed out before, there are many criminal cases occurring all over London. I appreciate that Lisa's involves more than just her; there's Melissa Greek as well, not to mention enough whispers of other disappearances that I should be sitting up and taking note of. But X is a Kakos daemon. Why would he care about a few humans when the vampires are on the brink of civil war? It just doesn't make sense.

The phone rings again. Without looking at the display, I answer it immediately. 'X,' I begin.

'Eh?' Rogu3 says. 'Ex what?'

Shit. 'Nothing,' I mutter.

'Uh, okay, then.' He's clearly confused but too excited by his own news to ask any more questions. 'I thought you'd be up. I was just contacted.'

My mind is elsewhere. 'Contacted by who?'

'Whom, Bo. Contacted by whom. And isn't it obvious?'

I snap back into reality. 'The tree people,' I breathe.

'That's not how they introduced themselves but, yes, the tree people. Their name is Tov V'ra. They want a meeting.'

I search the recesses of my brain. 'Good and evil,' I say slowly. 'That's what Tov V'ra means. It's Hebrew. It relates to the Tree of the Knowledge of Good and Evil. The one which Eve took the apple from.' A shiver runs down my spine. The graffiti Foxworthy told me about wasn't placed near religious buildings by accident after all. Any time criminal kooks use religion as their backbone, it spells trouble. At least we're finally getting somewhere. 'When do they want to meet?'

'The Whispering Gallery at St Paul's Cathedral at midday.'

I curl my fingers into tights fists. Shit. That's not a good time for a newbie vampire like me. 'You can't go,' I say, my mind racing. If I left now, there would be enough time for me to get to St Paul's before dawn then it's a simple matter of hiding out until the appointed hour. I won't be able to track Lisa's alleged kidnappers but I'll be able to identify them. That's a start at least.

'I have to go,' he says matter-of-factly. 'If I don't, they'll know something is up. Why else did we do all this in the first place? I've found nothing about them on the net, either with or without the tree image. If you want to know more about them, I have to go.'

'What happened to not doing any fieldwork?' I ask.

'This is for you. It's completely different.'

'No, it's not. I'm not putting you in any danger.'

'It's a meeting in one of the busiest tourist spots in the city, Bo. I'm hardly going to be in danger.'

'That's probably what Lisa Johnson thought,' I say drily.

'We don't know that she's in danger.'

True. It doesn't matter though. I've already put Rogu3 on their radar; there's no need to push the issue any further. 'Your parents would kill me. You've barely recovered from the last time. You're not going.'

'Bo...'

'Enough,' I say sternly.

'There's no choice.'

I pop my head round and glance at O'Shea. Kimchi has plopped himself on his lap and his weight is making the daemon's face turn red. 'There's always a choice,' I say with a half grin. 'In fact, I've got the perfect solution.'

~

St Paul's doesn't open its doors to sightseers until late in the morning but it does permit entry for morning prayer at a far earlier hour. Vampires aren't encouraged to attend. A church, even one on such a grand scale as St Paul's, doesn't actually forbid us from entering, after all they're not residential properties, but that doesn't mean we are welcome. There are no anti-vamp alarm systems – that would make the unfriendliness far too obvious – so as long as O'Shea's glamour holds, I shouldn't have a problem getting in.

I will have an issue if Tov V'ra want to go for a wander outside. Sunrise is less than an hour away. Despite the season, the clear sky suggests that it's going to be a glorious day. I can't even count on typically English cloud cover to get me through.

With five hours to kill before the meeting, I take advantage of the prayer ceremony. It'll be a good opportunity to test out how I look.

O'Shea grumbled a great deal when he disguised me as Rogu3, telling me that it's one thing to create a glamour of someone who's a similar shape and build, and quite another when there's at least a foot difference. I pointed out that he managed to create a glamour for himself that included breasts, so an extra bit of height shouldn't be too difficult. All the same, it's a strain for him to do it. He's no witch.

As I stroll inside, I realise why such glamours aren't more common. For one thing, it's damn uncomfortable. Every inch of my skin is prickling and I have to make a conscious effort to keep my arms battened down by my sides so that I don't scratch myself all over like a deranged creature covered in hives. For another thing, it's bloody awkward to walk. With Rogu3's physical mask covering my body, I feel as if I'm about to tip over. I'm forced to take small steps and my head swims. Perhaps it's the altitude.

An elderly gentleman who, despite his advanced age, is able to overtake me, peers at me. 'Are you alright, son?'

I try to smile and my mouth feels as if it's cracking wide. I give him a brief nod and remind myself to take care when speaking. O'Shea's skills at magicking glamour don't extend to the voice box. It's going to prove problematic – but not insurmountable. I croak, allowing my voice to come out as little more than a hoarse whisper. It's not perfect but it'll do.

'Flu,' I say.

He quickly withdraws, concern for an anonymous teenager overtaken by fear of germs. I wait for him to get some distance ahead of me then struggle up the aisle towards the small Middlesex chapel where morning prayers are held. I eventually grab a spot in a pew far back from the action.

The short service is surprisingly well-attended. There are quite a lot of smartly dressed people, no doubt on their way to work and taking advantage of the detour to pray for their sins. I also spot some tourists and entertain myself by guessing at their nationalities.

I'm just debating over a blond-haired couple, laying bets as to whether they are Scandinavian or German, when someone pushes past me and settles down next to me, so close that our thighs are touching. I give an involuntary grimace. I had perched right at the very end of the pew to avoid this very situation. Despite the number of people here, this is a damn cathedral – there are plenty of other places to sit. Now I have the choice of getting up and moving or being squashed into the uncomfortable wooden armrest. The former will only draw attention to me, so I decide to suffer in silence, although I throw an irritated look at my unwelcome companion. I'm playing the part of a teenager, so I figure I can get away with it. When I realise that I'm sitting next to a witch – and one who is proudly displaying both black and white on her cheeks – my resolve goes out of the window. I can't be in such close proximity to one of those things.

I start to rise, just as the organ music stops abruptly and the minister appears. He catches sight of me and frowns, gesturing at me to sit down. On any other occasion I'd have ignored his silent command but I can't afford to be examined too closely. I curse to myself and do as I'm told.

'Sweetie?' the woman asks, pushing a wrapped humbug in my direction and garnering me another frown from the minister.

I shake my head. Leave me alone. Just keep quiet and give me peace. She shrugs and noisily unwraps one, popping it into her mouth and sucking it with more fervour than even Kimchi would manage.

'I'm Doris,' she mumbles.

Good grief. This is supposed to be prayer time, not 'meet a stranger and chat to them' time. I force a smile and keep my eyes trained ahead.

'It's good to see a young person caring so much about prayer,' she continues. 'I don't normally come on weekdays myself but after what happened last night I told myself, Doris, you have to do something. You can't let those bloodguzzling monsters have all the power.'

Help me.

'That Medici isn't too bad,' she continues, completely ignoring the fact that everyone else's heads are now bowed as the minister leads the prayers. 'At least he's keeping his freaks in line. Did you see the rest of them though? Staring at him as if they wanted to murder him?' She tuts to herself. 'It's just not on. They need to be stopped. That Montserrat Lord is the worst of them. Uses his greasy good looks to act as if he's all noble. Well, I can tell you that he's not.'

I grunt non-committally, wondering if it's possible for this to get even worse. I try to turn away from her, to cross my legs and use my body language, if not my mouth, to make it clear that I want her to shut the fuck up and leave me alone. That's when I remember I'm supposed to be male. That gives me an idea.

I open my legs ever so slightly. Without realising it, the witch shifts over an inch. I open my legs wider, splaying them out more and more. She keeps moving until my legs are fully apart: I'm giving every appearance of a man asserting his dominance by displaying his junk to the world. I feel ridiculous but it works. The witch barely seems to notice. She just keeps chattering away, ignoring the reason why we're all supposed to be here.

'They don't expect us to fight back,' she informs me. 'That's the problem. Those devil worshippers think we're going to meekly accept them as our lords and masters.' She snorts. 'Well, they're in for a surprise. One day they'll get their come-uppance, just you wait and see.' She seems to take my silence as agreement. She nudges my side and beams. 'You seem like a sensible lad. You wouldn't let one of them get the better of you. Neither would I.'

A worshipper a few rows in front turns round and throws her an evil look and hushes her. Doris flips her middle finger. My mouth drops open. That was the last thing I expected in a place like this, even from a witch.

'Tight arse,' she mutters. She nudges me again. 'I can tell you agree.' She drops her voice. 'Don't let on to anyone, but I'm more dangerous than any of this lot realise. In fact, I gave them guzzlers what for just last week. Guess what I did?' Her smile stretches so wide I think her face is going to crack. 'Go on, guess.'

I grunt. Please, please, shut up.

She points to her cheeks. 'I'm a witch, see?'

No shit. I look like a teenager, I don't look like I'm blind. Or act like I'm half-witted.

'I cast a spell,' she informs me triumphantly. 'Any guzzler comes into my neighbourhood, they're going to be surprised.' She lets out a cackle which makes even more people turn and glare at her. The minister, who was keen enough to frown at me, simply lets her get on with it. She's obviously a regular and probably often does this kind of thing. Hell, he's probably terrified of her. She jabs her elbow in my ribs again. 'Yep, one of them vampires comes into my street and they're going to be sick in their own mind. It's an old hex passed down through my coven. They'll take that sickness and go crazy. They'll go back to where they belong and won't be able to help themselves. They'll end up attacking their own.' She leans back with a self-satisfied smirk. 'They won't know what hit them.'

I slowly turn my head to look at her. Hexes are notoriously unstable, much like this witch seems to be. It's as likely to affect a human as it is a vampire. Either way, if it works even slightly, it could cause a lot of damage. This witch is as stupid as she acts. Unfortunately, there's pretty much only one way to get rid of hexes. Even if she wanted to, she wouldn't be able to remove it.

The minister finishes up, bowing his head while everyone starts to file out. That felt like the longest twenty minutes of my life. I wait until the rest have gone then stand up and politely step to one side to allow the witch to go ahead of me. She pats me on the arm. 'You're a good boy. Maybe I'll see you here again tomorrow.'

The one thing I'm absolutely sure of is that she won't. I nod to the minister, who takes the chance to finally bestow a smile on me, then follow on her heels. I'm not going to let her out of my sight.

Early sunlight is already trickling in from the vast stained-glass windows but it's easy enough to dodge. When it's clear that the witch is going to leave straightaway, without taking any detours, I make a decision.

'Excuse me,' I ask her, as huskily as possible while pointing off to my left, 'but what's that?'

'The crypt, of course!' she says, staring at me as if I'm mad. 'Haven't you been here before?'

I shake my head. Come on witch, I think to myself. You know you want to.

'You won't be able to get down there for another hour,' she says. 'It's closed off to the public till then.'

I look as disappointed as I can. Thankfully it works. She casts her eyes around, registers that we're alone and gives me a conspiratorial grin.

'I'm here all the time. They won't bother me if I go down with you to take a quick peek.' She waggles her finger at me. 'We can't be long, mind.'

I gaze at her admiringly. In response, she pats her hair and preens. Apparently the less I say the better. I'll have to remember that.

With one final look around to make sure we're in the clear, we trot over to the crypt's entrance. I estimate there will be less than ten minutes before the cathedral staff come to get ready for the day's many visitors. I'll have to act quickly.

I use the suggestion of Rogu3's long legs to keep the pace fast. The truth is that it's remarkably hard for me to manage. I'm virtually running down the corridor, all the while looking like I'm out for nothing more than a gentle stroll.

'That's Lord Nelson,' Doris says, pointing to an ornate sarcophagus. 'He was a good man,' she sighs. 'He didn't like bloodguzzlers either.'

'No,' I say, using my normal voice and enjoying the look of

confusion, then alarm that spreads across her features. 'But you know what his last words were, don't you, Doris?'

'You...' she stammers. 'You...' She turns on her heel to flee but I grab her arm and hold her fast. She starts to chant a spell but there's no time for her to complete it and she knows it. If she had been prepared for such an attack, she might have had some success but she's not as good a witch as she likes to make out. I twist her arm and she squeals in pain, the sound echoing down the empty crypt.

'Come on, Doris,' I coax. 'What were Nelson's last words?'

She gasps, still trying in vain to free herself.

My eyes dance. 'I might let you go if you get them right.'

'Kiss me,' she yelps. 'Kiss me, Hardy!'

I shrug. 'Alright then. My name is Bo though.' Then just as the fear in her expression changes to outright terror, I let my fangs lengthen and I sink them deep into her papery skin, piercing through to the overly sweet blood underneath.

I have no intention of letting her live. It's not just because her stupid spell is targeting bloodguzzlers; it's that it could go wrong and affect all manner of people. That's what I tell myself as I drain her completely dry, leaving little more than a husk behind. When I'm done I lift up her almost weightless body and take her to Nelson's sarcophagus. It would be the ideal hiding place if it weren't sealed shut. There's no way even my vampiric strength is going to get the thing open. In the end I'm forced to take her to a lesser-known tomb where I slide the heavy stone aside and throw her in.

I apologise to the body inside. Hopefully Hubert Cruick-shank, whoever he was, won't have to spend the rest of eternity listening to her prattle on. I return the stone to its original position, dust off my palms and leave.

CHAPTER 17

PREMATURE
EJACULATION

I wasn't lying to pathetic, dead Doris. I've lived in London all my life and I don't think I've ever been to St Paul's Cathedral before, unless it was on some long-forgotten school trip. I suppose that's what happens when you live in close proximity to lots of places of interest; when they're right on your doorstep, you never bother to visit them because, well, they're always there. It's a different story when you're on holiday when you pack in as many landmarks as you possibly can.

I spend half the morning trailing around after groups who have probably seen far more London sights in their three-day-two-night stays than I have in a lifetime. I wonder for a moment whether my grandfather has been here, then quickly quash the thought.

When noon approaches, I make my way up to the Whispering Gallery. It's almost the perfect place for this kind of meeting; there are remarkably few hiding spots this high up. The gallery visitors may be watched constantly by the frescoes of watchful saints but there's nowhere for a surreptitious tail to eye their quarry without being seen.

206

I suppose it would be possible to watch from the ground. Edging over, there's a remarkable view of the cathedral below but it's a long way down. Even if someone did hang around and peer upwards for any length of time, they wouldn't see much – although they'd get a damn sore neck for their efforts. As for the much-vaunted whispers – the ability to whisper into the wall and for it be heard round the other side of the gallery – that feat is next to useless as well. There are too many people doing exactly that so that what occurs is a mesh of woven whispers, too many to be distinct.

I shrug and act like the teenager I'm supposed to be, pasting on a sullen look and hanging myself over the balustrade with my mobile phone in my hand.

Whoever the Tov V'ra group actually are, they are certainly punctual. Bang on midday, someone appears by my side. The action is too deliberate to be a coincidence. I don't look at them; instead I concentrate on my game of virtual Sudoku.

'All these people,' my new companion murmurs, 'scurrying around with wide eyes taking selfies instead of focusing on what's right in front of them. As a nation, we've become blind to reality.'

It's the kind of opener designed to fully engage a disaffected teenage hacker. I maintain my slumped stance; it wouldn't do to look too eager. Besides, I'm worried that any sudden movements will cause O'Shea's glamour to slip.

'Most people think that they're safe from the bloodguzzlers when they're inside the house of God. You know differently though, don't you, Alistair?' There's a pause. 'Or should I call you Rogu3?'

At least they've done their homework. I turn my head slightly. I'm faced with a youngish-looking man, not so old that I'm likely to consider him a threat or an unwanted authority figure, and not so young that someone like Rogu3 would dismiss him. Tov V'ra know what they're doing. He is wearing jeans and a carefully ironed T-shirt with a fish on it – one of those Christian emblems. It's a shame he's not using the Tov V'ra tree then I could ask him about it.

He chuckles. 'Yes, we know who you are.'

No, you really, really don't. He holds out his hand for me to shake. When I ignore it, he shrugs and drops it. My lack of manners doesn't appear to bother him.

'I'm Isaac.'

I grunt.

'That was quite some show you put on the other night,' he remarks. 'We were under the impression until then that you were fully bloodwashed.' He leans in slightly closer. 'That's what we call those who've allowed the vampires to fool them.'

I clear my throat, doing what I can to portray a little belligerence. I deepen my voice and pray that the croak I'm injecting into my tone is convincing. 'Who says I don't still think that?'

Isaac raises his eyebrows. 'You did put on quite a show.'

'I was having a bad night.' I say it casually. Acting relaxed helps me feel that way. It looks like my weak attempt at sounding like Rogu3 is going to pass muster but I'll have to keep my sentences brief.

'You weren't saying anything that the rest of us aren't already thinking.'

'Bullshit. All those protests have stopped.' I cough. 'People don't care.'

I'm rewarded with the faintest gleam in Isaac's dark eyes. 'Perhaps the protests have stopped for a reason,' he says enigmatically. Then he frowns. 'Aren't you feeling well?'

I realise I've been scratching vigorously at my arm. I drop my hand and mutter, 'Virus.' For good measure, I add, 'You should keep away.'

He laughs. 'I'm not afraid of getting sick but I am afraid of the monsters, the ones with smooth smiles and pointed teeth. They've fooled people for generations into believing that they're benevolent. That they're trustworthy.' He spits out that last word. 'But they're not. They're showing their true colours by upping recruitment. The government, the police, everyone, is sleeping with their eyes open. One day they'll wake up and we'll be nothing more than food for our bloodguzzling over-lords. We'll be caged like animals. A dying breed of nothing more than prey. Just you wait and see.'

It's a ridiculous supposition. Much as I despise Medici for breaking with tradition and turning more humans into loyal little vampire followers, his numbers are still tiny. The other Families could match him bloodguzzler for bloodguzzler, and the vampires would still be a tiny drop against the ever growing flood of humanity. It occurs to me that I'm making Michael's argument for him and my mouth twists invol-untarily.

Isaac smiles. 'I see you think the same.'

I shrug. 'Doesn't matter,' I mutter. 'We can't do anything about it even if we want to. They're too powerful.'

His eyes narrow and I think I might have given myself away and said too much. I shouldn't have worried. He's so wrapped up in his beliefs that his thoughts are on the hordes of vampires that he seems to think are lurking round every corner rather than the one right in front of him.

'That's where you're wrong,' he says. 'To thine own self be true, as the Bible says. We are going to be true to ourselves and we have a plan.'

My lip curls. That's not a quote from the Bible, that's Shake-speare. This guy isn't nearly as focused on his religion as he likes to think he is. I choose to ignore the quotation for now and focus on his other words. 'We?'

He holds my gaze, reaches into his jacket and pulls out a small white rectangle. A business card. Seriously?

Isaac pushes it towards me. With a display of reluctance, I take it and glance down. There are no words on it, not even a phone number or an email address. In fact, there's nothing except the tree emblem that Lisa Johnson had dangling around her neck.

'We are the Tov V'ra,' he intones majestically. 'We know the vampires are an abomination against nature. Against God. And we are going to stop them.'

I snort. 'That's your gig?' I roll my eyes and turn away. 'Waste of time.'

He grabs my arm. His grip is insistent but not tight; even if I were simply a teenage boy, I'd be able to break away from it easily. 'No, it's not. We have the people, the money and the resources. And we have a plan. We could use someone of your abilities, Rogu3.'

He's using my name – or Rogu3's, at least – to get me to trust him. His words are smooth but he's not given me enough information yet. 'No.' My voice is flat. I turn back and face him. 'You can't win. Not against the guzzlers.' I tighten my jaw. 'I know that much.'

'You don't know what we know.' A smile plays around his thin mouth. 'We don't just have a plan to destroy the bloodguzzlers. We can offer you a lot more. Ever had a girlfriend, Alistair? Or are you still in the locked-bathroom-door-and-soggy-sock stage?'

Yuck. I don't demean myself – or Rogu3 – by answering. I don't have to; Isaac is on a roll.

'We can give you girls. Willing, warm, pretty. Blondes, brunettes.' He exudes smarm. 'You name your type and we'll provide it. If you prefer boys, we can help you out there as well.'

I scowl at him and he laughs. 'If you'd rather have money, that can be arranged. We can pay off your parents' mortgage. Send you to university.' He watches me carefully. 'You don't want that though, do you? I can see it in your eyes.' He gives me a knowing smirk. 'It's losing those cumbersome V plates that's whetted your interest.' He lowers his voice to a whisper. 'I tell you what. To show you how far we are willing to go to prove what we can give you, I'll give you a little taster of what's on offer.' He snaps his fingers.

From the other side of the gallery, a blonde peels herself away from the wall and makes her way round to us. She's dressed much like the other people here but the glazed look in her eyes sets her apart. Unfortunately, she's not Lisa Johnson – but it could be her.

'This is Molly.' Isaac's smile broadens. 'Molly meet Alistair. You want to get to know him better, don't you?'

She places a hand on my shoulder. It's all I can do not to recoil. 'Yes,' she murmurs, her voice matching her dreamy expression.

'Take him to the restroom,' Isaac orders. 'Show him how well you want to get to know him.'

Good grief. Is this really happening? Isaac laughs at my expression. My mind is racing but I can't think of what else to do other than let Molly lead me away.

It's only when Molly and I are some distance away and I'm free from Isaac's suffocating gaze, that my thoughts start to clear. He's made no demands of me yet; no doubt those are to come. He's dangling the carrot first and the stick will come later. I need to work out a way to accept the carrot while maintaining a sliver of integrity. Not to mention O'Shea's glamour. This is going to be interesting.

As all this is clearly planned, Molly knows exactly what she's doing. She leads me straight to a disabled bathroom, reaches round me to close the door and locks it. Then she coils one arm round my neck and leans in, her lips parted.

I could negotiate with her, make some kind of deal whereby she gets out of this sleazy scene and keeps her mouth shut into the bargain, but somehow I don't think that's going to work. Whatever drugs are in her system, they have a hold on her that's going to outweigh anything I can say or do. And the expression on her face suggests that she believes this is her duty as a member of Tov V'ra.

I do the only other thing I can think of.

When her lips brush mine, I take hold of her waist then I gasp, willing my cheeks to flush red. Imagining the look on Michael's face when he watched me reach for him helps with that. Then, with one swift jerk, I pull myself away and grab my groin. I turn my back on her and hunch my shoulders as if I'm embarrassed. If Rogu3 ever hears of this, he'll probably kill me. Several times over.

Molly lightly touches my back. 'It's okay,' she whispers. 'It happens.' She gives me a pat. 'Next time will be different.' I can't tell without turning round whether she's relieved or not.

'Go,' I growl. When she doesn't immediately move, I deepen my voice. 'Go!'

She pulls away, unlocks the door and slips out. When I hear it bang shut behind her, I swallow hard. I hope Isaac buys it.

Taking a few moments to compose myself, I go to the sink and splash my face with water. I grip the edges of the ceramic and lean in to the mirror. My face wavers for a moment and becomes blurry. I blink, trying to focus. Shit, the glamour is slipping. I'm going to have to finish things up with Isaac before it vanishes entirely.

He's outside the door when I go out, leaning against the wall with his ankles crossed. Molly has completely vanished. He claps me on the back and winks. 'Good man!'

I avoid his gaze. He obviously knows what just 'happened' but he's choosing to keep me on side by pretending it didn't. That suits me; the less we talk about that little episode, the better.

'There are a lot more girls like Molly,' he boasts. 'And they all have the same agenda that we do. Things like that are the perks but they don't beat the real reason Tov V'ra exists.'

'Which is?' I manage to croak.

'Bringing hellfire and brimstone down on the head of every vampire in this country, of course.' He laughs at my expression. 'I know you don't believe me yet but you will. It doesn't matter how powerful you think the Families are, Alistair. We are going to destroy them.'

My skin is itching more than ever and I can feel time slipping away. Isaac has to get to the point soon or I'm stuffed. Instead of a lanky teenager, he'll be confronted with a short vampire. Admittedly it would be fun to see the look on his face.

'You can't.'

'Oh, we can. I'll prove it to you.' He ducks his head as a gaggle of chattering schoolgirls passes us. 'At three o'clock a new bill is going to be introduced into Parliament. I know that watching Westminster live on television isn't the most riveting programme in the world but you should watch. When you're done, call the number on the card.'

Isaac whirls and joins the schoolgirls. He's quickly swallowed up in their midst and I'm left frowning after him. There is no damn number on the card.

It's not easy getting out of the cathedral. My original plan was to wait until nightfall but I need to see what this parliamentary bill is about, so I can't afford to wait until then. The itching is becoming almost uncontrollable and, as I wait for O'Shea in one of the quieter side chapels, I start to feel both dizzy and nauseous. I end up sitting on the marble floor, resting my head and back against a stone plinth.

It takes O'Shea an age to arrive. When he does and beckons me inside his oversized overcoat for cover, I'm on the verge of passing out. The glamour has completely vanished and I'm back to plain old Bo.

'This isn't going to work,' I tell him. 'That coat is not going to stop the sun from burning me.'

'Relax. I borrowed it from Michael. It's UV proof. Just watch your ankles and stick close to me.'

I don't have the energy to argue. I hunch underneath and we shuffle out. Even with the coat's protection, I can still feel the sun's rays searing me. My chest is tight and it's becoming hard to breathe. Just when I'm sure I can't take it any more, I hear a car door open and O'Shea all but shoves me inside. I collapse onto the seat and take short, shallow breaths, willing myself not to throw up.

My skin is prickling; I can't tell whether it's from my brush with daylight or the last vestiges of the glamour spell. The uncomfortable sensation ends as soon as I feel a cool hand on the back of my neck. I jerk upwards and my eyes meet Michael's.

Although my chest tightens in delight at the sight of him, I also feel my stomach give another lurch. 'Shouldn't you be in crisis management?' I ask softly.

He gives me a crooked smile. 'I think I am.'

I sigh. O'Shea shrugs. 'You didn't give me much time to put together a rescue mission. I knew big, strong and handsome here would have all the necessary equipment.'

I'm glad to see that O'Shea is returning to form. His banter doesn't have quite the edge that it used to, but he's getting over the loss of Connor. I wish I could say the same. I can't focus on myself, however; there are far more important things to worry about.

'Have you and the other Lords come up with a plan for Medici?'

The warmth in Michael's expression is replaced with tension. 'Three nights from now. It's probably better if you don't know the details.'

I frown. 'Why not?'

He brushes a tendril of loose hair from my cheek. 'Because you'll jump in to the fray and I'll spend the entire time worrying about you instead of doing what I should be doing.' I open my mouth to speak but he hushes me. 'I know you can look after yourself. I know that you are big bad Bo. Just please,' he says, looking strained, 'let me have this.'

I subside. 'What about the rest of it?' I ask, referring to what was essentially his demand that I share my life with him.

He sighs. 'We'll deal with that later when the rest of this mess is cleared up.'

I try not to let my relief show. At least I'll have some time to persuade X – or to walk away from him. 'And what if *you* get hurt before then?' I ask softly. 'What will I do?'

He relaxes into a smile. 'I can look after myself.'

I can't stop myself from smiling back at him. My insides feel all gooey.

'You two make me sick,' O'Shea complains. My eyes turn to him, worried, but there's a grin on his face. Before I can stop him, he leans forward and taps the driver on the shoulder, murmuring something in his ear. I freeze.

'Devlin!'

He blinks. 'What?'

'You just gave him my address!'

His brow furrows. 'So?'

My mouth works uselessly, flapping open like a fish. Michael's eyes are hooded. 'Is it really such a big secret?'

'We've been through this,' I hiss, finding my voice.

'No, we haven't, Bo. Not really. I still don't understand why you're so determined to keep your new life secret from me.'

I slump down miserably in my seat. X is going to freak. Forget Medici, X may very well destroy Michael out of pure spite before Medici can lift a finger. Shit, shit, shit. Even if I keep Michael out of the apartment, X will know the truth. The damage is already done and I won't be able to keep it from leaking into my thoughts.

O'Shea stares from me to Michael and back again. 'What's the problem? Is it because of the guy you work for? Maria told me about him.'

The blood drains completely from my face while Michael goes completely still. 'You work for a ... guy?' he asks, speaking in a low, dangerous tone.

'He's my employer,' I say through gritted teeth. 'Don't start with the jealousy thing.'

'Why would I be jealous?' He crosses his arms behind his head in a deceptively casual position. I know better. 'You've simply failed to mention that you're working for someone. Why would you do that, Bo?'

I throw my hands up in the air. 'Confidentiality is part of our agreement, that's all! He's...' I look at O'Shea. 'What exactly did Maria tell you?'

'That he's some big internet whiz. I imagine Rogu3 is creaming his pants.'

I relax slightly. At least she kept the Kakos daemon part out of the equation. 'He's shy,' I finish, looking back at Michael.

His eyes narrow a fraction. 'And Maria?'

I start. 'Huh?' I'm beginning to see why Michael is pissed

off. He doesn't know anything about what I've been up to, other than what's been advertised in the tabloids. 'She's a kid. I found her at some underage dive,' I explain. 'She's obviously in a bad way but I'm not sure what to do about her. She doesn't seem to have any family.' I take a deep breath. 'We keep having the same conversation, going round and round in circles. My employer is off limits. He pays for my accommodation so that falls under the same caveat. Ask me about anything else and I'll tell you.'

'Is he living with you?'

'No. In fact we usually communicate by phone. I don't see him face to face all that often. Other than that, I can't talk about him.'

Michael looks away. 'When was the last time you killed someone?'

Bugger. 'Isn't there something else you'd rather know? Honestly, I'll answer just about anyth...'

'Bo.'

I mutter a curse. O'Shea gapes. 'That's your question? Mikey, honey, you can ask her anything at all, and you go with what the gutter press are spreading about her? Bo doesn't kill people. She might beat them up and take away their lunch money but she's not evil.'

Thanks a bunch, O'Shea. I sigh. 'This morning, alright? I killed someone this morning.'

The air in the back of the car crackles. O'Shea's astonishment is so obvious that it's almost comical; in contrast, Michael doesn't look surprised at all. 'For him?' he grounds out. 'Your employer?'

'I told you he's off limits,' I say. 'But for the record, no. This one was all me.'

'You really are evil,' O'Shea breathes. Without warning, he wraps his arms round me. 'I'm so proud!'

'You don't even know why I did it.' My words end up muffled in his chest but I think he heard me.

'I don't need to know.' He pulls back and chucks me under the chin. 'I'm sure you had good reason.'

I sneak a look at Michael. 'I'm not sorry. I just did what had to be done. It wasn't pleasant but it was necessary.' Maybe. Probably.

He still won't meet my eyes. 'I can't judge you on this, Bo. I have killed in the past.'

'Damn,' O'Shea whistles, in an obvious attempt to lighten the atmosphere. 'I'm the only death virgin. I'm going to have to do something to keep up. Maybe we can pull over here. Look, there's someone wearing pink and orange together. That's a heinous crime against fashion. I'll get out here and...'

'Enough.' Michael's tone brooks no argument.

O'Shea's attempts at levity were making the situation worse, not better. All the same, I touch him lightly on the arm to show I appreciate the effort. He smiles at me but there's a strain to his mouth that wasn't there before. He put on a good show of dissembling but does he really think I'm a monster?

I swallow. His loyalty in the face of the overwhelming evidence against me makes me feel like a shit. I left him to get over the loss of Connor on his own; I should have been there by his side. Then I damn myself for weakening. I'm a better investigator and a greater force for good when I don't let shit like this get to me.

CHAPTER 18

LOOK FOR WHAT ISN'T THERE

There is no longer any reason to keep Michael out, so I lead both him and O'Shea up to my apartment. Michael doesn't say a word and his expression is nigh on impossible to read. I decide I can't worry about what he's thinking. Instead, I walk past Maria who is curled up on the sofa and staring at us with her strange green eyes, and flick on the television. It takes me some time to find the right channel; it's not as if I'm usually tuned into Parliament TV.

'What's this about?' O'Shea asks.

I shake my head. 'I don't have a clue. Not yet anyway.'

When the camera turns to Vince Hale, rising out of the back benches with his shiny suit and an obvious statement to make, I feel the first flicker of dread. As soon as he starts to speak, Kimchi comes careening out of the kitchen where he was gnawing on goodness knows what. He growls at the screen. Maria jumps about a mile and cowers behind a cushion. The rest of us watch in stony silence.

O'Shea frowns. 'I know his face.'

'He's anti-vampire,' Michael explains.

'But potentially pro-Medici,' I add.

O'Shea's eyebrows shoot up his forehead. 'Really?'

'Hush.'

'As the Right Honourable Ladies and Gentlemen are no doubt aware,' Hale begins, 'recent vampire activities are a particular cause for concern.'

There's a rumble of agreement from the assembled politicians. Honestly, they sound more like a playground rabble than this country's democratically elected representatives.

'I wish to propose a new bill ensuring that vampire numbers are capped. For the good of this country, we cannot permit the five Families to continue to besmirch the name and reputation of the good people of the United Kingdom. Although I hesitate to use the word, the bloodguzzlers' activities are unhealthy. The members of my constituency are demanding that action is taken and, frankly, I agree.'

The Speaker of the House, a sleek whippet of a man, peers over his half-moon spectacles. 'Are you suggesting that we revoke the binding law of 1532 and remove the vampires' current legal status?'

'Legal status?' Hale scoffs. 'They have no legal status. They act with absolute impunity. The law provides absolute immunity and we have only their word that they act to punish offenders.'

Parliament rises up again with a growing chorus of 'hear, hear'. All of us lean forward. Even Maria pays attention, forgetting her fear that Kimchi will slobber on her.

'Maybe he's not as keen on Medici after all.'

I shake my head. Something else is going on here.

Enjoying his audience, Hale waits for the hubbub to die down before speaking again. 'However,' he booms, 'that is not something I wish to address. In recent days we have seen that the Medici Family is at least prepared to prove their mettle and address their inadequacies.'

Inadequacies? Is that what he's calling those three blood-guzzlers who Medici executed? I gape in disbelief.

'No,' Hale remarks in the grand-orator fashion of someone who knows this moment will be played out across television screens for days, months and years to come. 'What I propose is that we return the cap on their numbers. There is no good reason why they are recruiting and we should put an immediate halt to it.'

'Hear, hear!'

'That's a good thing, isn't it?' O'Shea asks by my side.

I bite my lip. 'Wait.' Somehow I don't think Hale is finished.

'And we should demand a return to the original numbers of five hundred vampires per Family,' he says. 'No more and no less.'

I clench my jaw. 'There it is.'

O'Shea scratches his head. 'That doesn't make any sense. Is he proposing what I think he's proposing?'

As if he were in the same room with us, Hale answers O'Shea's question. 'Let's face it, anyone who has willingly signed up with the Families has already proved that they are prepared to take their life in their hands. Forty-two per cent of all new recruits do not even survive the turn.' I blow air out in a silent whistle. He's made that statistic up; not even close to that many die before making the turn. 'Their very nature means they are already diseased. Let us not forget that vampires originate from a blood infection! Any vampire who was turned after each Family reached a population of five hundred should be put out of their misery and put down.'

The room erupts. I turn to Michael, who is standing rigid. The only sign that he's heard Vince Hale's words is the bitter cold emanating from his eyes. I shiver involuntarily. Hale is a braver man than he realises; I wouldn't want to go against that many vampires.

'What he's proposing is genocide. No one will let that pass.'

Michael takes a long time before answering. When he does speak, his tone is stiff and awkward. 'Public opinion will be with him.'

'The protests have died down,' I begin.

'You know how people feel, Bo. We've still not done enough to reverse the damage that Nicky caused.'

I pinch the bridge of my nose. What a fuck up – but it doesn't mean that a bill of this sort would ever be passed. There's no chance. Besides, it takes ages to enact laws. I've listened to my grandfather complain about that on many an occasion.

'He's just grandstanding,' I insist. 'It's tied into this group I've been investigating. Tov V'ra. I think they've absorbed most of the protestors into their ranks.' I think of Molly, the young seductress I met today, and shudder. 'They're a distasteful bunch. No one will take this seriously.'

'I hope you're right.'

'I am.' I'm insistent. To imagine this kind of thing could ever go ahead is insane.

Michael's phone beeps. He pulls it out and answers it. 'If you're calling about that prick in Parliament then I already know.' He pauses then momentarily explodes. 'Fucking hell!'

I take a step backward. I've never seen Michael react like that. He grabs the remote control and tries to change the channel. Instead of the familiar sight of Westminster, we're faced with what appears to be a yellow animated square with a cheesy grin.

'Damn it! Where's the news?'

Maria edges over and takes it from him, finding the right channel with quick fingers. Suddenly I feel very old. I'm about to thank her when I see who is now on the screen. Medici. Again.

'I've been watching the events in Parliament today,' he says. 'Despite my earlier words, I fully agree with Vincent Hale's sentiments. Vampire numbers are out of control and I am prepared to accede to his demands. The Medici Family will return to the capped population of five hundred. It will be a painful experience for all, but one we are prepared to undertake for the good of the country.'

'No,' I whisper. 'He can't do this. He's the one who started increasing the population in the first place!' Not to mention that he was trying to pass himself off as a hero for 'saving' all those poor humans from themselves.

'He's a frozen-hearted bastard,' Michael says. 'He can do it and he will. He also knows that the rest of us will refuse to follow suit. We'll be weakened and he will come out on top. It's as if he's planned this from the start.'

I can't help feeling that Michael is right. Medici is too calculating for this to be some spur of the moment decision. 'It's murder.' I ignore the looks I receive from both O'Shea and Michael. What I do is far less cold-blooded than what Medici is proposing. I grit my teeth. 'It's also too pat. Not just in the planning.'

'What do you mean?'

I point at the television. 'He started his own statement less than five minutes after Hale did his thing. Yesterday, their roles were reversed: Medici executed those three bloodguzzlers and Hale was talking about it within minutes.'

'You think they're working together?'

I nod. 'I do. They're not perfectly in tandem. After all, yesterday Medici was acting proud of his recruitment drive. They don't want to appear too closely knit – but I don't think there's any doubt that they are. The question is why.' Medici, Hale and the Tov V'ra – a triumvirate that seem not only to be in cahoots but also to have a carefully planned agenda. This is not good.

Medici refuses to take any questions from the assembled press, whirls round and heads back into the safety of his Family fortress. The camera flicks back to the news anchor who repeats what just happened with unmistakable glee. I nudge Maria and she turns off the television.

'The other Family Heads are going to want to meet again and discuss the new development,' Michael says.

'It seems to me,' I snap, 'that there's a whole lot of discussing going on and not much action.'

'What would you have us do, Bo? Burn down Medici's house with everyone inside it?'

It's not a bad idea. I shrug helplessly at Michael. It seems that through the course of our relationship, he's grown less decisive and softer and I've grown harder and more willing to allow for inevitable casualties for the sake of the greater good. It's not a thought that sits well with me.

The tension is broken by a sharp knock at the door. All of us jump, with the exception of Kimchi who clatters towards the front and starts leaping up in delight at the unexpected caller. His claws scrape against the panelled woodwork. Whoever is on the other side starts thumping; apparently knocking simply isn't enough.

'Blackman! Open up!'

I frown. I know that voice. Maria vanishes while O'Shea and Michael watch me march over and nudge Kimchi out of the way. I open the door, revealing the rage-filled features of Rogu3's father.

'Mr Jones,' I say. 'What a pleasant surprise.'

He barges past me. Kimchi launches towards him with a lolling tongue but Jones scowls at the dog with such ferocity that Kimchi actually falls backwards in mid-lunge. I'll have to try that technique myself.

Rogu3's father looks round the room. When his eyes land on Michael, he sneers. 'I might have known he'd be here as well. Is he involved in a plot to turn my son? Is that what this is all about?'

'I'm not quite sure what you're referring to,' I say. It's not exactly true; I think I know what he means – I just don't want to be right.

'You promised me you'd keep away from him!' he yells.

Damn it. I should have known better than to take Rogu3 at his word. I should have taken a few minutes to call Mr Jones and check that it was alright for the boy to start working with me again. Shoulda woulda coulda.

'You need to go,' I tell Michael.

He glances from me to Mr Jones and back again. I'm obviously not in any danger, regardless of how irate Jones is. And Michael does have far more important things to do. He gives me a terse nod and strides out. I watch him go, my stomach tightening at his jerky movements.

I don't yet know how I'll manage it but I'm going to make things better for Michael. It's the least I can do. I need to see him smile again, even if it kills me.

'Are you even going to look at me?' Rogu3's dad rages.

I turn back to him. 'I'm sorry. I thought that everything was...' My voice drifts off.

'Everything was what?'

I shake my head. 'Nothing. I won't contact Rogu3 again.'

'It's too late.'

'It's never too late, Mr Jones,' I begin, but he takes a threatening step towards me. Despite the situation, I'm impressed. He will do almost anything to protect his son, even stand up against a vampire with a reputation like mine.

'There's a man outside my house.' He balls up his fists. 'Outside my home. He refuses to leave until you appear.'

I pause. Isaac. It has to be. Sudden fear rips through me. He must have discovered the truth somehow about our meeting at St Paul's and he's going to use it against us. If Rogu3 gets hurt, even slightly…

'Just because he's wearing a suit, doesn't mean I can't tell he's up to no good!' Rogu3's father yells. 'You don't have to be a scary prick to dress like a reject from the Hells' Angels.'

O'Shea shoots me a nervous look as if I'll take offence at the insult against my dress sense but that's not what I'm worried about. Isaac didn't strike me as the kind of person who would wear a suit. Besides, I only saw him a couple of hours ago. Why would he have changed his clothes? I was wrong; this has to be someone else.

'Mr Jones,' I say carefully, 'I need you to be more specific. What does this man look like?'

My phone rings. Normally I'd ignore it but, with everything else going on, I don't think I can afford to. I answer it, keeping my eyes trained on Rogu3's dad. 'What?'

'That's not a very friendly way to answer the phone, Bo,' X chides.

'This isn't a good time. I know we need to talk but…'

'You're perfectly right we need to talk. Stop arguing with the man and get over here before I get hungry.'

I freeze. Oh no. 'You. You're the one outside Rogu3's house.'

'Got it in one,' he tells me cheerfully.

'But you like him. You want to give him a job. Why would you…'

'You know why. Get here, Bo. Now.' He hangs up.

'What is it?' O'Shea asks, clearly alarmed at my suddenly white face.

'I have to go,' I mutter.

'Who was that?' Mr Jones demands. 'What do they want?'

I ignore his frantic questions. 'Where's your wife?'

'With Alistair at home.'

'Did you call the police?'

'No.' His face pales. 'Should I have?'

'No. It's good that you didn't.' If X wanted to, he could make mincemeat out of any coppers who showed up. They would only serve to piss him off. I know he's a Kakos daemon but this is a hell of a way for your employer to show displeasure. Surely a note in my file would have sufficed?

I grab my jacket and shrug it on, heading straight for the door. The sky has darkened enough that I should be safe to be outside. If I take the motorbike, I can get to Rogu3's place quickly.

'I'm coming with you,' Mr Jones says.

I glance back at him. His emotion makes him a liability. 'Make sure he doesn't leave for the next hour,' I tell O'Shea.

'Bo, do you really think this is a good idea?'

I soften my voice. 'Please.'

O'Shea's shoulders drop. 'Okay.'

'You can't keep me prisoner!' Mr Jones yells. 'You can't...'

I stride out, leaving him to shout and scream all he wants. I've got more important things to deal with.

'I'M NOT VERY IMPRESSED, BO,' X says, shaking his head at me. 'I don't ask much of you, just don't tell anyone about me and go after the criminals I point out. All you had to do was to sort out Lisa Johnson's disappearance. Instead, you're wilfully breaking all my rules.'

'It's not my fault!' I burst out.

He clicks his tongue. 'I thought it was a good thing when

you stopped being so frightened of me.' He steps forward, for a moment revealing the writhing black tattoos that twist and turn across his skin. 'Now I think that was a mistake.'

I calm myself down. 'I haven't told anyone about you. Read my thoughts – you know exactly what I've done. I haven't broken any of your damn rules.'

'You brought the half-breed to the apartment. To *my* apartment. *He* brought the vampire. I think I made my feelings on that matter pretty clear, even for someone like you.'

I fold my arms. 'There's no need to insult me.'

'It appears that there's every need.'

'Rogu3's father showed up at my door less than fifteen minutes after Michael came in. There's no way he got across town that quickly. You must have been here at least an hour before then.' I take a deep breath and force myself to meet X's harsh gaze. I'm not afraid of him; I'm not afraid of him; I'm not afraid of him. 'What gives?' I demand. 'Is fortune-telling one of your skills as well? Because if it is, please, tell me how all this is going to end. It'll save me some time. There's a lot going on, you know. Medici and some politician called Vince Hale are involved with the Tov V'ra. Medici is on the verge of killing more than two thousand newbie vampires just because he feels like it. If you want to tell me off, then get in line. Right now you are low on my list of priorities.'

Something flashes in X's face that almost – but not quite – has me running down the street as far away as I can get from him.

'I instructed you to stay away from witches.' Shit. Doris. I'd forgotten about her. 'You failed, little Bo. I also told you to stay away from Medici and concentrate on Lisa Johnson.'

'Didn't you hear what I just said?' I say, growing bolder because I was still standing. 'They're all linked.'

'You don't want to annoy me, Bo,' he says silkily. 'I don't

have many faults but I can, on occasion, be a bit petty. Cross me and you'll suffer the consequences. Leave Medici alone. Concentrate on the Tov V'ra and rescuing Lisa.'

'Why do you care so much about one human girl?'

His dark eyes swarm over me. 'Every life is important.'

'This coming from a Kakos daemon,' I scoff. I tilt up my chin. 'I'm not making another move until you promise me that you will leave Rogu3 alone.'

'I fail to see why you insist on using that ridiculous moniker.'

'It's the one he's chosen. And I mean it, X, you know I do. I will walk away right here and right now unless you give me your word that you won't go near him again.'

X regards me silently for a moment. 'Do you know,' he says eventually, 'I think you mean that.'

'You can read my mind. You should know.'

He runs his tongue along his bottom lip. I catch a glimpse of his sharp white teeth and only just repress a shudder. I'm aware that I'm treading on dangerous ground here but I've had enough of X and his demands. I'm not his plaything to jerk around as he pleases.

'Very well,' he says. 'I vow that I will not approach Alistair Jones again. My word is my bond, Bo. I never break it.'

I let out the breath I hadn't realised I was holding. 'Thank you.'

He holds up his palm. 'There is one other thing, though.' He smiles. 'I also vow that if your Michael finds out who I really am, I will take revenge. There will be no more wheedling and no more bargains.'

The only other person who knows X's true nature is Maria. I'm confident I can impress upon her how vital it is that she says nothing. She'll understand. X's smile broadens. 'Very well,' I snap, repeating his capitulation back at him.

He crooks his finger at me. 'Lisa Johnson. Her, and her alone.'

I open my mouth but he shakes his head and starts to walk away. Fine. I trust Michael. Regardless of how idiotic the other Family Heads are, I know he'll come up with a decent solution for Medici's vile proposal. The rest I can manage.

I walk towards Rogu3's familiar house and rap on the door. There's a long wait and then his mother opens it, her pale face peering out at me. 'Good evening, Ms Blackman.' Her eyes dart across the street.

'He's gone,' I say. 'He won't be back.'

Her hand flies to her throat. 'Are you sure? Who is he?'

'No one you need to worry about, I promise.' I pause for a beat. 'I apologise for involving Rogu3 – I mean, Alistair – in my business once again.'

'It's okay. He told me about it.' She swallows nervously. 'We decided not to tell his father.'

Then I suppose Rogu3 had some parental permission to come to me. It doesn't make me feel better. 'Can I speak to him? It won't take long.'

She nods jerkily. 'He's in his room – it faces away from here. He doesn't know what was going on outside. We thought it was best.'

I try to smile. 'I'm sure it was.'

'I'll go and get him.' She disappears for a minute.

Although I've been invited into their house on a previous occasion, it's clear that this time I'm going to be left cooling my heels on the doorstep. I could barge my way inside but I don't think that would be a wise move.

When Rogu3 appears, surprise lights his features. He asks me inside but I quickly decline. 'You should have told your father you were working with me.'

He shrugs. 'My mum knew.'

'You told me both your parents were on board.'

'So I lied. Don't tell me you never have.' His insouciance bothers me, probably because it's too much like my own. 'Anyway, how did it go today? Did the Tov V'ra show up?'

'They did.' I take out the card which Isaac gave me and show it to him. 'I'm supposed to call the number on there, except I don't see any number.'

Rogu3's brows snap together. He turns it over in his fingers several times before his expression clears and he lets out a short laugh. I frown. I have yet to find anything amusing about any of this.

'You need to look at it differently,' he says. He holds it up between his thumb and forefinger. I squint. I still can't see anything apart from the bloody tree.

'Branches. Trunk. A few leaves.' I shrug. 'What am I missing?'

'Don't look at what's there,' Rogu3 says. 'Look at what *isn't* there.'

That doesn't make any sense. I'm about to tell him so when suddenly everything slides into place and I see what he means. 'The white space,' I breathe. 'It's not the tree that's important. It's the space between the branches.'

He nods. 'It's difficult to spot unless you know what you're looking for. The white space creates the shape of a number between each branch. There's your phone number.'

'Damn stupid way to communicate your details,' I grumble. I check my watch. It's already gone eight; Isaac will be wondering why I've not been in touch. I draw out my phone and quickly dial then I pass it to Rogu3. 'You've got a cold,' I whisper before the rings cease and someone picks up.

He nods. 'Hello?' He coughs and clears his throat, changing the phone to speaker. 'This is Alistair.'

'I'm glad you called.' It's Isaac. 'What did you think of the show?'

Rogu3 frowns at me. I lean forward, keeping my voice low. 'Politician. Vince Hale. At three o'clock, he...'

He bobs his head. I guess he saw it too. 'Impressive,' he murmurs into the receiver. 'That was your doing?'

I hold my breath.

'You could say that,' Isaac answers. 'I assume you're calling because you realise we have more power than you thought. We really can bring the Families down.' He laughs. 'Either that, or you want to see more of Molly.'

Rogu3 glances at me, puzzled. I dismiss Isaac's words with a quick wave and hiss at him, 'Find out what happens next.'

'What now?' Rogu3 says. 'I'm interested in what you have to offer, so what do I do now?'

'Well, you're satisfied as to our desirability,' Isaac says. 'Now we want to prove your worth.'

I knew it. I wait, curious to hear what he's going to demand.

'What do you want?'

'Oh, it's pretty straightforward. We want your friend.'

'Eh?'

'Bo Blackman. Give us Bo Blackman and we'll give you everything you've ever dreamed of.'

My mouth suddenly goes dry. Well, I wasn't expecting that.

CHAPTER 19
WHO'S BAD?

The drop, if you can call it that, takes place at midnight, smack bang in the middle of Piccadilly Circus. I don't think Tov V'ra have really thought this through. My face is well known and if anyone spots me being bundled into the back of a van then I'm pretty sure it'll be headline news.

But Tov V'ra is slicker than I give them credit for.

Rogu3 has arranged to meet me here ostensibly to apologise for his little show in front of Medici. At least, that's what Isaac thinks he's arranged to do. Instead, Rogu3 is going to stay at home and I'm going to be 'kidnapped'. Hopefully. If they decide they just want me dead, we're going to have a bit of a problem.

The one good thing about the plan is that Rogu3 isn't going to be present. I've made him promise to stay home, no matter what. With his father back on his case, I don't think he'll disobey me. In theory, Tov V'ra will contact him tomorrow when they're convinced of his loyalty. By then it won't matter.

Even at this hour of night, the street is busy. I wear my trusty leather jacket and make sure I'm not disguised in any way. I'm meeting someone I trust – why would I try to hide? I paste a bored expression on my face and scowl at pedestrians who consider approaching me. It doesn't take much: a flash of my fangs and they're quick enough to back off.

A few minutes before the magical witching hour, a scuffle breaks out directly in front of the statue of Anteros. A lot of people mistakenly think he's Eros but Anteros is far nastier; he's the god of requited love. In other words, he punishes those who refuse to accept everything that love has to offer. I watch the action for a moment or two. Anteros, were he to exist, wouldn't have any beef with me, not now. I've told Michael that I love him; it's only X's stupid rules that keep getting in the way. Those, and the fact that I seem to be turning into a homicidal maniac.

I'm prepared to ignore the display of arrogant fisticuffs but when I see that one of the fighters is a witch – and a black and white witch at that – I change my mind. This is too good an opportunity to miss. It niggles me that X doesn't like me focusing my energies on them but, in this scenario, the only person he's likely to punish is me. And it's not as if I went out looking for them, I reason. I'm here on his orders because this is about helping Lisa Johnson.

I ignore the traffic lights and dart across the road. A couple of cars beep their horns but when I turn and they see my face, their expressions go from irritated to comical horror. I snarl at them and keep going.

There's already a crowd forming around the fight. If Tov V'ra are going to show up and do whatever dirty deeds they have in mind, this lot might put them off. I don't want to have to cool my heels for yet another night.

Just as the witch raises her hands, a telltale gesture signifying she's about to let loose a nasty spell, I leap into her path and smile.

'Good evening.'

She blanches. I wink at her then lunge forward, grabbing a

hank of her hair and pulling. She screeches in agony. I twist round to throw a questioning look at whoever she was fighting. The weedy human takes full advantage of my intervention and pushes through the watching crowd before disappearing into the distance. The crowd continues to capture all the action on their phones.

Keeping one hand on my new witchy companion, I swipe in the direction of the nearest voyeur, wrenching the phone out of his grasp. I throw it down and stomp on it hard then bare my fangs at the other spectators. They take the hint and, within seconds, all the filming ceases. It's not the photographic evidence that bothers me – there are plenty of CCTV cameras around here to 'protect' the tourists – it's the notion that I'm public property and will allow any passerby to upload my image to YouTube. I have a reputation to maintain. The meaner I appear to be, the easier the rest of my work becomes.

'So,' I coo, twisting the witch's hair harder so she squeals. 'You thought you could perform a magical attack in the middle of one of the city's busiest areas, did you?' I tut. 'You should know better than that. Especially when you are so easy to bring down.'

She doesn't answer. I'm debating whether to nick her flesh with my teeth or break her nose when I catch a movement out of the corner of my eye. Bugger it. Two uniformed police officers are heading straight for us, no doubt alerted by the crowd. I should just let the witch go but then I might be forced to answer a bunch of daft questions in a cell instead of continuing my mission.

I drag her away from the police and the gawking people. All I need is a side street where I can knock her unconscious as quickly as possible, then I can circle round the back and return to my spot. The trouble with Piccadilly Circus is that it doesn't have many shady alleyways.

'Anyone follows me,' I growl over my shoulder, 'they can join her in her grave.'

The crowd flinches, like some strange amorphous whole. Good. I march the witch away from the people and into the quietest street I can find. She's not putting up much of a struggle; I suppose she's already given in to the Bo Blackman inevitable.

Aware that I have little time, I yank her up and spit into her face. 'Why the fight?' I demand. I shake her. 'What exactly were you up to?'

She stares at me with her wide eyes. At first I think she's merely scared but a second or two later, when she starts to laugh, I realise it's something else.

'You,' she says simply. 'I was paid fifty quid to fight you.'

Before I can say or do anything, and completely ignoring my hold on her hair, she reaches into her pocket and draws out a damn taser. Great. Rather than try to jerk away, I reluctantly let her zap me. At least that's what I tell myself, as pain surges through every vein and artery in my body. This is what I came for.

I WAKE UP IN A CAGE. I have no way of knowing how long I've been out for because there don't appear to be any windows and the room is completely dark. I have very little room to manoeuvre — and someone is hiding in the shadows and watching me. For now I pretend that I'm oblivious to their presence. There's no point in giving away all of my secrets just yet.

I pick myself up and massage my aching neck then edge towards the bars. Gingerly, I reach out to touch one; the tip of my finger merely scrapes the metal but I'm still thrown backwards. Ouch. That hurt. No doubt it's another Magix creation. I should have done more to bring down that corporation when I had the chance.

There's a soft chuckle. I make a show of spinning round. 'Who's there?'

I'm not sure who I was expecting to see: Isaac perhaps, or some other fresh-faced Tov V'ra plonker. But it is Vince Hale. This time I don't have to fake my look of surprise.

He offers his usual smooth, practised smile which I've already seen via a hundred different cameras. 'I see you recognise me. Fame does make introductions far less complicated, doesn't it? Although in your case it's more infamy. You are a naughty girl.' He clears his throat. 'Forgive me. You're no girl. You're a bloodguzzling freak.'

I narrow my eyes into slits as Hale takes mincing steps towards the cage. Someone should give him lessons in deportment; he looks like a baby giraffe with a hot rod stuffed up its arse. 'I don't normally come to see any of the bloodguzzlers we capture,' he muses. 'But you're a special case. In the end, you were disappointingly easy to get hold of. You might put on a good face but you're still just a weak newbie.' He leans forward. 'Can you stand sunlight yet?'

I snarl. Rather than being intimidated, he simply laughs. 'Oh, how the mighty have fallen.'

'Why are you doing this?'

He twinkles at me like a benign dictator. 'Isn't it obvious? You're an affront to God. You shouldn't exist, your kind shouldn't exist. I'm going to make sure that's exactly what happens.'

I need him to tell me more. I get as close to the bars as I dare. 'You'll never succeed,' I goad. 'We're too strong. Any plans you put in place might bring down one or two vampires, but you'll never get us all.'

His eyes brim with amusement. 'Do you think,' he says

softly, 'that this is the part where I reveal all my plans to you and then you manage a daring escape? I don't have the time and I don't care enough about you to talk to you. I just wanted to see the look on your face when you realised it was all over. No one's coming to rescue you. No one cares. Your little hacker buddy gave you up with barely a second thought. How does that feel, to be completely abandoned by someone whose life you saved?'

I play along. 'Rogu3 wouldn't do that.'

'He would and he did.' Hale draws his fingertip along the edge of the cage. 'You're not getting out of here. We've tested it on numerous subjects and most of them far stronger than you. You, Ms Blackman, are well and truly screwed.'

Before I can say anything else, he turns on his heel and disappears. This time, he doesn't hide in the corner, he actually leaves. I'm left alone in pure darkness. Fortunately, that's the best kind.

I look around. I've been a vampire for long enough that my night sight is fairly good. I can't quite pierce the far corners of the room, of which Hale was no doubt aware, but I can see enough to tell that I'm in a smallish space. There's one door and whitewashed walls. There are even a few blood splatters dotted around but they're probably there for effect. They want me scared and quaking in my boots. It's probably part of the fun.

I can't see any cameras but that doesn't mean I'm not being watched. I take a deep breath and fling myself at the bars, just in case. It's agony. When I fall back onto the stone floor, I let my hand fall to my ear. When I feel the small nub still there, I relax. They must have searched me but they weren't looking hard enough. Embedded close to my skull is a tiny tracking device that Maria helped me insert earlier. It helps that I have unbelievable healing powers; a few hours after its insertion there's barely a scar. Sometimes, I reflect, technology can be far more useful than magic.

I stay where I am, groaning occasionally. I'm not putting that part on for effect, I really am in considerable pain. I might be rather incapacitated but I enjoy the repeated shudders and spasms: they keep my mind clear. Between each one, I try to recoup my strength. I'm probably going to need it.

Despite the aftershocks of pain from my collision with the cage, I'm surprised Tov V'ra haven't done more to hurt me. I don't think it's because of any high-minded ideals; Hale is drawing this out for maximum effect. There can't be any other reason for keeping me alive. That was one of O'Shea's concerns: we could put as many plans and back-up plans into effect as we wished, but if I were dead then none of them would work.

I hope he's not going to take too long. Once the pain starts wearing off, this is going to become rather dull.

I'm not sure how much time has passed when the door re-opens. If I was expecting Hale to reappear, I'm disappointed. When I see who is there, I bite down on my bottom lip to stop myself smiling.

I lift up my head . 'Hello, Lisa.'

She flinches, her eyes widening. She looks over her shoulder as if she's seeking reassurance from someone behind her. When it doesn't come, she turns back at me helplessly and stands there, her shoulders dropping. Gone are the pretty clothes and make-up; she's wearing a white shift and looks rather ... sacrificial. Oh dear.

'How do you know my name?' she whispers.

'I know your parents.'

She continues to stare at me like a rabbit caught in headlights. 'You gave my dad your autograph.'

I nod. 'I did.'

'I didn't think you'd remember him. Or know who I am.'

'They're very worried about you, Lisa. They hired me to find you.' I watch her carefully for a reaction. Her eyes aren't glazed like Molly's were – I don't suppose there's any need to drug your followers when you can keep them inside your compound and completely under your thumb – but there is a dullness to her irises which wasn't in any of her photos. 'You didn't even tell them you were leaving.'

'I...' she licks her lips nervously. 'I wasn't allowed to.'

This isn't the same fierce young woman who marched for a hundred causes or who caught Adrian Leeman's heart. 'It's not all you thought it was going to be, is it? Joining the Tov V'ra, I mean. You thought you were going to save the world from the vampires and instead you're just a servant, passed around for sexual favours.'

Her mouth tightens. 'It's not like that. We're going to heal the world.'

You know when someone starts spouting Michael Jackson lyrics that they're done for. 'Not everything is black and white though, is it? Or the thriller that you were hoping for.' I stand up, ignoring the flare of pain that shoots down my legs. 'I'm bad but you really want to beat it out of here.' It's on the tip of my tongue to ask her if Billie Jean is also her lover but that might be taking things a step too far.

'Stop talking! You're just a monster! You're trying to get inside my head and twist my thoughts.' She backs away. 'It won't work!'

It already is. The sudden emotion she's showing is proving that. 'Your parents love you, Lisa,' I say, dropping my voice and holding her eyes. 'They're going crazy trying to find you.'

All the anger leaks out of her and she stares at me. I can't read her expression but it's definitely a step up from the zombie look she was sporting. 'Are they...' She pauses and swallows. 'Are they alright?'

'What do you think?'

Her shoulders sag. 'I had to come here. It's the only way. They told me I'd be part of something greater.'

'You're a sex toy, passed around from man to man.'

The abrupt flare in her eyes, which dies almost as quickly as it rises up, proves the truth of my words. She shakes her head vehemently though. 'It's not like that. What I do is for the martyrs.'

Every molecule in my body freezes. Martyrs? I don't like the sound of that at all. 'Who are the martyrs? What are they?'

'That's enough.' My eyes flash to the door. Isaac is standing there, a frown on his face. 'Lisa, do what you came here to do. We need Ms Blackman to look pretty for the cameras.'

Lisa glances at him and then at me. Her tongue darts out to lick her lips and, for a moment, I think she's going to refuse the order, whatever it may be. Then the dullness returns. She nods and, while Isaac watches, takes out a small knife. The blade is sharp and catches the weak light streaming in from the door.

I glare at Isaac, throwing as much malevolence as I can at him. 'This isn't necessary,' I growl.

He laughs. Gone are the relaxed features and easy smile of the boy I met in St Paul's Cathedral. This is pure menace. I sigh. He thinks he's dealing with a monster. He doesn't know what I do though; to know that, you need to become a monster yourself.

'Oh, Ms Blackman, it's very necessary. We don't want the watching public to think that we've hurt you.' He smiles. 'At least not yet. After all, you're going to be the face of the revolution. Lisa is simply going to help you gain the strength you need to sit up straight and form coherent sentences.'

I gesture at myself. 'As you can see, I can already manage both those things. I don't need her blood. I prefer to drink from willing donors.'

The snort Isaac emits is extraordinary. 'Yeah, right. That's why you drain the blood from half of the people you capture.'

Shit. 'That's different.'

He raises his eyebrows. 'Is it.' It's not a question. 'Come on, Lisa. Chop chop. We don't have all day.'

'Look at me, Lisa,' I say softly. 'And think. Who's the bad guy here? Who's making you bleed? Because it's not me.'

'Now!' Isaac barks.

Lisa flinches, drawing the knife across the pale skin of her arm. She thrusts it through the bars of the cage and all three of us watch her blood splatter onto the cement floor. My stomach rumbles, loud enough for them to hear. Isaac chuckles while Lisa looks terrified.

I cross my arms. 'I do have some self-control. I'm not doing this.' No matter how delicious the scent of her is, this isn't going to add a bloom to my cheeks. I was right about the cameras and it's the reason he's staying in the doorway. He needs footage of me with blood dripping from my mouth and he wants to stay out of shot. He needs me to look like the vampire I am, not the hero the rest of the world sees. I'm not going to give him that kind of satisfaction.

Isaac clicks his tongue. 'Mr Hale thought you might prove difficult. Fortunately there's more than one way to skin a cat.' He snaps his fingers. 'Bring him in.'

My stomach drops. No longer sure what's going on, I look behind him. A man appears from the corridor outside. His tree tattoo is proudly displayed for all to see. I recognise him from the little coffee shop and my heart sinks. That's nothing compared to what happens when I see what – or rather who – he's holding.

He has a long chain made out of shiny metal that looks similar to the stuff the cage is made of. He gives it a sharp tug and there's a vicious snarl. Lisa whimpers. I ignore her and focus on what's at the end of the chain. There's a sudden flurry of movement and it darts forward, all white incisors and sharp, gaunt features. A vampire. He lunges for Lisa and she jerks back. The man cackles, pulling sharply on the chain again and bringing the vampire to heel.

His features ring a bell. I sift through my memory, alighting on the images that Michael showed me. The man is one of the missing Montserrat bloodguzzlers.

Judging from the crazed look in his eyes, he's been here for some time. He's also obviously starving. Whoever he was originally, that person is long since gone; this creature is just an animal, reduced to its baser instincts. I spy a network of criss-crossing scars and fresh welts across his body. He's been hurt and hasn't healed. Whatever happened to him, it certainly wasn't pleasant.

'Be thankful that we're on a schedule and don't have time to do the same to you,' Isaac murmurs in the same cheerful tone. 'We were going to use him for this little show but when your hacker mugged up for the cameras, Mr Hale was smart enough to see a different opportunity.'

I understand. 'Why use a vampire who no one recognises when you can have the Red Angel?'

He smiles. 'Just so. You're the one guzzler, the one freak, who everyone thinks is a hero. If we can change their opinion of you, they won't blink when they see what we do next. If the public can't trust you, they can't trust any vampire.'

Lisa's blood is continuing to drip. He points at her. 'Drink from her or you know what will happen. I will order his release and it will be a bloodbath.' He shrugs. 'Either way, we will get what we need. It just depends whether she survives or not.'

'She's one of you. Why would you sacrifice her?'

'There are necessary casualties in every war,' Isaac intones, as if he's repeating a well-worn mantra. 'Lisa understands.'

I'm not so sure about that. Lisa is shaking from head to toe. Her face is getting paler and paler and it has nothing to do with blood loss.

'Let's forget the cage,' Isaac murmurs. 'We'll get a better shot without it.' He produces a key from his pocket and steps over, nudging Lisa roughly out of the way. He unlocks the door and it swings open, then he wags his finger at me. 'No funny business.'

I take in the situation. I could probably bring both Isaac and his goon down but it wouldn't be easy and Lisa might end up as collateral damage. I need to play the long game here. I make a decision, step out and grab her arm, raising it to my mouth. I lick the blood and the coagulant in my saliva seals her wound. Isaac raises his hand.

'Not so fast,' I growl. 'I just prefer the jugular.' I pull her back towards me and let my fangs sink into the flesh of her neck. Then I drink.

CHAPTER 20
WE ALL HAVE OUR DEMONS

I must have put on a good show because, once I've taken my fill, Isaac leaves me in peace. Part of me was concerned that Lisa's blood might be tainted in some way, laced with a drug to weaken me, kill me or turn me into a rabid animal, like the poor bloodguzzler who was dragged out of here still snapping at his chain. She tasted clean, though. Whatever Isaac has up his sleeve, he wants me completely compos mentis.

Still, he's given me more information than he probably intended to. Tov V'ra's original plans obviously didn't include me. Hale, Isaac and whoever else is in charge of this outfit have altered their set-up to include me. They might think they're being clever but last-minute swaps often don't pan out. It means they've not had time to consider all the variables. I smile in the darkness. Variables like me.

Even so, I'm not stupid. I hunker down in the centre of the cage and hug my knees, giving the impression of someone who's defeated. I've been in worse situations than this – and this time I'm better prepared.

I don't know how long I was unconscious for, so I don't

know what time it is. One of the less-advertised aspects of being a vampire is that our internal body clocks work differently after we've turned. Even in the depths of the cellar, I can feel that it's night.

I scratch my head for a moment and ponder. Given that the majority of London is asleep, Isaac must be planning to release his photos of me drinking from Lisa later on. He'll want a lot of people to watch them.

I understand that Tov V'ra's end-game is to destroy the Families once and for all, but I still don't get how they're planning to do it. And there's Medici to take into consideration: if he is working with Hale, how does he fit into all of this? Unless he's using Hale to rid himself of the other four Families once for and all without getting his hands dirty. Then his bid for power will be completely unobstructed. Considering the hatred in both Hale and Isaac's eyes when they looked me, it's possible that for once Medici may have bitten off more than he's realised.

I'm just dropping into a doze when there's a sudden buzzing in my ear. I slap at it reflexively.

'Bloody hell, Bo!' O'Shea hisses. 'This equipment is delicate!'

I drop my head further down so any cameras can't make out my lips moving. 'Sorry,' I murmur back. 'I wasn't thinking.'

'I'm not sure you're thinking about anything. This seems like a fool's errand to me.'

I tense. 'What do you mean?' If this place, wherever it is, is well fortified and well guarded, I could be in real trouble.

'These guys don't have a clue, is what I mean. Anyone can waltz up and say hello. It's like a goddamn American summer camp. So far I've spotted a barbecue, a café, volleyball nets ... you're not being held at Fort Knox, you're in Disneyland.'

I consider this. 'It makes perfect sense. Tov V'ra are setting themselves up as the good guys. They want to make it clear that they have nothing to hide. If they did have, someone would have popped by before now and asked whether their missing loved ones are having a game of rounders nearby. Hiding in plain sight is the smart way to manage it. No wonder no one's noticed them before. They've not advertised themselves but they've not hidden themselves either. Guards would cause the outside world to ask questions.'

'Well,' he says, 'there have been plenty of people doing that. Until about eleven o'clock there was a steady stream of journalists wandering in and out. I guess they've changed their minds about keeping quiet. Lots of pretty photos being taken of blonde children and happy couples.'

I nod. 'They're selling the ideal human life.' I suppose I should be grateful that Isaac didn't make me drink from a kid – although Lisa is attractive enough to make an effective anti-vampire poster child.

'Do you know what they want with you?' O'Shea asks.

'They're going to use me as an example to prove to the world that vampires are evil.' I shrug. 'It's not a bad idea. Despite my best efforts to the contrary, I still get a lot of publicity.'

'Then what will they do?'

I grimace. 'I don't know.'

'I could call the police. I'm sure Foxhunt would come running if I phoned.'

'His name is Foxworthy and he's not hugely impressed with me at the moment. Besides, I think this is one of those matters that's best kept in house. So to speak.'

'Suit yourself.'

I wet my lips with the tip of my tongue. 'Are you inside?'

'Nah. I wanted to get the lay of the land first. Should I head in? It wouldn't be hard, I can just stroll in through the front gates.'

'Do that. Don't involve yourself in anything though – just watch.' Better to be safe than sorry. I pause. 'How big is this place?'

'Pretty massive. There are a lot of people milling around.'

'Any idea where they might have taken me?' I ask. 'If they're lax about security, they're going to have me somewhere nondescript so they don't arouse suspicion. I'm not the only vampire here so it's probably a pretty big building, either underground or somewhere with no windows.'

'Most of the buildings are wooden huts. There's a big stone structure in the middle with a huge cross on the top.'

'Well,' I say, 'they will want to make sure their strong religious values are displayed to the world.'

'They're believers?'

'Actually, I don't think they are. It's just an excuse to do what they're doing. They're fanatic, certainly, but they're not as Christian as they pretend. Not the ones in charge anyway.' I tell him about Isaac's misquote.

'Figures,' O'Shea says.

I think about Isaac's mention of his 'schedule'. 'They're planning something big. Can you see signs of any movement? Large groups of people entering or leaving or equipment being moved around?'

'Other than a maypole they've just erected in front of the church building, nope.'

I frown. Maypole. Huh. That's an interesting construction for the middle of winter. It's also pagan – and paganism has far more connections with vampirism and daemons than with humans.

'Okay,' I say slowly, mulling over everything. 'Is everyone else okay?'

'Hunky dory. Maria is back at your place with Kimchi. Mikey baby is holed up with his Family.'

'Medici?'

'The same. Everyone's keeping inside.'

'The calm before the storm,' I muse. 'You should probably go, Devlin. Don't exert yourself too much in the meantime. You're going to need your energy for later.'

There's a long pause. 'Okay. You called me Devlin though.'

'I'm aware of that. It doesn't mean anything.'

His voice is quiet. 'I hope not. I need you, Bo. You're my friend. What happened to Connor wasn't your fault.'

I suck in a breath, trying to ignore the ache that rises up without warning in my chest. He keeps saying that but repetition doesn't make it true. 'Thanks,' I grunt. Saying what I really think is pointless.

'Michael needs you too. He might be too butch to say it but he does.'

It takes me a moment to speak. 'I need him too.' It's the truth. 'But I really do prefer it when you're less serious. I'm not in mortal danger. This will all turn out fine in the end.'

'Sure.' He doesn't sound convinced. 'Listen, Bo, about that other daemon, the one you've been working with. Is he the guy Maria told me about? Did he send you in there?'

'Someone's coming,' I lie, 'I have to go.'

'Bo, wait...'

'Shh.'

Thankfully, he takes the hint and the transmitter clicks off. Small mercies and all that.

It's still night when they come for me. I count twenty-one of them in total. Clearly, Tov V'ra isn't taking any chances, even with all of the anti-vampire Magix toys they have to play with. I don't resist; I'm too curious to see what they have planned. I don't make things easy for them either. To bring me along they are forced to drag me. Maybe I'll get lucky and they'll think that I've given up – or that I'm too weak after my collision with the magicked cage, regardless of Lisa's blood.

If I'm expecting fireworks and pizzazz, I'm sorely mistaken. Instead they haul me down a long corridor, up two flights of stairs and outside. It's a clear, crisp night, with a myriad of bright stars twinkling down at us. It takes me only a second to work out where I am. Behind me is the stone building designed to look like a church and in front is the odd maypole which O'Shea described.

Standing a fair distance away is a large crowd. Many of them are wearing the same simple white clothing as Lisa but there are some who are dressed differently. I scan everyone in turn, trying to work out which is O'Shea. He damn well better have seen what's going on and made his way here to join them.

I'm so focused on the people that it takes me a moment to spot the cameras. There are four of them, encircling the maypole with their dark lenses pointed directly at it. Once I see those, I also see the chains wrapped round the maypole. Okay. I guess I have more of an idea about what they're planning to do with me now. If they're all going to stick to the Bible, perhaps it'll be some sort of stoning affair. That'd probably kill me, I reflect; there are enough people to manage it, especially if I'm completely immobile.

That could be another reason why Isaac wanted to make sure I was fed first. It means I'll be able to heal myself so the stoning itself will be longer and more torturous. I don't see any stones, however, and it's probably too brutal for television viewing. These guys don't want to look like monsters – that position is reserved for me and me alone.

I chew on the inside of my cheek. No, they're going to want

to do something to make me appear unnatural and evil. To be honest, that really shouldn't be so hard.

I'm dragged over to the pole. From several metres away I can smell the fresh paint. Whatever they're planning to use the pole for, I'm going to be the sacrificial lamb that has to test it out – sacrificial in more ways than one.

It takes five of them to pull my arms behind my back and place handcuffs round my wrists. Considering I'm not doing anything to get away or stop them, it's hard not to roll my eyes. Tov V'ra are bringing new meaning to the phrase 'better safe than sorry'. Unfortunately, it's not the first time I've been forced to wear cuffs such as these. They're specially designed to work against bloodguzzlers; they don't just restrain us, they also sap our strength. Even if I wanted to do something, I'm not sure I'd be capable of it.

Before they can attach me to the pole, there's a rippling of applause from the assembly which grows louder and louder. I turn my head, expecting to see Hale's irritating swagger once more but it's not him; instead, four figures are striding out from the church. The one on the far left is Isaac, the others I don't recognise.

'Where's Hale?' I shout. 'Where's Vince Hale? Doesn't he want to be here to witness your little show?'

'Don't be so stupid,' sneers one of the four, an older man with a weak chin and flabby jowls. 'He's far too important for this.'

It's not that he's too important, it's that he's too concerned this might still go tits up. If this staged execution – as I assume it is meant to be – doesn't receive the public support Tov V'ra hopes for, Hale will want to make sure he has deniability. And these guys are calling *me* stupid? This time I do roll my eyes. Almost immediately, I'm rewarded with a hard slap across my face.

'Stop it, Abraham,' Isaac hisses irritably. 'We can't afford for her to be bruised.'

'Yeah, Abraham,' I taunt. 'You don't want to damage the merchandise.' The words are barely out of my mouth when Isaac sucker-punches me in the stomach. I wheeze and double up.

'No one's going to see those bruises,' he tells me. Then he turns and beckons to someone outside my line of sight. I crane my neck until I see Lisa. 'Come here,' he commands. 'You deserve to witness this up close and personal.'

I watch her approach. 'She doesn't look very keen,' I murmur.

Isaac ignores me. I can tell from the stiffening of his shoulders that he heard me – and he knows I'm right. The expression on Lisa's face suggests that she'd rather be anywhere else. This I can use.

'Before you slit my throat or chop off my head or do whatever it is you're planning to do,' I say conversationally, 'I don't suppose you could tell the cameras where Melissa Greek is. Her family and friends are desperate.'

'Shut up.'

'She was about Lisa's age,' I continue. I let out a small laugh. 'In fact, and you won't believe this, Lisa's doctor used to know Melissa Greek. Dr Bryant? Nice lady.'

Lisa's eyes fly to mine. Good. I've got her attention.

'Melissa was part of Tov V'ra. I know because she had one of those little trees as jewellery. Did you use her for sex? Pass her around and then kill her off when she decided she didn't like being treated like an empty vessel for your sperm?' I look around. 'Or is she here? Is she out in the crowd watching this happen?'

'There's no one called Melissa here,' Isaac snaps, more for Lisa's sake than mine.

'Ah,' I say, nodding as if everything is now clear. 'So you *did* murder her.'

Abraham gets up into my face. 'Stop talking or I'll disembowel you,' he hisses.

I smile and open my mouth ever so slightly, letting him see my fangs. He backs off hastily and I laugh. I'm aware the sound has an edge of madness; I should probably not do that.

'Turn on the cameras,' Isaac orders.

Four people break away from the crowd. They're obviously nervous but they're also drones – what Isaac commands, they will do. I realise that this isn't some avenging anti-vampire crusade; the sex, the people, even the damn clothing ... it's just a brainwashing cult.

With Abraham watching me, Isaac watching Lisa, the other two Tov V'ra leaders watching the camera operators and the crowd watching all of us, they complete their preparations. I stop paying attention to them and search again for O'Shea. I did tell him to get some sleep but if he's curled up somewhere and missing all this action, I'm going to be pissed off. And possibly dead. I scan each face. He's in full glamour, that much I know. It is pretty much a given that no tribers will be welcome here, whether they are vampires or not. The problem is that I don't know which face or body he's got on. He couldn't choose one until he saw who was in Tov V'ra.

There's a crackle of nervous energy in the air and all the mindless people are feeding it. Some are shifting from foot to foot, some are scratching or twitching or murmuring to friends. There's only person who's standing as still as a statue: a young man of dazzling good looks. When my gaze meets his, he gives me a minute nod. Ah ha. It figures that O'Shea picked someone young and handsome. I almost grin then I remember what's going on and manage to stop myself.

The taller of the other two Tov V'ra leaders looks at his watch. 'It's time, Isaac. You're up.'

Isaac gives a terse nod of acknowledgement and clears his throat. I can only see two of the cameras from here and both of them show steady green lights. Here we go. I half lean forward, curious despite myself.

'We all know what sort of world we are living in today,' Isaac intones. 'The sort of world where freaks of nature – monsters – rule the streets. They treat us like food and we let them. They pretend that they are kind and benevolent but they're not. They are evil through and through.' He points at me. 'They are vampires.'

I almost expect a drum roll to follow. It's a shame when there's nothing. I smile for the camera; I'd give a little wave if my hands weren't bound. My mouth might be working just fine but my body is heavy and sluggish. Thank you, Magix, I think sourly.

'What most people don't realise,' Isaac continues, 'is that vampires are evil even before they are turned. The vast majority of the Families recruit only criminals.'

I stiffen. That's a well-kept secret. For a second, I wonder who's been blabbing but it's obvious – it has to be Medici. Prick.

Isaac tuts sadly. 'They also use a human façade to stop us from fearing them. The true face of a vampire is far more terrifying.'

He jerks his head. The crowd turns dutifully, looking not at me but at the shape being dragged out from the church. It's the crazed Montserrat vampire from earlier. He's dressed in midnight blue to advertise his original allegiance. Everyone knows I was Montserrat as well; Isaac is linking me to him and vice-versa.

The look on the bloodguzzler's face is even more vicious. Being taunted by the promise of blood which is then snatched away from you will do that. He strains at the leash around his neck, his veins bulging, while his eyes roll and writhe in his skull. Whatever sense of humanity he once had is long gone.

One camera tracks his progress towards us, the other stays focused on Isaac. 'We've let the Families get away with murder,' he says. 'Even when a tiny defenceless child called...' He frowns. 'Damn it. What was that kid called?'

'Tommy Glass,' someone from the crowd provides helpfully.

He nods. 'Edit that later,' he instructs, beginning again. 'Even when a tiny defenceless child called Tommy Glass is slaughtered in his own garden, we let the vampires get away with it.' He shakes his head then his fist, then his head again. He's wasted here – he should start his own dance troupe. 'This is what a real vampire looks like,' he yells, pointing at the unfortunate insane bloodguzzler. 'Not this!' he turns his finger on me.

I don't look at him. The Montserrat vampire, whoever he used to be, is snapping and snarling. The metal round his neck is bulging. Each time he snarls and jerks, it shifts, expanding and contracting. I'm pretty certain it's not supposed to do that. The Magix techies apparently aren't as clever as either they or I thought. The slave collar is about to give way and no one, apart from me, realises.

'Isaac, look at the vampire.'

Isaac ignores me and continues his anti-vampire diatribe. I look at Abraham. 'Listen to me. The bloodguzzler over there is about to break free. You've starved him. He's completely insane. If he breaks out of that leash, there will be a bloodbath.'

'Shut up, bitch.'

Good grief. Does anyone around here have any sense? I grit my teeth, ready to try Lisa, but it is too late. There's a creak, followed by a snap as the collar finally gives way, then the bloodguzzler launches himself towards Isaac. It makes sense – he's the nearest.

The crowd screams. They turn to run, tripping over each other in a frantic bid to get away. 'Release my handcuffs!' I shout. 'I can take him on!' Abraham turns, fear getting the better of him. Bloody wanker. 'Isaac!' I scream. 'Let me go!'

Isaac has faster reflexes than I gave him credit for. Rather than use them to set me free so I can help, he grabs hold of Lisa and thrusts her in front of him. Then he throws himself down on the ground, flattening his body against the grass. The vampire is almost on her and there's nothing I can do.

I squeeze my eyes shut, drawing up as much energy and strength as I can muster with the energy-sapping handcuffs wrapped round me. Then I fling myself in front of her. The vampire collides with me, falling backwards. He lets out a howl of frustration and picks himself up, fangs gleaming.

'Don't do this,' I whisper. 'You're going to regret it. You're better than this.'

He doesn't hear me. He's nothing more than an empty shell filled with the animalistic desire to kill and eat. I could probably take him on but my hands are tied behind my back and I can barely move my legs. This is going to be interesting.

From out of the corner of my eye, I see O'Shea's glamourised form move towards us. I shake my head frantically, not looking directly at him but praying he gets the message. There's another way. There's always another way.

'Lisa,' I say quietly. 'On a count of three, I need you to move left. That camera is heavy. Give it one sharp shove towards the vampire and with luck it'll fall on him and trap him.' It won't hold him for long but it'll give me enough time to end this.

She doesn't say anything but she suddenly grips my upper arm. She gets it, she knows this is her only chance – after all, the bloodguzzler will only kill me to get to her. It's her he wants.

'One,' I say, watching the saliva drip from his mouth and his gaunt muscles tense. 'Two. Three!'

She darts over. At first I think the camera is too heavy for her to topple then with one great shove she does it, just as the vampire swivels and leaps. The camera crashes into him and he falls to the ground. I'd like to say I run over, but it's more of a shuffle. I fling myself down. He's pushing at the camera and gnashing his teeth.

'I'm sorry,' I whisper into his ear. Then I use my teeth once more. Unfortunately ripping out throats with my fangs is becoming my thing.

Under normal circumstances an older vampire like this one would be able to heal from this kind of wound. The Medici one didn't because I threw her off a roof; this one doesn't because he's already too weak. Isaac and the rest of Tov V'ra have a lot to answer for.

When it's clear that he's safe, Isaac picks himself up. 'You see!' he bellows into the nearest camera. 'You see what vampires are capable of!'

'For fuck's sake. He only did that because you turned him insane.'

Isaac's face twists into an angry snarl. Interestingly, it matches the look the Montserrat vamp had on its face. He marches over and pulls me up by my arm then starts dragging me backwards.

'We are running out of time,' he shrieks. 'Get back here!'

He yanks me to the maypole, grabs hold of the heavy chain and uses it to bind me firmly to the pole, looping it round my ankles, my torso and my shoulders. He's in a hurry. I frown. That's when I feel the familiar prickle across my skin. Oh. Dawn.

Some of the crowd who stayed behind, including O'Shea, press forwards. Isaac stares into the camera.

'Sunlight is God's gift!' he yells. 'It gives us life!' His voice now has an edge of hysteria. 'It's also proof that vampires are unnatural. If they can't stand sunlight, that's our sign that they are not meant to be!'

This isn't going as smoothly as Isaac had hoped. His three fellow Tov V'ra leaders, Abraham included, are nowhere to be seen. The watching crowd, helped along by O'Shea's mutters, is growing uneasy.

'She saved us!' one of them calls out hoarsely. 'She stopped that vampire!'

'Yeah!' someone else chimes in. 'Bo Blackman isn't evil. She's the Red Angel!'

The chorus is growing but my time is running out. The first streaks of light are appearing in the sky. It was a clear night, I think dully; it's going to be a beautiful day. At least I'll get to see the sun one last time.

'No!' The word rips out of O'Shea and he strides forward, shoving Isaac to one side. He's maintaining his glamour but the expression on his face is all Devlin. 'She's not done anything wrong.'

I have, I want to say. I've not been a good person. I feel my skin burning. O'Shea drops to my feet and starts fumbling with the chain.

'Hang on, Bo,' he says. 'I've got this. I've got you. I'm not going to lose you as well.'

I feel like I'm on fire; any second now I will be. 'Get away, Devlin,' I croak. 'It's not safe.'

He starts to unwrap the chain. 'You might be a bitch some-times, Bo Blackman, but you're my bitch. Shut up.'

'Stop it! Leave her!' Isaac shrieks. 'She deserves to die! She's a monster!'

Can't really argue with that. I tilt my head back and feel the first rays of sun on my upturned face. This is it. There will be blisters and burning and then, at the end, there will be nothing left. It's a hell of a way to go – and it will really bloody hurt.

O'Shea loosens the chain completely and I hear it clank onto the ground. He tugs frantically at my body. There's a shout. I open my eyes to see Isaac flinging himself at O'Shea, fists flying in all directions. Several members of the crowd break away. They'll tear him apart. If I can just save O'Shea before I spontaneously combust then it'll be enough.

The magic of the handcuffs is too strong. I trip over the damned chain and fall flat on my face. I roll to my side. I have to get up, there are only seconds to go, I have to get up…

'Bo.'

There's a click. All of a sudden I feel a rush of energy as my body returns to normal and the handcuffs fall away. I turn to see a man standing there. I've never seen him before in my life and he's brazenly displaying a Tov V'ra tree, tattooed on his neck for the world to see. I blink in confusion and he looks away. 'You're not all bad,' he mutters.

'Bo.' It's O'Shea. The watching humans didn't try to hurt him, they *helped* him. I take in Isaac's crumpled body. O'Shea is standing next to him, his glamour fading. The Tov V'ra followers are staring at him in surprise but he's only staring at me.

'It's daytime. You're still here.'

I smile sadly at him. No, I can't withstand sunlight yet; I'm not strong enough. I'm burning up.

I look down at my arms: they're fine. Then I reach up and touch my face. O'Shea is right.

'You're not a newbie any more,' he says. He looks round at the others. 'And she's not a freak or a monster either!'

Isaac starts to laugh. He's on the ground, completely defeated and quite possibly staring his own death in the face, and he's laughing.

Lisa stares at him with hatred in her eyes. 'I believed in you. I believed in this cause. At least the vampires have an excuse, but you were prepared to let one of them kill me just so you could be headline news.'

I struggle to my feet. That's when I notice she's holding a knife. Her hands look slick with sweat but her grip is tight. I know exactly what she's planning and there's no way I'm going to let her do it. Ignoring the pain coursing through my body, I lurch over to her and put my hand on hers.

'Don't,' I tell her. 'It's not worth it. He's not worth it. Don't turn to darkness because of this place or because of these people. You might never come back.'

'He deserves to die.'

'He'll be dealt with.'

It's touch and go. I can see the desperation in her eyes and how badly she wants him to hurt. This has to be her decision; I'm not going to make it for her. I can only guide her to the right one like Michael once tried to do for me.

Eventually, her shoulders sag and she drops the knife and it thuds to the ground. I leave it where it is and turn to O'Shea, who's silently watching the proceedings. If I choose to end Isaac here, he'll let me. He won't even judge me for it. I don't know what he went through in those black weeks following Connor's death but I'm betting he's had to deal with his own darkness too.

'Call Foxworthy,' I tell him. 'He can round up the others and deal with this mess.'

He quirks up an eyebrow. 'Are you sure?'

I nod. I bend down and take Isaac's phone from him, putting in a number I know better than my own.

'This is Michael Montserrat.'

'It's me.'

There's a pause. 'Where have you been? I was worried.'

'I'm fine.' I glance down at the sun dappling across my skin. 'I'm really fine.'

He exhales. 'I don't like it when you don't keep in touch, Bo. It makes me … anxious.'

I can't stop myself smiling. 'I love you. I know I said it before but I want to make sure you heard me. I love you. You're an overly responsible megalomaniac with the weight of the world on your shoulders but I still love you.'

'And you're a hard-headed, stubborn witch who doesn't know what's good for her, and who thinks she's all alone out there in the big, bad world when there are all sorts of people who care about her more than she realises.' He chokes slightly and I blink, taken aback. I made Michael Montserrat choke. 'I love you too,' he says.

'I should beat you into a pulp for calling me a witch,' I growl.

He laughs.

'Listen, something's going on. Hale and Medici are up to something and I don't know what. They want to bring down the Families and I think they're planning something huge. There's something about martyrs.' I curse. I wish I knew more. 'They want to hurt you, Michael.'

'We figured something was up. Don't worry, Bo. The four Families are staying inside until we get a handle on exactly what's going on. We're not about to make any stupid moves. It'll be fine.'

I glance round at the assembled people. Some look shame-faced, others frustrated. Things had to come to a head between the humans and the vampires; they've been heading towards boiling point for months but now it feels as if the valve has been released. We can all go back to the way things were. I meet O'Shea's eyes again. Most of us anyway.

CHAPTER 21

BLOOD IS THICKER THAN WATER

Lisa looks uncertain. She turns her hands over and over again, glancing to me for reassurance. 'Do you think...' she pauses. 'Do you think I should ring the doorbell?'

I'm about to suggest that's a good idea, rather than give her parents a heart attack by strolling in, when the door opens. Alison Johnson's face peers out. She takes in me first then her gaze drifts to Lisa. As if in slow motion, her hand goes to her mouth and her eyes widen. A beat later, her surprise is overtaken by delight and she throws herself out of the door, clutching onto Lisa as if she can't believe she's real.

'You're here! You came back!' She hugs her tightly. 'Jonesy! Jonesy! Get out here!'

There's a thump and the station caretaker appears. His reaction is virtually identical to his wife's. He's holding a mug of tea which slides from his hand, splattering all over their cream carpet. He doesn't even notice me, he simply rushes towards her, enveloping both Lisa and his wife in an embrace.

'Lisa!' He starts to cry. 'Lisa!'

I take a step back. I don't belong here; this moment is for them and I'm intruding. Jonesy looks up for a brief second and mouths a thank you in my direction. I give him a brief nod and move away.

Alison starts wailing. 'I thought you were dead. I thought you were never coming back!'

As I turn away, I reflect on my suspicions when I first came here and the way I'd picked up on Alison's use of the past tense. It wasn't that she had wanted her daughter to be a corpse, she hadn't dared to allow herself to believe otherwise. Her subconscious knew how dangerous hope can be.

Family will do that to you; you might argue and fall out and even spend periods of your life hating your blood relatives, but there's no stronger link. There's no one more important.

I clench my teeth to try and stop my tears from flowing. It doesn't work. As my vision is blinded and my chest begins to heave and wrack with sobs, I start to run.

~

THE HOSPITAL IS bright and busy with white-coated people. The woman at the front desk raises her eyebrows when she sees me. It's obvious she knows who I am. I don't need to stop and ask her where to go – I know exactly where I'm heading.

I turn to the lifts and hit the button. After several seconds, I give up on waiting and head for the stairs, taking them three at a time. I sprint down the corridor, ignoring the surprised heads turning towards me.

He's in a room of his own; he'll be pleased about that. In fact, I can just imagine his voice my head: 'Can't mix with the hoi polloi, Bo. That simply wouldn't do.'

I half smile, wiping away the last of my tears, and step over to my grandfather's bed. There's a cumbersome ventilator by the side helping him to breathe. He doesn't look like he's asleep, he looks like he's dying.

My knees give way and I clasp his hand in both of mine. His skin feels like paper and his fingers are thin and bony.

'I'm sorry,' I gasp. 'I'm so sorry. I should have been here. I shouldn't have left your side for anything.'

His chest rises and falls with unerring regularity. If I concentrate, I can hear the bustle outside: beeping machines, hushed voices, concerned visitors... It all fades away. As far as I'm concerned, it's just my grandfather and me.

A sharp pain abruptly lances my calf. I let out a half screech and scoot away, tripping over my legs in a bid to extricate myself from this new threat. Whoever it is, I won't let them hurt my grandfather though. I raise my hands and my fangs lengthen. I'll kill them.

The damn cat meows then starts washing itself. It pauses to look up at me with slitted eyes, as if to ask me where the hell I've been. I rub the spot on my leg where it bit me and smile ruefully. I guess I deserved that. Although how in hell the vicious beast managed to gain entrance to a sterile hospital, I have no idea. If my grandfather were awake, he'd have told the administration in no uncertain terms that he needed his cat to assist in his recovery, but for the life of me, I can't imagine who else would have that kind of clout.

Then I pause. I slowly pick myself up from the floor and look at him. He still looks remarkably ill but his eyes are open and they have that familiar ferocious glint of intelligence in them. He's awake.

He opens his mouth and whispers something but I can't catch it. I lean down and ask him to repeat it. 'You are a Blackman,' he says huskily. 'Blackmans do not writhe on the floor, no matter how dire the situation may be.'

I can't help myself, I start to laugh. Then I hug him but immediately pull back because I'm afraid I might hurt him. The cat leaps onto the foot of his bed and curls into a ball. It keeps one eye open, fixed on me just in case I try any funny business. For once I don't care; the bloody thing can do whatever it wants.

'We've not had much luck in getting hold of your grand-daughter,' a woman says, her shoes squeaking as she walks into the room. She catches sight of me and halts, then smiles. 'I take that back.'

I lick my lips. 'How ... how is he?'

My grandfather clears his throat. 'There's no need to talk about me in the third person. I'm not dead, you know.' He grunts. 'Much as this woman here is trying to change that.'

The nurse rolls her eyes. 'Now, Mr Blackman, you know those blood tests were for your own good.'

'I don't see how jabbing me repeatedly with a needle is for my own good,' he grumbles.

She smiles at me. 'We were having trouble finding a vein.'

There's yet another mumbled protest. 'I'm still here, you silly woman. You don't have to speak about me as if I'm a child.'

I raise my eyebrows. Happiness fizzes through me but I'm concerned about the effect his words will have on the nurse. She takes it all in her stride. I suppose she's used to curmudgeonly old men.

'I should have been here,' I tell them both. 'When did he...' I pause and look at him. 'When did you wake up?'

'Late last night,' the nurse says.

At the same time, my grandfather speaks. 'It was thirteen minutes past one. I know because the damned clock was annoying me.'

I frown. 'What clock?'

The nurse leans in towards me. 'He pulled out his IV and threw its pole at the wall. Smashed the clock in one move. Not too shabby for someone who's been in a coma for months.' The corner of her mouth lifts. 'You know we'll still charge you for that, though.'

I sink down into the chair by his bed. 'I'm sorry,' I whisper, barely noticing the nurse make a discreet exit.

'For what?'

'I wasn't here when you woke up.'

He tuts. 'Don't be ridiculous. It was the middle of the night. I'm sure you had better things to do.' He pauses. 'It's not night-time now.'

'No.'

'How did you get here?'

'I guess I'm past the newbie stage of vampirism,' I say softly. 'I can withstand the sun.'

He manages to smile, although I can tell it's an effort. 'Well done you.'

'I think it's down to the laws of nature rather than anything I did myself.' I take his hand. I have to tell him what a crappy granddaughter I've been. He deserves the truth.

I suck in a breath and meet his eyes. 'I didn't come and visit,' I admit. 'Not once.'

He wheezes. Alarmed, I stand back up, ready to scream for the nurse again. He's not in difficulty though – he's laughing. 'And why,' he gasps in between laboured breaths, 'should you have come? I don't imagine I was scintillating company. Although I rather hope that you put down the bitch who put me here.'

'Not me. But, yes, she's gone. A lot has changed in the months you've been … sleeping.'

'Comatose, you mean.'

I shrug.

He raises his arm and I grasp his hand again. He struggles to prop himself up. I try to protest but he's determined. 'There's a hardness about you that wasn't there before.'

I drop my gaze. 'I've done some ... things.'

He emits another choking laugh. 'I can imagine.'

'No.' I bite my lip. 'You can't.' It's an effort to find the words. 'Connor died. I quit New Order.'

'And,' says a voice from the doorway, 'she's been working with a goddamn Kakos daemon.'

I freeze. I release my grip on my grandfather's hand and slowly turn. O'Shea bobs his head in greeting. 'Hey, old man,' he says. 'I knew you were too stubborn to stay asleep for long.' My grandfather mutters under his breath.

I still can't move. 'How did you know?' My voice is strangled. 'Did Maria tell you?'

O'Shea steps in. I notice that he's clutching a bedraggled bunch of flowers. 'Here,' he says, thrusting them forward. 'I nicked them from another room.'

'O'Shea!'

He glances at me. 'What?'

'How did you know?' Fear ripples through me. This is too much. X will go crazy.

He gives me a droll look. 'Seriously? How stupid do you think I am?' He pauses. 'Not as stupid as you, that's for sure. Bo, you can't trust those things. They're evil through and through.' I stare at him, slack-jawed. He sighs. 'You're working for a mysterious daemon who I don't know? Who has unlimited resources? Not to mention all that business with Rogu3 last year and killing a Kakos daemon live on television.' He scoffs. 'It wouldn't take a genius to work it out.'

'Devlin, this is important. You can't tell anyone, you need to keep your mouth shut.' I fling panicked eyes at my grandfather. 'It's a condition of our ... relationship. He'll kill anyone who knows the truth.'

For the first time, O'Shea looks nervous. 'Oh. You could have said.'

'How was I supposed to know you'd work it out?' I howl.

He shrugs feebly. 'Oops.' The cat starts to growl as he runs a shaky hand through his hair. 'What he doesn't know won't hurt him. Unless you tell him that I know, he'll be none the wiser.'

'He can read minds, you idiot!' I curse loudly. 'We need a guard here now. I can call Arzo. Foxworthy, too. I can…'

'Bo.' I look at my grandfather. 'Relax.'

'How can I relax?' I shake my head. 'You don't get it! He made it very clear that he would be forced to take action if I told anyone.'

'You didn't tell anyone.'

'But…'

'Shhhh. I've been unconscious for several months, you know. This is rather a lot to take in at one time.'

I fumble for my phone. I have to speak to X, I have to pre-empt whatever he's planning. Maybe if I offer myself up first… I dial his number, ignoring the tremble in my hands as I hold the phone to my ear. It rings and rings and rings. He's not answering.

'This is really bad,' I mumble. 'Really, really bad.'

My grandfather sighs. 'Honestly, Bo. The half-breed is right. Sometimes you really are stupid.'

'It's not like I sought him out,' I protest. 'He came to me!'

Sternness flickers across his expression. 'Not that. I've been around long enough to know that nothing a Kakos daemon does is without design. He sought you out.'

I stare at him. He's known more tribers and been involved in more tricky situations with them than I could ever be. That's what happens when you're fool enough to become head of MI7, the country's supposedly secret organisation that deals with all things triber. Despite all that, I had no idea he'd had anything to do with any Kakos daemons. Ever.

He sighs. 'This would have been planned all along.'

'What?'

'People would have found out about him eventually. Do you really think you could keep this a secret forever?'

'I *was* keeping it a secret though! I've known him for ages!'

'And he's probably disappointed that you've not let the cat out of the bag before now. This will be his end game. He'll be after one of us, after whoever ends up knowing the truth.'

'No. Sure, X is a Kakos daemon and I know I can't fully trust him but he's not all bad.'

'He's a Kakos daemon, Bo. *Que sera sera.*'

O'Shea swallows. 'Shit. This is pretty bad.'

I glare at him. 'You bet your skinny arse it is.'

His bottom lip juts out. 'My arse is pert and cute.'

'I'm glad someone can make a joke at a time like this.' I ball my hands up into fists. 'I have to find him. I have to explain.'

'He's not going to be found unless he wants to be.'

'That doesn't mean I can't try!' I throw back.

My grandfather sighs. 'Go. It won't do any good.'

'He's saved my life before,' I protest.

'Because he wanted to use you for his own ends.'

'So you're saying I should give up? Let him do whatever he wants because I broke his stupid rule?'

'No,' my grandfather says calmly. 'You need to find out what he really wants and take things from there. You can work it out.'

The nurse comes back in. Her beaming smile is inappropriate considering the dread churning in my stomach. 'He needs to rest.'

'*He* has done nothing but rest for months,' my grandfather snaps.

She's right: my grandfather doesn't need this. X will listen to me if I talk to him. I know what he's said before but there has to be a way out of this. There's *always* a way out.

I bend over and kiss my grandfather's cheek, smoothing his hair. 'I won't let him hurt you,' I promise.

'I've been in a coma, Bo. It's not me he wants.'

Our eyes meet for a second and I nod.

'Do you think it's me?' O'Shea asks shakily.

I look at him. 'I don't know,' I mutter. 'But I'm not going to let him take you either. Let's go. We can find him together.'

Despite his earlier jokes, O'Shea is clearly terrified. To his credit, he nods. 'Okay, Bo.'

'I'm really glad you're alive,' I tell my grandfather. 'I do love you.'

He smiles. 'I love you too, Bo. Don't do anything reckless.'

I bite my lip. Sure. No problem.

CHAPTER 22

REVENGE IS A DISH BEST SERVED COLD

I don't say anything to O'Shea as we stride down the hospital corridor. In theory, it shouldn't be hard for him to keep up with me; I do have remarkably short legs. But my determination to get out of here before X does anything rash makes me move at an incredible pace. We forego the lifts and run down the stairs. When we reach the bottom, O'Shea finally speaks up. 'You don't even know where he is, Bo! Slow down.'

'That's why we need all the time we can get to try and find him,' I say through gritted teeth.

'It'll be alright.'

'You don't know that,' I snap. At least O'Shea came here and told me. At least I might have a chance to find X. I stop in my tracks and turn. 'How did you know I was here?' I ask.

O'Shea frowns. 'At the hospital? I didn't. Michael asked me to come by and speak to that woman who was attacked. I was on my way to her when I heard a few doctors gossiping that the Red Angel was in the building.'

I ignore his remark about the gossip and focus on his reason for being here. 'Tara Wilkes. The woman Medici used as an excuse for his little execution party.'

He nods. 'That's the one. She's about to be sent home. I was going to ask her a few questions to see if we could find out more about what Medici is planning. It's unlikely, but maybe one of her attackers said something to her. It was worth a shot.' He points ahead. 'In fact, there she is.'

I follow his finger. Looking pale and sitting in a wheelchair, but otherwise alive and fairly well, is the woman in question. Damn it, O'Shea is right. It's not just X that I have to worry about.

I check my watch. This might be my only chance to speak to her. I'll have to spare a few minutes.

'Tara!' I call. I march over to her. She flinches dramatically. In theory that shouldn't be surprising considering why she's in hospital, but I'm hardly likely to be a rapist. I try to soften my approach but I'm not sure it works. 'I'm Bo Blackman. It's nice to meet you.'

Her eyes are wide and saucer-like. She doesn't say a thing. Is she a damned mute? As I frown at her, her head bows, her long straggly hair covering her face. Her fingers twitch at her loose cotton trousers as she turns her wrist. I watch her movements. She's checking her watch. I wonder if she's waiting for someone to come and rescue her from me. Then I see her other wrist. There, only just concealed by a hospital band, is a slim gold charm bracelet. It only has one charm – a tiny golden tree.

My body goes very still. 'Why are you afraid of me?' I ask.

Her head remains bowed. I try again. 'Tara,' I prod gently. 'You shouldn't be scared. I'm not going to hurt you.'

Other than jerking her fingers, she doesn't move. I lose my patience and grab her fringe, yanking her head upwards to force her to look at me. There are a few cries from people around us but I ignore them.

'You're supposed to be dead,' she snarls.

O'Shea starts. I lean down and hiss. 'Well, guess what? I'm not.'

She checks her watch again then she pulls her shoulders back as if mustering her strength. She looks at me again. 'It doesn't matter, monster,' she spits. 'Because everyone else will be soon.'

'What do you mean?'

She laughs and I slap her hard across her face. I see two security guards approaching me from the far corner. Just try it, guys. Just try to cross me and you'll see what happens.

She flashes a mixture of disgust and ire at me. 'The martyrs will be doing their job right now.'

My insides turn to ice. 'Tell me.'

She hawks up a ball of phlegm but, before she can do anything with it, I grab her neck and heave her upwards, dragging her out of her chair.

'Tell me!' I repeat.

'You're the only bloodguzzler out on the streets. Every other freak of nature is tucked away inside their fortresses, thinking they're safe. Medici made sure of that.' She smirks. 'They're not going to be safe for long.'

There's a sudden loud boom. At first I think it's a clap of thunder but thunder doesn't make the earth shake. It's not an earthquake either. My eyes meet O'Shea's and he whispers the same thing that I'm thinking. 'Bomb.'

I release Tara instantly. She collapses back into her chair but I don't waste time on her – I'm already sprinting out of the door. By the time I'm halfway down the street, I hear another boom from somewhere further across the city. My heart is pounding painfully in my chest. I have to get to Michael. I have to get to him now.

There's a screech of tires and a siren screams into action. An ambulance comes up beside me with O'Shea at the wheel. He doesn't stop it, simply reaches across to open the passenger door whilst the vehicle's still moving. I leap inside and slam the door shut.

'Drive,' I say breathlessly, 'drive.'

He puts his foot down. We careen down the street, twisting first one way then the other.

'It doesn't make any sense,' he says as he swerves to narrowly avoid a group of surprised office workers on their way to lunch. 'How could they bomb the Family houses? How would a bomb get inside?'

My mouth is dry. 'Because Medici made sure that all the Families were going to match his recruitment drive. They didn't have time to spare on security like they would usually. Even after what happened with Nicky, they cared about nothing more than matching Medici, bloodguzzler for bloodguzzler. Tov V'ra must have made sure that their people were inside.'

'Suicide bombers? But that's nuts.'

'Everything about them is nuts,' I say, fear causing my hackles to rise. No wonder Isaac was laughing: he knew he'd already won. I picture Michael's face, the way his hair flops over his forehead and the warmth in his eyes when he looks at me. There have only been two explosions so far. He might still be okay. Then there's another explosion, followed immediately by another.

'Faster!' I scream.

The Montserrat mansion comes into view. It's no longer the vast, proud edifice it once was; at least half of it has been turned into a pile of smoking rubble. Flames spring out from it. I feel like I can't breathe. I think I scream again but I'm no longer sure. All around us there are car alarms and screams and shouts and the noise is unlike anything I've ever heard before.

O'Shea slams on the brakes. There's a mess of twisted metal

from cars blocking the street. The ambulance isn't going any further.

Without waiting for O'Shea, I kick open the door and launch myself out. I can still get to Michael, I *have* to get to him. I jump over the charred mess of what was probably once a person and push myself faster. Adrenaline courses through my system; right now it's the only thing keeping me upright.

I wheel round, ready to plunge inside, find Michael and rescue whoever else I can. Matt and Beth and Nell and Ria and Ursus and everyone else.

A ring of steel latches round my arm and yanks me back. I stumble and fall. 'Let go of me!'

X's face blurs into focus. 'If you try to go in, you will die. You're not strong enough.'

'Fuck off!' I try to wrench myself away but he has me stuck fast. In one swift movement, he crouches and takes hold of my knee. Before I can say or do anything, he twists it hard and pain rips through me. He's broken my leg. I snarl in his face.

'It's the only way, Bo. You won't make it if you go in. You'll heal quickly – just not quickly enough.'

'X! You can't do this. You can't!'

There's another loud bang as the remaining windows blow out. Glass flies everywhere, a multitude of shards biting into my flesh. I ignore them.

'I beat them. I beat the Tov V'ra. This isn't fair!'

X sighs. His face looms closer. 'They're not who you were really up against, Bo.' A sad smile lights his face. He's not using any glamour; he's in full Kakos daemon mode, his tattoos writhing and twisting their terrible dark path across his skin.

'Come any closer, Devlin, and I will kill her!' he calls over my shoulder.

I stagger to my feet. I don't care if my leg is broken. X can snap every damn bone in my body. I'm going in.

He grabs hold of me again. 'I'm growing tired of this, Bo. Stop it.'

I look into his face. The billowing smoke makes tears run down my face. I stare at him and gasp. 'This was you. This was all you.'

He slides his gaze away. 'Yes and no. It wasn't just me, it was the Kakos daemons as a group. The Families have been using us as scapegoats for their actions for decades. They've been getting far too uppity. We decided it was time to do something about it.'

'This is why you were so desperate for me to find Lisa Johnson. You needed something to keep me away from Medici. You've been working with him.'

He shakes his head. 'No. I did need you to keep away from him, but we're not working with him. We don't work with anyone.' He gazes at me meaningfully. 'We manipulate everyone.'

Including me. 'There have only been four explosions, you prick! Not five.'

He holds up his index finger. 'Wait for it.' All of a sudden there's another one, coming from the east. From where Medici will be. A smile tugs at X's mouth, a goddamned smile. 'There's nothing worse than thinking you're home and free and then having everything you know completely wiped out,' he says softly.

I kick upwards with my one good leg, connecting with his groin. For once, he doesn't move away in time but I'm rewarded with little more than a pained grimace.

I start limping towards the huge house. I can still find Michael. He can't be dead yet, I would feel it in my heart if he were. Agony shoots through me but I don't care. I'm going to do this.

There's a heavy sigh from behind me. 'In about ninety

seconds, the entire building is going to collapse.' I ignore him. X continues. 'You'll barely make it to the front door.'

I keep going. It's only twenty feet further. The huge midnight-blue doors might be hanging off their hinges but I can still get inside; there are benefits to being petite. I don't think about the death and destruction I'm facing; I don't even think about X. The only thing on my mind is Michael.

'Bo. I do like you despite all your faults. I didn't necessarily approve of this course of action, you know.' I keep limping forward. The closer I get, the stronger the wall of heat is. The fires inside must be blazing at unbelievable temperatures. No, no, no, no, no. X speaks louder as though trying to cut through my pain. 'I can save one.'

One.

'I'm sorry,' he says. 'It's the best I can do. Name one person and I will get them. If they are still alive.'

Flames blast from the door, licking their way towards me as if they have a mind of their own. I'm thrown backwards once more.

'Name one, Bo.'

Matt. Nell. Beth. My heart screams in agony. There's only one choice. It's not even a choice. Michael. Save Michael.

'As you wish.' While my weak, traitorous body gives way and I fall forward onto my hands and knees, X's shape flies forward. The searing heat doesn't seem to bother him. Less than ten seconds later, there's a vast deafening rumble. As I scream, O'Shea grabs me under my arms and drags me away. Then, right in front of my eyes, the entire structure collapses.

~

I'M NOT QUITE sure what happens next. I don't faint or fall unconscious but it's as if everything fades into the background.

277

I'm aware of O'Shea murmuring things in my ear but I have no idea what he's saying. It's not until we're standing in the door of my apartment that I realise where I am.

'We can't be here. This belongs to X. He's killed them all, Devlin. He's...'

'Shh. We have to get Maria and Kimchi.'

'And me.' I look over to see Rogu3. He rushes towards me, wrapping his arms tightly round my body. 'As soon as I saw the news, I tried to come. I tried to get to the Montserrat mansion because I thought that's where you'd be. All the streets are blocked off. The only other place I could think of to come is here.'

'There is no Montserrat mansion,' I murmur. 'Not any more.' I pull away from him. Maria is in her usual place on the sofa but this time she is hugging Kimchi. He licks her face and whines.

'Look,' she says. She points the remote control at the television, turning up the volume. The images flit from Montserrat to Gully to Stuart to Bancroft to Medici. Every vampire stronghold is now nothing more than a pile of rubble.

'We don't know at this time,' intones the news anchor over the live feed, 'whether indeed any vampires have survived. It's possible that in one fell swoop they have been completely obliterated.'

'*Que sera sera*,' I whisper. Then I walk over to the television and put my fist through the screen. Everyone flinches. 'We have to get out of here. Now.'

'Where are we going to go?'

I shake my head. 'I don't know. But this place belongs to a Kakos daemon and Kakos daemons are responsible for this. We have to get out of here and hide.'

Rogu3 coughs. 'Bo.' I glance up but he's not looking at me. Something or someone is behind me. X.

I turn. Kimchi whimpers and buries himself further into the crook of Maria's arm. 'Even my dog knows what you really are. I am going to kill you.'

'No, you're not, Bo.' He looks down at the body in his arms. 'I told you before, none of this was my decision. And I can't apologise for what was inevitable.' He sighs. 'But I did promise revenge if anyone discovered my identity.' He sweeps a look round the tiny assembly. 'I am a man of my word. And I did tell you I was petty.'

X kneels, placing Michael's limp form on the floor. I rush forward, falling down by Michael's head and cradling his face in my hands. At first I don't see it. Then I freeze and lean over him. His breath is hot against my cheek.

'He's alive.' I clasp my hand over my mouth. I can't believe it. 'He's alive!'

X sighs. 'I am sorry, Bo.' He places a hand on my head, a gentle pressure. 'I did promise you my revenge and here it is. It's going to be worse than you could have imagined.'

I consider stabbing him in the gut but he simply laughs. He doesn't sound amused, more sad. A moment later he's gone.

O'Shea kneels down at the other side of Michael. I smooth my fingers over Michael's face, still unable to believe what I'm seeing. Nothing good has come out of this day but if he's still here, there is hope.

'Bo,' O'Shea says. I don't pay him any attention. 'Bo, look!'

I frown. 'What?'

'Can't you see it?'

Alarm bells start ringing inside my head. 'See what?'

O'Shea reaches over and gingerly lifts up Michael's right eyelid. His iris and pupil are only just visible. 'Now do you see it?'

I stare. My mouth drops open as Michael starts to cough

and splutter, coming slowly back to consciousness. He groans, his features twisting in terrible pain.

'Oh God,' I whisper. 'X. That's his revenge. That's what he meant.'

Michael's eyes focus on me. He wets his lips. 'Bo. You're still here.'

I try to smile. I look into Michael's now-human eyes and I really do try to smile. He's alive. That's what matters.

ABOUT THE AUTHOR

After teaching English literature in the UK, Japan and Malaysia, Helen Harper left behind the world of education following the worldwide success of her Blood Destiny series of books. She is a professional member of the Alliance of Independent Authors and writes full time, thanking her lucky stars every day that's she lucky enough to do so!

Helen has always been a book lover, devouring science fiction and fantasy tales when she was a child growing up in Scotland.

She currently lives in Edinburgh in the UK with far too many cats – not to mention the dragons, fairies, demons, wizards and vampires that seem to keep appearing from nowhere.

* 9 7 8 1 9 1 3 1 1 6 5 0 7 *